DAUGHTER OF SERPENTS

DAUGHTER of SERPENTS

THE VALLEY OF SCALES SAGA

SYDNEY WILDER

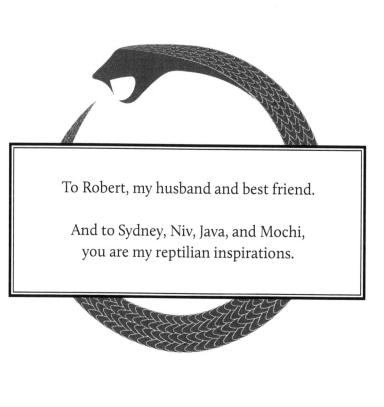

To Robert, my husband and best friend.

And to Sydney, Niv, Java, and Mochi,
you are my reptilian inspirations.

Table of Contents

Daughter of Serpents

Prologue

THE CHILDREN HAD FINALLY GONE TO BED.
Beatrice Thorburn pulled her graying almond hair out of its stiff bun and felt a wave of relief wash across her scalp. It was nine o'clock, the time when the boisterous evening melted into the stillness of night, and the head-mistress of the Thorburn Estate, an orphanage tucked deep in the forest near the village of Vale, finally had a chance to relax.

Running an orphanage was no easy task. Raising a single child was a lofty undertaking—let alone twelve of them. Twelve bodies to clothe, twelve mouths to feed, and twelve pairs of hands to make little messes every-where they went. Beatrice sighed as she wiped bread-crumbs off the embroidered fabric of a couch cushion.

Twelve children. But until earlier that day, that number had been thirteen.

She gazed out a large window into the wilting remains of her garden. Behind a small cluster of trees lay an old storehouse. Its single small window was musty with mildew, and the wood was beginning to rot at the base, splintering apart like cracks in a shattered mirror. Beatrice hadn't ventured into the building since the girl left.

I wonder if she'll be alright on her own.

She had pleaded to stay, and considering her situation, Beatrice nearly obliged. But Beatrice had always been strict about her rule that children must leave the orphanage once they turned eighteen. Otherwise, her twelve mouths to feed could easily double or triple. *She's an adult now,* Beatrice reasoned, *and she must learn to fend for herself.*

But she was no ordinary girl. Beatrice knew that by making her leave, she was casting the girl into a life of extreme hardship. She was destined to live alone, an outsider on the very edges of society, not fitting in no matter how hard she tried. That had always been her fate from the moment she was left on the doorstep eighteen years ago.

But there was also a matter of safety. As the girl grew, so did the level of danger. Beatrice could never forget the horror on Jack's face when she had bitten him. It was a miracle that he had even survived the attack.

Gods forbid anyone ever finds out her secret. Or worse, someone discovers what sort of horror I'd been raising all these years and comes after me.

Beatrice had promised her husband that she would look after any child that showed up, no matter who they were or what circumstances they came from. "Every child deserves a loving home," he had said. But it had been nearly twenty years since his passing, and as both her husband's money and her composure dried up, keeping that promise became harder every day.

And as much as Beatrice wrestled with her disgust and resentment, she had raised the girl her entire life and prayed that she would find a way to survive. There was no avoiding the truth; if she was discovered, she would be killed.

Beatrice shook her head. She couldn't let these worries consume her mind every night. Taking care of the children was difficult enough—she needed to use her few precious hours alone to decompress. She ventured over to a wall-length bookshelf and plucked an aging hardcover from the very bottom. Nothing relaxed her more than a good book. In the dim light of a heavily shaded oil lamp, Beatrice was so immersed in the novel, her eyes softly skimming each line of text, that she didn't hear the rustling outside until it was nearly at her front door.

She bolted upright. *Intruders? Or perhaps just a wild animal?* She stood up and placed the book on the couch, her eyes locked on the front door. She crept toward it, her arms outstretched to defend herself. *I need a weapon.*

There's a letter opener in the kitchen... no, there's no way that little knife will do me any good.

Her eyes flicked toward the upstairs, where her husband's old blunderbuss was locked away in a cabinet. *Dammit, I don't even know how to fire a gun.*

The rustling was right outside the door. The shiny brass handle rattled from the outside.

There's no time to prepare. Whatever it is, it's comi—

The door burst open. Beatrice bolted her hands over her mouth, refusing to scream for fear of waking the children. At the worst, she had expected a burglar or maybe a vagrant ... something human, at least. What she had not expected were two massive reptilians, each over six feet tall, with the wiry scaled bodies of lizards and an army of spines trailing down their hunched backs. Their long teeth hung jagged from their gums, and in each one's spindly claws was a sharply pointed spear.

Varan?

The lizardfolk race lived further to the northeast, a substantial journey from Vale. The small village didn't border their territory.

Good gods, what are they doing here?

Beatrice didn't have a way to ask questions. Reptilians were silent creatures, except for the occasional hiss. They communicated without words in a way that humans had never managed to comprehend. Some humans believed they didn't communicate at all, and they acted on little more than animal instinct.

Beatrice had never seen a reptilian in person, but she could tell by the intense gazes in their amber eyes that they weren't mere beasts. *They planned to come here.*

The Varan didn't seem interested in harming Beatrice, but they did warn her with a wave of their spears to stay out of the way. As she cowered on the couch, the Varan began scouring through the house with little regard for the fact that they'd just invaded a peaceful home, in a peaceful village, far away from their native lands. Beatrice watched in alarm.

"Wait! What are you doing!?" Her voice rose in panic as one of the Varan opened a tall cabinet and its contents spilled onto the floor. Her grandmother's antique novels scattered across the hardwood in a flurry of gold-trimmed paper, their spines splayed and their yellowed pages bent at odd angles.

The Varan peered up at her, one of the hardcovers still clenched in its claws. It hissed, tossed the book at Beatrice's feet, and continued its ransacking.

I'm an idiot. They can't understand me.

As the two lizards continued searching, a third figure appeared in the doorway. Like the Varan, this creature was so large that it had to duck through the doorframe like it was crawling into a cellar. The massive snake's mottled black-and-brown scales glittered in the dim light of the parlor. Its slitted eyes, a glossy shade of bronze, seared into Beatrice's soul. Its large, muscled arms held no weapon, but Beatrice was more terrified of the fangs that she knew lurked behind its serpentine lips. Naga venom was deadly to humans, scorching them from the inside out in a matter of hours.

I... I don't understand. What is a Naga doing here with two Varan? What do they want?

But with no way to communicate and the tips of the Varans' spears looking very sharp, Beatrice could do nothing but stand aside as the Naga joined the Varan in their search.

Until the Naga decided to head upstairs.

"No!!!" Beatrice flung herself toward the stairwell. The Naga hissed softly, a look of disdain on its face, before slithering its way past her. But just as the reptilian made its way into the dark hallway leading to the childrens' bedrooms, he felt a sharp pang of alarm in his head.

<Boss! Down here!> The reptilian thoughts flowed through his mind without a sound, but their intent was as clear as a spoken voice. <We found something!>

The Naga quickly slithered back down the stairs and past the stunned headmistress. His Varan companions stood outside in the estate's withering gardens. The trio of reptilians ventured to the edge of the estate, where one of the Varan pointed a clawed finger at a rotting wooden building.

<In here.>

The storehouse was musty and dark. All they could see was a rusty pile of gardening tools slumped into the nearest corner. The Naga lit a nearby oil lamp, and the rest of the room flickered into view. The shed was illuminated in a soft orange light that cast deep shadows across an old twin bed with a rusting metal frame and a lopsided bookshelf that held a few dusty paperbacks. The Naga's serpentine eyes narrowed, and he wondered what unfortunate being was cursed to live in such a dilapidated place.

A Varan tapped on the Naga's shoulder. In the lizard's scaly palm were two small pieces of snake shed, no larger than a human fingernail. The yellowed skin had crumpled like old parchment in the stagnant air of the storehouse.

<She was definitely here,> he remarked.

<Well, now she is not,> the Naga grumbled as he plucked the snake shed from the Varan's claws. His yellow eyes, each with a haunting sliver of a pupil, gazed out at the bright moon. The thought of her living in such squalor made his reptilian heart, already blighted by nearly two decades of anger, flare up even more.

He held the translucent, papery skin up to his mouth and flicked his forked tongue. <This is fresh. She was here less than a day ago. This is clearly her home, so where could she have gone?>

<Aren't humans weird about children?> the other Varan piped up. <They typically make them leave when they become adults. Such heartless creatures. How old would she be now?>

The Naga sighed. <About eighteen years, more or less.>

<In that case, she's probably gone. She could be anywhere, and I doubt that quivering harpy inside is going to be much help.>

The Naga held up his palm and curled his scaled fingers into a fist around the crumpled bit of snake shed. <It's so small that the scent coming off this is faint, but I'll try my best to track her. I'll search every village in this damn valley if I must.>

<But sir, what if she's within the city, through the gates? We'll never get past those.>

<Not yet, we won't. But for now, we'll track her scent and continue our search through the villages. Onward, we have a lot of ground to cover. Like you said, she could be anywhere.>

The reptilians trudged back through the gardens, trampling the withered flowers beneath their heavy, scaled bodies. As they slipped around the front of the orphanage and prepared to descend into the village at the base of the hill, the Naga gazed longingly back at the storehouse.

<I swear, no matter where in Squamata you are... I will find you.>

Chapter 1

MARISSA SAT ALONE, HUNKERED UNDERNEATH a shoddy tin awning outside the busy inn's back storeroom, twirling a plump rat over a tiny roasting spit that she desperately tried to keep lit. A thick blanket of rain poured down just inches from her crackling fire, which was nothing more than a few handfuls of sticks piled in a pyramid shape. The flames demanded more fuel as they broiled their way through the spindly twigs, but every potential bit of firewood beyond her tiny shelter was now soaked.

This is, without a doubt, the worst birthday I have ever had.

Marissa had seen this coming, but it was still a difficult reality to grasp. She knew Beatrice's rules about adults leaving the orphanage, but she thought the gruff but occasionally kind-hearted headmistress might make an exception. *I won't cause any trouble. I'll stay in the storehouse and fend for myself. You won't even know I'm here.*

Her pleas had nearly worked. But as the morning of Marissa's eighteenth birthday arrived, Beatrice's sympathies hardened into a firm adherence to the rules. Marissa was given a few copper coins, a cloak, a scarf to hide her identity, and a brief, callous farewell. By three o'clock, she walked out of the musty old storeroom that she called home and plodded down the village road toward an uncertain future.

Marissa pushed up the sleeves of her light brown cloak, and a deep, unsettling anger ran through her body. With her arms fully exposed and her mottled black-and-brown scales glowing in the faint light of the fire, she was reminded why she would never be normal. Because behind her hooded cloak and the black scarf that covered the lower half of her face, she was a monstrous combination of human and snake. A half-Naga.

She stretched her arms out and rubbed her freshly shed skin, which felt smooth to the touch as it rippled under her bare palms. Her scales trailed down her arms and legs, ending just before her wrists and in the middle of her calves. Her stomach and chest were almost entirely reptilian. She had a womanly hourglass figure clad in soft white belly scales but no discernable breasts. She crudely trimmed her long black hair so that her thick bangs helped hide the scales that spread across the edges of her forehead above her reptilian nose. With her arms and legs covered, she could pass for human.

Until she had come across the inn, Marissa had been wandering down the main road for hours, her mind too numb to comprehend her situation. She paced aimlessly, not knowing or caring where she was going. Beatrice had warned her that the outer villages were littered with bandits, so she crept into the nearest town once the sun had set. Marissa peeked down at her belt and sneered at the tiny, rusted dagger that Beatrice had given her. *Like that'll do any good.* Marissa was barely five foot two, small even by human standards, and through childhood incidents, she'd learned that her half-Naga venom wasn't powerful enough to kill a human. She was no match for any ambushers that wanted to steal her meager copper coin.

Marissa had heard the cacophony of activity flowing out of the inn all night, but thankfully she hadn't heard anyone bustling around in the storeroom, and no one had tried to open the back door. She despondently listened to the joyful music and banter like a woeful puppy chained in a backyard. She had spent most of her life isolated and alone, and the raucous laughter overflowing out of the tavern made her longing heart sink. She huffed and shook her head, determined not to let futile emotions muddle her perseverance.

Because she now had a plan. While cooking her meager dinner, she'd been listening in on the patrons' faint conversations. They spoke of all sorts of normal trivialities that floated through Marissa's ears without another thought.

But a few discussions piqued her interest. Several customers had mentioned the vast, beautiful kingdom of Brennan, which lay farther north beyond the quaint idleness of the outer villages. Marissa had heard of the Valley of Scales' central kingdom her whole life. When she was young, one of the newer arrivals at the orphanage claimed to be from there. He spoke of towering buildings made of perfectly chiseled limestone, cobblestone streets lined with shops full of whimsical toys, and in the center of it all, a massive palace with spires that seemed to touch the clouds. It sounded magical and, more importantly, much safer than the bandit-riddled dirt roads that snaked through the outer villages. She knew that the kingdom would be full of reptilian-hating humans, but being in a busy city would make her feel less isolated. She just had to keep her distance.

A sharp, gamey smell filled her nostrils, and Marissa removed her meal from its makeshift spit. Normal humans found roasted rat repulsive, but for her, it was an abundant source of food. Beatrice wouldn't always remember to bring Marissa's dinner out to the storeroom, and as a growing half-Naga, she was always hungry. She'd taught herself how to hunt as a young child, with her venom finishing off her prey in a matter of minutes. She just had to be careful that Beatrice never found the discarded bones. She was already wary of the half-snake child, and discovering that Marissa had succumbed to her reptilian instincts would've likely sent the headmistress over the edge.

CHAPTER 1

At least, unlike full-blooded snakes, I prefer to cook my food and not swallow it in one gulp.

Marissa picked the last bits of rat meat off its scrawny bones and carefully buried the remains in the soggy dirt. The rain had stopped, and Marissa pressed the back of her head against the aging wood of the back door. She closed her eyes and let the soothing sounds of the bustling inn sweep across her ears like joyful music. She needed to rest, and in the morning, she would head north; the main road led straight to the kingdom gates.

I must stay hopeful. Who knows what awaits me there? It can't be much worse than living in an old storehouse.

THE TOWERING GATES THAT GUARDED THE southern entrance to Brennan were the largest structures Marissa had ever seen. Her head tilted upward in awe as the dense forest that surrounded the main road faded away and the massive, intricately patterned iron barriers loomed into view. On either side of the gates, a thick limestone wall nearly fifty feet high cascaded across the horizon, bordered by a field of bare grass that separated the kingdom from the murky, tangled swampland. As enchanting as humans made the kingdom seem, Marissa knew the sinister reason for such extraordinary fortifications—to keep the native reptilians out.

Or half-reptilians. Marissa pressed her scarf against her face as she approached the gates, making sure it was wrapped tightly around her head and neck. She swallowed heavily, trying to appear inconspicuous as she lingered among the small crowd waiting for the gates to open. She noticed that she was the only one traveling on foot; the other visitors had arrived using horses, either mounted in saddles or perched atop humble wooden carts. The sounds of flared nostrils huffing and scraggly tails whipping away flies swept through the air.

The mounting tone of impatience melted into relief as a woman dressed in purple-and-gold regalia chimed a bell from a guard tower atop the limestone wall. The bulky gates heaved open with a slow whiny creeeeeak, and the restless crowd filtered in through the opening, jostling past each other as they went. Marissa hung back, not wanting to be trampled by stomping hooves or rolling cartwheels. Instead, she took in the impressive sight that lay beyond the gates.

Brennan was nothing like the outer villages, which consisted of small towns scattered in sparse clearings between thick swaths of forest. The main road that Marissa had been traveling on was nothing more than a sandy path surrounded by an endless canopy of trees so dense and overgrown that it nearly blocked out the sunlight. But the land beyond the gates was wide open, a sprawling city square of cobblestone bordered by rows of limestone buildings several stories high. Marissa's eyes widened as she caught a glimpse of an immense church, at least a hundred feet tall, decorated with a stained-glass window several times her height. She admired the way the colored glass pieces gleamed like gemstones in the vibrant sunlight.

The clamorous crowd had dissipated, and Marissa wandered through the towering gates just before they creaked shut as noisily as they had opened. Not only was the city square more open than the surrounding wilderness, but it was also a lot busier. She stood awestruck in the middle of the square, observing the roar of activity that swept past her. A pack of children chased each other near a large fountain, weaving in and out of the dozens of adults that strolled through the street. Their squealing voices sailed through the air, echoing faintly in Marissa's ears.

I've never seen so many people in my life.

The ordinary yet exuberant scene reminded Marissa of the lively inn the night before. *People chatting, laughing, shouting...* a deep melancholy washed over Marissa, and she felt an urgent need to scurry away from the square as fast as possible.

She slipped into an empty alleyway, away from the bustling activity, but the deep sadness only intensified. She sighed and pressed herself against a building, the chill of the limestone seeping through the back of her cloak. It was early October, the time when the typical swampy heat of the valley began to crisp up into a season vaguely resembling fall. Marissa knew that normal humans loved this time of year, but her half-reptilian blood preferred the humid warmth of the summertime.

She crept through the alleyway and found herself on the other side of the city square, surrounded by a sea of buildings separated by a cobblestone road. It appeared to be some sort of religious quarter—churches, monasteries, and shrines were scattered between the storefronts. Her reptilian nostrils flared underneath her scarf as a warm, alluring scent overwhelmed her senses. It smelled sweet and yeasty, and her stomach responded with a ravenous rumble.

Bread.

It was nearly noon, and Marissa hadn't eaten yet. Her reptilian half didn't mind subsisting on rats, but she would still sometimes succumb to her desire for human delicacies. The scent was deeply nostalgic, as it reminded her of when she was young and still lived in the main orphanage. She would awaken on Sunday mornings to Beatrice pulling a rack of warm blueberry muffins from the oven, fresh steam wafting off their perfectly browned tops.

Marissa spotted a bakery sign hanging from one of the storefronts, and her body tightened in defiance. *No. I'm a snake. Snakes eat rats. They certainly don't waste what little coin they have on sweets.* She huffed and stomped away, determined to hunt down a cheaper but significantly less appetizing source of food.

CHAPTER 1

IT HAD BEEN TWO HOURS, AND EVEN WITH HER heightened reptilian senses, Marissa hadn't managed to track down a single rat.

She slumped against some crates in an alleyway, her previously ravenous stomach now screaming for food. She buried her face in her palms, trying to drown out the gnawing hunger pains with sheer mental determination. But her resolve was quickly fading. As her unruly stomach continued to complain, buying a pastry from the bakery became even more tempting.

Faint chirping sounds echoed from further down the alleyway, and Marissa saw several small yet plump pigeons flittering around a cluster of trash cans, their pointed beaks plucking breadcrumbs from the cracks in the cobblestone. She ignored her human half telling her she was insane and dove for the group of birds. Marissa had the sharp reflexes of a full-blooded snake, but the pigeons still scattered in a flurry of flapping wings long before Marissa could reach them.

Damn it. They're a lot quicker than rats. And they can fly.

Past the alleyway, Marissa saw the ever-tempting sign for the bakery in the corner of her view. *I'm going in circles. These city streets all look the same.* She didn't know how much longer she could keep up the rat chase. She was so hungry that she was beginning to feel dizzy, and she feared that passersby would be horrified if they caught her scampering around the alleyways trying to catch vermin.

She pulled her meager copper coin out of her cloak pocket and grimaced. *One pastry. Then, I either need to find some rats or become faster than those birds.*

The scent of sugar and fresh dough became even more intoxicating as Marissa walked through the bakery door. Within the cozy shop, which contained long wooden shelves full of knickknacks, potted plants, and mysterious glowing stones, was a glass display case full of huge sweets. Their crusts were puffy and crisp, and their various toppings and glazes glistened under the dim lighting.

"May I help you?" a woman asked, her elbows plopped on the register counter.

"Y-yes." Marissa eyed the display case, overwhelmed by the options. "What do you recommend?"

"Well, it is October, so our pumpkin doughnuts are the most popular right now." The woman pointed to the top shelf, which contained fluffy rings of rich orange batter, glazed over with a shiny, sugary coating. Marissa bit her lip and swallowed heavily as her mouth watered.

"How much?"

"We're closing soon, and I need to get rid of these last ones, so two copper each?"

Marissa pulled her scant bit of change from her pocket. *I only have five copper. One doughnut would be almost half of my money...*

She realized that the cashier was watching her stare hopelessly at the few coins in her palm. Marissa quickly shoved the change back into her pocket, embarrassed. Marissa's dirty cloak and barely soled shoes were an obvious giveaway of her current situation. To Marissa's surprise, the cashier's glance was not one of disgust but sympathy.

"I'm gonna let you in on a little secret." The cashier's voice lowered to a near-whisper. "The owner throws the leftovers away when we close. It's a terrible waste. I can't give you everything, but take the rest of the doughnuts. I'll just tell him we sold out."

Marissa was so shocked that she could barely sputter a "Thank you." She left the bakery with a bag of four pumpkin donuts and the first bit of happiness she'd felt in months. She waited until she could creep into a nearby alleyway to enjoy her prize, and when she pulled her scarf down below her lips and took her first bite of one of the doughnuts, all her anxiety dissipated. Her whole body felt weightless, like a carefree child, and she pressed her head against the limestone bricks and took a deep sigh of relief.

She knew the feeling wouldn't last long. Even with a bag full of sweets, she was still a lost soul, a vagrant with no home and very little money drifting aimlessly through the kingdom. But today, she'd gotten four doughnuts for the price of one, and she knew that to endure her new life, she had to enjoy the little victories.

She tossed the last bit of doughnut in her mouth and repositioned her scarf over her nose, admiring the setting sun creeping below the rows of limestone buildings. She needed to ration the other three sweets, and she held the bag close to her chest like a prized possession.

Damn... I still need to find a place to sleep tonight.

Chapter 2

Marissa's joy was short-lived. At night, she would search for some semblance of shelter until exhaustion took hold, and she was forced to sleep in whatever dark alleyway seemed the least dreary. She would pile wooden crates around the dumpster into a makeshift fort, but it was always futile. At least once per night, she would be jolted awake by the stomping hooves of the city guards' horses with the same tiresome declaration; that she couldn't stay there and needed to leave.

Where the hell else am I supposed to sleep?

Two days later, she had no money, no stable source of shelter, and very little energy. The consecutive nights of interrupted sleep seemed to compound on her fatigued body as she stumbled through the kingdom streets. She had reached the center of Brennan, where the majestic royal palace loomed over the immaculately trimmed gardens that sprawled in all directions. The buildings on the edges of the bordering district seemed minuscule by comparison. Marissa couldn't help but lift her weary head to admire the massive structure. *The spires really do seem to reach toward the clouds.* But her sense of wonder and magic had dried up with her souring mood, and all Marissa wanted was a decent night's sleep.

And food. Marissa had become accustomed to the everlasting pang of her hungry stomach. She was occasionally able to find a rat scuttling through the alleyways, but the kingdom was kept remarkably clean. The cobblestone streets felt a lot more sterile than the wild mess of the swamplands, and even in the alleyways where the shopkeepers' trash cans lurked, there were few signs of vermin.

The doughnuts were long gone, and the severe lack of rodent prey had forced Marissa to spend the remainder of her copper coin when the hunger pains became unbearable. Marissa clasped her stomach and plopped down on the rim of a decorative fountain. Once again, she was in dire need of food, but this time she had no way of paying for it.

The soft, tranquil sound of trickling water filled Marissa's ears. She spun around to face the fountain, which contained three tiers topped with a small, spouting geyser. Marissa peered around. She was in a new, unfamiliar part of Brennan; some sort of merchant's district, judging by the elaborate storefronts, and the streets were quiet. She made sure no one was looking before cupping her palms and dipping them into the base of the fountain.

The water was cool and refreshing as she took in deep gulps, but it did little to soothe her ravenous stomach. She quickly wiped her mouth and slipped her scarf back over her face. But she had noticed something sparkle at the bottom of the fountain when she scooped a handful of water. She peered back down, and her eyes nearly popped out of her skull.

The objects were blurred by the rippling water, but the familiar color and glint were unmistakable. Copper coins. At least a hundred of them scattered across the bottom of the fountain.

I don't understand ... people threw money in here ... for what purpose?

For someone as impoverished as Marissa, the concept of passersby tossing coins into a fountain was baffling. She shifted forward, her eyes locked on the glittering coins. *They're just sitting there...*

Marissa's head spun wildly around the square. *No one is looking... certainly, the owners of these coins didn't need them...*

With her eyes still darting around for onlookers, she stuck a shaking hand in the water and frantically fished around the bottom of the fountain. Her fingers curled around a handful of coins, and she jerked her hand back and shoved the wet bits of copper into her cloak pocket.

She exhaled a deep sigh of relief. *Now all I must do is find a nearby alley to count these coins, and...*

"HEY!"

Marissa's head shot up in the direction of the harsh shout. A pair of guards on horseback about fifty feet away at the edge of the square were pointing at her, their faces tense with disapproval and scorn. Marissa froze, blood souring in her veins. She bolted as soon as the guards' horses took a step toward her.

She fled at a wild pace; her legs pumping and her body flooding with adrenalin as the sound of stomping hooves leered in the distance. Marissa didn't dare look behind her, but she knew that they were getting closer. *I can't outrun a horse. Think like a snake. How would they escape a predator?*

Marissa didn't have the long, slender body of a true serpent, but she could still squeeze into places where a towering horse couldn't fit. She stopped, her squalid shoes scraping against the cobblestone, and dove down a gap between two buildings, barely a foot wide, too small to even be considered an alleyway. As she ran down the dark, narrow path, she heard the hoofbeats come to a stomping halt. She peered over her shoulder and saw the guards grimace and take off at a hard canter farther down the street.

The maneuver would only buy her so much time. All that the guards had to do was circle around the remainder of the block to reach the other side, and at the horses' swift pace, that wouldn't take very long. She emerged on the other side of the gap onto an unfamiliar street, and her head darted ferociously around the quiet road. No sign of the guards, but the faintest stomping of hooves against cobblestone echoed in the distance.

When snakes can't out-slither their prey, they hide.

With little time until the guards rounded the city block, Marissa dove up the stairs of the nearest lit storefront. The door swung open wildly on its hinges, a brassy bell at the top of the doorway rattling with a metallic chime. She shuddered, but luckily no one in the shop seemed to notice her. Out the store's wide display window, she saw the two guards sweep obliviously past as their horses slowed to a trot.

She took a deep breath and attempted to regain her composure. *I hope they give up. Certainly, they have better things to do than punish a vagrant for stealing a few coins from a fountain.*

She warily stepped away from the window, then she felt a hard thump against her back. Startled, she spun around and locked eyes with a tall, wiry man, easily a foot taller than her. He appeared to be in his early twenties, with light chestnut hair and a pair of thin glasses sitting atop the bridge of his nose. He wore a loose white shirt topped with a light brown vest and a long, chocolate-colored tailcoat jacket. Marissa shuddered, afraid he'd be irritated by her clumsiness. But he only smiled.

"My apologies. I wasn't looking where I was going." His voice was deep, yet soft. Marissa gulped, too afraid to speak. He was the first human to smile at her in a long time. "Anyway, welcome to The Menagerie. Are you looking for anything specific?"

The ... Menagerie? Marissa gazed past the man, and her eyes widened as she realized the contents of the store she'd walked into. The large room was littered with cages, tanks, and plush beds containing creatures that Marissa had only heard about in fairy tales. Cat-sized dragonlings, fluffy hatchling phoenixes, and fox kits with multiple bristling tails filled the store with a symphony of yelps, caws, and hisses. Marissa even noticed a three-headed dog lying beside the register, its six eyes casually flicking across the onlookers. She knew little of the lands beyond the Valley of Scales, but she hadn't realized the extent of their magic.

The man noticed the astounded wonder in her eyes, and he chuckled.

"They're beauties, aren't they? Anyway, feel free to browse. My name is Arthur. Let me know if you need anything."

Marissa nodded, not taking her eyes off the array of fantastical creatures. The man, Arthur, smiled and stepped out of the way, resuming his place behind the register.

Marissa wandered through the store, her eyes carefully scanning each enclosure. She jolted as something rustled behind her, and she spun around. A giant black-and-white lizard stomped toward the front of its enclosure, its clawed front feet scraping against the glass. Marissa's gaze darted upward, and she realized a group of bearded dragons was doing the same thing. They frantically pressed their bodies against the glass, wanting to get out.

Marissa took a step back. The back half of the store was full of reptiles, and she noticed the wall on her right had nine embedded tanks arranged in a three-by-three grid. Marissa realized that the tanks were full of snakes. And every single one, from the baby corn snakes to the heavy-bodied pythons, was sitting at the front of its tank, staring at her with intense gazes from their unblinking reptilian eyes.

They know.

"Wow, they're looking right at you," Arthur remarked. He was sitting by the register, his elbows propped on a spread-out newspaper. He seemed both amazed and ... concerned. *He knows something isn't right about their behavior. He's also probably wondering why my face is covered...*

"I... I have to go." Marissa stumbled backward, nearly bumping into a display case full of metal name tags. Arthur gave her a quizzical look, and Marissa's nerves fluttered. She took a deep breath and calmly but swiftly exited the shop without another word.

MARISSA SAT IN A QUIET ALLEYWAY, CLUTCHING A small bag of candied pecans in one hand and her four remaining copper coins in the other. The sweet, earthy nuts were pleasant, but Marissa missed the comfy richness of a hot meal. She couldn't spend more than one or two copper on a single meal, which limited her to snacks from bakeries and cart vendors scattered throughout the district. She closed her eyes and pressed the back of her head against the cool limestone bricks, her mind reminiscing on the home-cooked dinners that Beatrice used to make. Even when eaten alone in the damp confines of an old storehouse, they were a luxury that Marissa now sorely missed.

She'd been tucked away in the alley for several hours, only sneaking out to buy pecans from a vendor pushing a metallic cart down the cobblestone streets. They were only one copper per bag, and while they were filling, they left Marissa's stomach with a roiling discontentment. She considered scouring the rest of the alleyways for rats, but she was concerned that the guards who chased her down earlier would return. She didn't know how severe of a crime stealing coins from a fountain was, but she didn't want to find out.

The sky was darkening. Not only was it almost six o'clock, but murky gray clouds lurked in the distance, overtaking the hazy orange sunset and filling the air with the damp tension of incoming rain. *Sleeping in an alleyway isn't going to be an option tonight.* She needed to slip out into the streets and find some petty bit of shelter where the guards wouldn't harass her.

She tossed the pecan wrapper in a nearby trash can, carefully pocketed her remaining copper coin, and slipped into the narrow road behind the main storefront. As she walked, attempting to find a suitable place to sleep in the limestone jungle, her mind flicked back to The Menagerie. The kind shopkeeper's smile had made her lonely, dejected heart flutter, but what truly seared into her soul were the penetrating glances of every snake in the shop.

She had always known she had a connection with reptiles. As a child, she'd spend quiet afternoons hidden away from the other children, basking in the warm sun behind the storehouse with her dark scales absorbing the soothing heat. Occasionally she'd come across a stray corn snake or scrub lizard hiding in the brush, and against their natural instincts, they would go after Marissa like an attention-seeking puppy. But the incident that burned in her memory the brightest was the time she came across a huge cottonmouth coiled in the dirt.

Even though it was a venomous snake, one of the largest native to the Valley of Scales, Marissa felt nothing but peace as it slithered toward her. She studied its mottled black-and-brown scales and shiny copper eyes, mesmerized at how similar it looked to her. As it wound its body around her arms, its tongue flicking the inside of her wrist, Marissa realized she could *feel* the snake's contentment. Unlike the more humanoid reptilians, true reptiles were simple creatures, and Marissa could sense their faint yet palpable emotions.

CHAPTER 2

But the feelings she sensed from the horde of snakes in The Menagerie were far more powerful than anything she'd ever experienced. Their emotions had melded together into a tidal wave of staggering strength, echoing in Marissa's head until her temples began to throb. Though they weren't capable of complex thoughts, Marissa knew that, despite the limitations of their primal emotions, the snakes were trying to tell her something important.

Marissa couldn't decide if she was desperate to return or if she never wanted to visit the overwhelming shop again. *It is only a few blocks away... I could go there again tomorrow...*

She shook her head and huffed. *Enough about the pet store. Focus on finding shelter.*

As she stepped past the back door of a storefront, she gave it a second glance, and her eyes widened. It was unlocked, cracked open, so a tiny sliver of dim light crept through the slit. Marissa leaned toward the door, peering through the gap with a single eye. The main storefront was stripped of furniture, and the windows were clouded over with grime. It had clearly been abandoned for a long time.

Marissa took a deep breath and pressed her fingers against the door, pushing it with great hesitancy. The old hinges creaked loudly as the door swung open, but nothing else happened. No one popped out of the emptiness to chase her away. *Which means no one will mind if I sleep here tonight.*

She decided to settle upstairs in the cobwebby loft, as it was higher up and had fewer windows for passersby to notice her through. Not long after she settled in, the clouds finally erupted in a heavy pitter-patter of rain that pounded against the building. *Yet, I am safe.* Marissa closed her eyes as a soothing warmth washed over her. As a child in the leaky old storeroom, she'd never been completely sheltered during a storm.

For the first time since she left the orphanage, Marissa felt safe and comfortable enough to pull her one treasured possession out of her cloak pocket—an old paperback of her favorite book, *Nim's Forest.* The worn spine was splayed, and the pages yellowed, but its story was just as magical as when she was a child.

She sighed. *Tonight, is a good night*—she was fed, warm, and dry. But the rest of her copper coin would only last a day or two, and she didn't know how long she'd be able to sleep in the abandoned storefront until someone kicked her out. The worst part about being homeless was the insecurity, spending every day just trying to survive.

She shook the heavy existential thoughts out of her mind and focused on her book. But through her mental sorrow, she decided she was going to seek out every bit of happiness she could find. *And that means returning to The Menagerie tomorrow.*

Chapter 3

A FAINT CHIME ECHOED FROM AN ORNATE clock perched above the register. Arthur looked up from the newspaper sprawled across the counter and sighed. *Six o'clock.*

He knew he should've been paying more attention to the customers. He'd left much of the interactions to his cheery assistant, George, who was currently guiding a new bearded dragon owner through potential enclosures. Instead, Arthur had buried his attention in the day's newspaper. Specifically, the massive phrase blotted across the front page:

ROGUE NAGA HARASSES OUTER VILLAGES, BREAKS INTO HOMES.

He'd combed through the article several times over, anxiety mounting in his throat with every word. His blood chilled at the final sentence of the article:

> "In response to the recent ransacking in Vale, His Majesty King Gabriel III has dispatched a unit of his best-trained members of the royal guard to de-escalate the situation."

De-escalate. Arthur huffed. He was familiar enough with the royal guard to know how trigger-happy some of its members could be. While the guards were highly trained in calmly handling even the most difficult situations, Arthur knew that all went out the window when it came to dealing with the reptilians. To the royal guard, they were savage beasts, less than human, and the guard would gladly put a bullet through the Naga's chest to get the situation over with. And the worst part was that the entire kingdom would hail them as heroes for doing so.

Arthur sighed, folded the newspaper into a dense square, and shoved it in his breast pocket. He stood up and walked over to George, tapping him on the shoulder.

"It's time for me to head out," Arthur announced. George's customer was currently fawning over their new pet lizard, which gave Arthur a moment to speak with his assistant. "Are you all set?"

"I'll be fine. There's only two hours left, and I know how to close up shop."

"Excellent." Arthur smiled. George had been a frequent visitor to the shop for almost a year, and since he'd recently turned eighteen and wanted to be a herpetologist, Arthur hired him as his assistant. This was George's first time handling the shop alone, and Arthur had to calm his shaky nerves. The Menagerie was his life's work, his dearest treasure, but he knew that if he wanted to help that Naga, he would have to learn to trust the shop in his assistant's hands.

Besides, it was only two hours until closing, and the shop was quiet. Arthur brushed past the few browsing customers and pushed open the heavy front door, the crisp October breeze hitting him in the face as he exited. The Valley of Scales was a beautiful place, a dense swampland full of the world's most fascinating reptiles, but during the summertime, it was so hot and humid that the city streets felt like a sauna. Arthur had been looking forward to the cooler weather for months.

When Arthur was expected at the palace, his parents would send a royal carriage. Arthur wasn't a fan of such pompousness, but the shaded vehicle was always a relief from the sweltering streets. But this time, Arthur's presence would be a surprise, and now that the autumn breeze swept through the air, he preferred to travel on foot.

The sky was a brilliant, fiery blend of color as the sun melted over the tops of the limestone buildings that lined the streets. In the distance, a heavy cluster of gray clouds signaled that it would be a rainy night, but for now, the evening air was calm. The entire kingdom was cast in a hazy orange glow, which seemed to give the cheery shoppers and boisterous children that moved through the streets a magical aura. Arthur smiled as he walked past them and appreciated that they were oblivious to his presence. When he traveled by royal carriage, people tended to stare in awe, which always made Arthur uncomfortable.

But despite the beauty of the serene fall evening, the Naga's fate was heavy on his mind. Arthur knew nothing about him or why he was breaking into villages. But no one had been harmed, and as a herpetologist with a deep admiration of the reptilians, he couldn't just stand by while the royal guard hunted the snake down.

Arthur's love of reptiles was complicated by the fact that his father was King Gabriel's cousin, and even as a distant member of the royal family, he was expected to abide by their beliefs. And those beliefs had never included sympathy toward the Valley of Scales' natives. Despite growing up in the palace, he had been kicked out a year ago and stripped of his position as a royal herpetologist. He huffed. *My knowledge of reptiles is only relevant when it fits the king's needs.*

This arrangement wasn't all negative; he was able to start his dream business, and the ruddy old apartment above his shop was far more alluring than being under the royal family's nose. But it also meant that he couldn't keep up with their affairs—he wished he'd known about the Naga before the royal guard was dispatched. But either way, he knew he had an enormous challenge in front of him. Convincing the king to do *anything* was difficult; the most powerful man in the kingdom was generally too stubborn to heed the words of others. *But if it means resolving the situation peacefully and allowing that Naga to live, it's worth a try.*

Beyond his worries about the Naga, in the back of his mind, he thought about the strange girl that had wandered into his shop earlier that day. She was young and timid, and the lower half of her face was mysteriously covered by a black scarf. But what was even more perplexing was her effect on the snakes at the back of the shop. Arthur couldn't believe his eyes when every single one of them, regardless of age or species, slithered to the front of their tanks and stared at the girl like she was their leader. Arthur had spent many years around snakes, and their reaction to the girl's presence was far beyond the bounds of their natural behavior.

Arthur's eyes widened. *Is it possible she ... can communicate with them?*

He stopped. He's been so deep in thought, so lost in the recesses of his mind, that he hadn't realized that he'd reached the palace. The stiff-postured guards side-eyed Arthur as he stepped up the enormous flight of stairs that snaked up to the palace doors, but didn't say a word. Arthur took a deep, reassuring breath as the massive doors, nearly two stories high with each side containing a carved image of a prancing stallion, groaned open with a loud creak not unlike the city gates.

Maybe I'll see her again. He pondered hopefully as he paced through the glittering foyer, his shoes squeaking on the polished floors. He could hear the faint beginnings of rain pound against the colossal palace walls. *Maybe, if I don't scare her off ... I could talk to her.*

"Arthur?"

He spun around. In the cavernous hallway, a tall, wiry man with thinning chocolate hair and a thick mustache had his eyes locked on Arthur. In his arms was a towering stack of hardcover books, some several inches thick.

Arthur sighed.

"Hello, Father. Yes, I came for a visit."

"Well, you're a little late." The man set the heavy stack of books at his feet and stretched his tired arms. "We just finished up dinner. We were celebrating—as I told you in my letter, Ramsey just joined the royal guard. It's a shame you couldn't make it."

Arthur exhaled sharply, trying to hide his agitation. He didn't want to listen to his father prattle on about his perfect brother's latest achievement.

"I need to speak with the king," Arthur stated curtly.

His father's face dropped into a frown. "We haven't seen you in weeks. You don't show up to your brother's celebration dinner, and now you march in here demanding to see the monarch on a whim? I thought I raised my son better than that."

Arthur chewed his lower lip, his face burning red. *I probably should've at least shown up to Ramsey's dinner.* And even if Arthur had requested to speak with the king beforehand, he knew his ruling relative wouldn't have been pleased to see him. In fact, he may have made an extra effort to make himself unavailable.

"Look, Father, I'm sorry. I admit that I should've come to dinner. But this is urgent. Please, let me speak with him."

His father gave a long, heaving sigh. "You know as well as I do that Gabriel rarely takes unannounced visitors. I'll let him know you stopped by, but—"

"He's in the library, isn't he?" Arthur's eyes flicked down to the pile of books on the floor. "You're bringing him those books from the archives."

His father's mouth hung open, but he didn't respond. Arthur shook his head and briskly brushed past his father, heading down the hallway toward the royal library.

"Arthur! Arthur!!"

He ignored his father's indignant shouts and increased his hastened pace, nearly running toward the dark wooden doors at the end of the hall. He ignored the guards on either side of the immense structures and hauled them open himself.

As the heavy doors swung back with a slow groan and the quiet, dimly lit ambiance of the library came into view, Arthur took a deep breath. He knew that if he was going to visit the king unannounced, he needed to at least have a calm demeanor. The royal library was a serene place of knowledge, the greatest in all of Brennan, with bookshelves two stories high lined with thousands of titles on every possible subject. The room was dark, with a few heavily shaded glowstone lamps providing bits of shadowy light next to plush velvet reading chairs. And in one of them, tucked away in the back corner, King Gabriel sat with a wafting pipe clutched in his fingertips as he spoke to a dark figure seated across from him.

As Arthur got closer, he realized the figure was his brother Ramsey, dressed in a fine vest and jacket with his chin propped on his palm. He and the king caught a glimpse of Arthur's approach, and their conversations ceased mid-sentence. Their flat expressions contained traces of surprise and displeasure.

"Hello, Brother," Ramsey greeted dully. "We missed you at dinner tonight."

"Yes, I sincerely apologize. I've just been so busy with The Menagerie, I lost track of time." Arthur turned toward the king, suddenly remembering to bow. He did so in a quick fumbling motion, and the king gave a small nod. "Your Majesty, sir, I know my presence is sudden, but would I be able to have a moment with you tonight?"

The king raised an eyebrow, and his expression lightened.

"Certainly," he responded, much to Arthur's surprise and Ramsey's chagrin. "In fact, have a seat. Your brother and I were just discussing his decision to join the royal guard."

"Yes, congratulations." Arthur forced a smile as he perched himself in a nearby chair. It was simultaneously very dense and incredibly plush. His teeth gritted at the thought of having to have this conversation with his brother present, but he had to take advantage of the rare opportunity to speak with the king. "I'm sure Father is very pleased with you."

Ramsey opened his mouth, his brows furrowing at the subtle jibe, but Arthur quickly cut him off.

"So, Your Majesty, I wish to speak with you about the Naga that has been traveling through the outer villages."

"Ah, of course. I knew it was only a matter of time until you came marching down here to voice your opinion on the matter." The king's voice was low. "And that Naga has been breaking into and ransacking homes, terrifying our people. I wouldn't call that 'traveling.'"

"Yes, you are right," Arthur agreed. He knew he needed to put his sympathies for the reptilians aside and handle the conversation with more poise. "It's wrong for that Naga to be scaring the villagers. But Your Majesty, the Naga hasn't harmed anyone, and dispatching the royal guard is only going to escalate the situation."

The king frowned. "So, what do you suggest we do? Ignore the Naga while it gathers up a small army and continues causing trouble? You say it hasn't harmed anyone yet, but what happens when it does? What happens when someone dies? I know you have an inexplicable love of those beasts, but you need to have some common sense."

Arthur's face fell as the king's painful yet true words rang through his head and rattled his conviction.

"Let me find the Naga and persuade him to back down without violence."

"Persuade?" the king huffed. "And you are aware that they can't speak?"

"Yes," Arthur sighed. "Somehow, I'll find a way to communicate. Please, Your Majesty, let me do this. There's no downside for you. If I am unsuccessful, let your guards do what they need to do. But if I can persuade the Naga to return to its territory, we can end this without risking a war."

The king took a long draw from his pipe, his eyes narrowing. Arthur tried not to gag as a plume of wispy smoke wafted in his direction.

"I understand the logic of your proposal, but those reptilians cannot be reasoned with, and I will not ignore conflict for the sake of keeping peace. My men will track down that Naga and put an end to this, and you are not to intervene."

"But Your Majest—"

"No, Arthur. My word is final."

Arthur's shoulders dropped. He knew that getting into an argument with the king would only further cement his family's irritation with him. Ultimately, the king was the sovereign, the sole ruler of Brennan, and Arthur was powerless to change his mind. Arthur's eyes flicked over to Ramsey, who had a deep frown buried behind his palm. *And, of course, my pretentious older brother is watching me fail. He's definitely going to tell our parents about this.*

"Very well." Arthur kept his face firm, refusing to show disappointment or anger. "Thank you for your time, Your Majesty. I wish you both a pleasant evening."

As Arthur left the library, venturing down the towering hallway and out the palace doors into the crisp autumn air, he felt an overwhelming sense of apprehension. He knew that obtaining the king's permission to track the Naga down would be difficult, but he was still surprised that the king hadn't heeded his request. *We should try to resolve this without violence. Why must the king always escalate things?*

He wandered down the mountain of steps toward the palace gardens, the air damp with the remnants of rain. Beyond the sprawling, immaculately trimmed landscape, the glowing lights of the encircling districts glittered like a sea of yellow stars. He had a backup plan, but it came with far greater risk.

I'm still going to track down that Naga. I just need to reach him before the royal guard does.

ARTHUR WAS PERCHED ON THE EDGE OF HIS BED, dressed in silk pajamas with one of his juvenile boa constrictors coiled in his lap. It was nearly midnight, and he was too anxious to sleep. Instead, he peered out the window at the dark limestone buildings framed by an indigo sky, rubbing his palm over the smooth scales of his nearly six-foot-long pet snake.

His mind was made up; he was going to track down the Naga. He'd already written to a longtime friend in the outer villages, packed a week's worth of essentials, and plotted out his journey on an old parchment map. With or without the king's permission, he had a hefty mission in front of him. *Maybe impossible,* he worried. He'd have to track down an elusive Naga and its band of Varan, and once he did, he'd have to find a way to communicate with the silent creatures. Many humans in the kingdom believed they were too unintelligent for language, and even if Arthur could convey his message, he had no idea how the Naga would react. If the snake was breaking into homes, even without violence, it probably wasn't friendly. And despite Arthur's love of reptiles and years of study, he was still a human, and reptilians hated humans.

Just like how humans hate reptilians. Arthur sighed. The worst part was that as much as he wanted to pack up and venture toward the outer villages in the morning, he still had to run The Menagerie. He'd stopped by George's apartment on the way home, and his assistant said that he would be happy to mind the shop for a few days, but tomorrow he was going to visit his ill father and wouldn't be able to start until the day after.

Arthur was frustrated, but he decided not to push the matter. As much as he needed to find the Naga before the royal guard did, The Menagerie was still his responsibility, and he had to tend to his collection. He knew he'd be on edge the entire day, but at least there was one perk of spending one last day at the shop. *The snake girl.* As he lay down on the bed and closed his eyes, he couldn't keep her out of his mind.

It's a long shot, but I hope she visits tomorrow.

ONE WEEK EARLIER

*T*HE WHOLE VILLAGE WAS SOLEMN.

The Naga could feel the sadness and tension in the air as he slithered up to the Varan guards. Typically, he wouldn't be welcome in Varan territory, especially the capital city of Komodo, but this time he had been summoned by the chieftain himself. The Naga had been escorted by two of the lizardfolk, and the guards greeted them with a firm nod and stepped aside.

Down a soft sand path, a few hundred feet away, the sprawling huts of Komodo came into view. They were small structures, their frames made from cypress logs and the edges of their palmetto thatch roofs rustled in the gentle breeze. On a typical evening, the community would be bursting with activity. But now, it was nearly deserted. Fresh animal carcasses were piled next to the remnants of smoldering fires, and colorful, woven-grass baskets were scattered outside the huts. Everyone had gathered at the towering pyramid-shaped temple in the center of the city for the funeral.

Although Varan typically buried their dead, the girl's remains had been cremated and placed in an elaborate woven urn in the center of the temple. It was raised several feet up on a platform surrounded by the carved circular symbol of the reptilian god Sauria, a snake biting its own tail. The outer edge of the symbol was lined in ancient reptilian—a series of hieroglyphs depicting the journey through reincarnation. The girl's family had decided on cremation because her killer had stripped her body of her scales.

The Naga stood silently in the corner of the temple, his clawed hands clasped together. As the Varan chieftain sang reptilian prayers that echoed through the minds of the funeral goers, the Naga closed his eyes and lifted his head to the ceiling.

Oh, great Sauria... he whispered. *Please be with her. Please guide her through the great lands of Reptilia, far beyond this life and into a new one.*

The Naga knew that this funeral was especially painful. Not only was the daughter of the Varan chieftain murdered by a poacher, but the loving father feared that his child would be unable to reincarnate without her scales.

CHAPTER 4

After the ceremony, one of the guards pulled the Naga aside.

<Follow me.>

Behind the temple was another palm hut, much larger than the others, decorated with vibrant flowers and strands of carved shell beads. The chieftess was too distraught to speak—her wails could be heard across the entire abode. The chieftain stood, patting his sobbing mate on the shoulder, and managed to calm himself enough to pull the Naga aside for a conversation.

<Don't listen to them,> the Naga remarked, gesturing toward the temple. <Scales or no scales. We are reptilians to the very depths of our souls. Your beautiful daughter will be born again. I am certain.>

The chieftain smiled sadly, appreciative of his words, <Thank you, Ezrinth. It is good to see you again.>

<The pleasure is also mine, Rathi. I give you my deepest sympathies.>

<Please, let's go out to the gardens and have a seat. We have much to discuss.>

They ventured outside. Beyond the palace was a sprawling landscape of swampland, crowned with clusters of shrubby trees and patches of tall, thick reeds interspersed with shallow ponds. The water's calm surface stood dark and glossy, highly reflective, like a mirror. It was still and serene, framed by the melting sun slipping over the horizon.

<I know when you first came here, I turned you away, and for that, I do apologize. I always thought vengeance

was a foolish, hateful ploy.> Rathi sighed. <But that was before I lost my only child. My dear Mikara ... it feels like she was just here yesterday. I can't believe I will never see her again. She was so young... she'd only just turned eighteen...>

Ezrinth sighed. *Eighteen years old. They're the same age.* He placed a hand on Rathi's shoulder, patiently waiting for him to regain composure.

<My apologies.> Rathi cleared his throat. <I appreciate your attendance at the funeral, but as you know, there is a reason why I summoned you here today. I know we've always been ... wary of you, Ezrinth. We must respect Orami and the Naga.>

Ezrinth's body tightened at the mention of his father.

<But I cannot stand by while the humans continue to kill reptilians. As of tonight, we are with you, Ezrinth. We will join your cause. Let us reclaim Squamata once and for all.>

Ezrinth smiled, exhaling with relief. He felt overjoyed and honored at the chieftain's decision. Behind them, a small band of Varan warriors, clad in simple yet colorful regalia, marched up to the gardens. They stopped curtly in front of Ezrinth and offered a deep bow of solidarity.

<I will fight,> Ezrinth declared. "For all of us. Let us reptilians finally unite and prevail above the humans. But first...> he looked over at Rathi, and back at the Varan. <Dear warriors, I have another mission to

complete. There is someone I must find, and I need your help.>

A LOUD, BOOMING CHIME ECHOED FROM THE large antique cuckoo clock that the previous tenants had inexplicably left behind. Its alarm rattled through the upper floor of the abandoned storefront, where Marissa sat cross-legged next to a tiny fire smoldering inside the brick fireplace, munching on a roasted rat. *Seven o'clock.* The ornate timepiece, nearly as tall as Marissa and too heavy to easily move, was the only piece of furniture in the grubby room. A few small windows let in beams of soft, warm light that illuminated the thick layer of dust coating the aging hardwood floors. It was old, bare, and dirty, but for Marissa, it was a secure place to stay hidden.

She had spent much of the morning and evening in the empty room, mainly catching up on sleep. The dust-coated floors weren't as soft and inviting as an actual bed, but they were still an improvement over the rough, cold alleyways. *At least here, the guards can't chase me away.*

But once the clock struck noon and Marissa had recovered from her many nights of subpar sleep, her stomach began to rumble. She only had four copper coins left, but a bold yet treacherous idea popped into her head. *What if I venture back to the church district and find that bakery again?* It was a substantial walk through the most crowded parts of Brennan, but if the generous woman was at the register, maybe she would offer Marissa some extra sweets.

Marissa decided it was worth the risk and made the long trip back to the bakery. But upon arrival, she was disappointed to find that the kindly woman had been replaced by a sour-faced, elderly man that took one look at her dirty clothes and threw her out of the shop.

She bit back the urge to curse at the man as the door slammed behind her. It was nearly two in the afternoon, and her hungry stomach was now throwing a rumbling temper tantrum. She grumbled, reluctantly spent two of her copper at a nearby pretzel cart, and stomped her way back to her makeshift home in the merchant's district.

When she was nearly home, she managed to catch a glimpse of a rat scurrying down an alleyway, and she bolted after the creature, gaining ground on the frightened rodent until she was able to deliver her finishing blow of venom. She grinned as she held up her catch by its naked pink tail, her chest pounding from the adrenalin rush of the hunt. Her head darted around as she made sure no one had noticed her strange behavior, and she discreetly hid the rodent in her cloak pocket.

She'd managed to find some matches in a downstairs closet and some dry twigs dropped by the manicured trees that lined the cobblestone sidewalk. Marissa was hesitant to use the ash-coated old fireplace, but she didn't want to risk being caught cooking her meal outside. *A normal human won't react well to a vagrant roasting a rat over a fire.*

But it was now seven o'clock, and Marissa had one hour until The Menagerie closed. She wanted to wait until late in the evening to return to the store, as there would be far fewer visitors. She peered out the musty window. The sun had disappeared, and the deep indigo of the night was setting in. The streets were mostly empty. She picked the last of her meal off its spindly bones, patted an old rag over the warm embers until their reddish glow faded, and dove downstairs to the back door.

The hazy cobblestone streets of the merchant's district glowed a bright orange under the bulbous lamps that lined the road. It was quiet, except for the occasional clip-clop of a distant carriage or the soft footsteps of a lone traveler. Marissa passed by many unique shops and inns, all filled with whimsy and charm. She'd seen wealthy patrons visit during the day, collecting whatever baubles they fancied, but nearly all the shops were closed now that the sun was down. She only had a few blocks to cover, and it was a quick journey.

As Marissa approached The Menagerie, she admired the little shop's display window. A young dragonling, too small to even fly, was fast asleep on a soft pillow. It seemed oblivious to the constant caws of the brilliantly plumed phoenix on a perch not even a foot away.

An anxious voice crept into her head. *Are you sure you want to do this?*

Her entire life, the isolating instinct to avoid human contact had been drilled into her mind. It was such a major part of her psyche that even passing by pedestrians on the city streets put her nerves on edge. She knew the shopkeep's innocent smile the day before was dangerous. *Don't get too comfortable. Be polite, but distant. He can't know who, or what, you really are.*

The brassy bell chimed at the top of the doorframe, and the large three-headed dog boisterously bounded its way up to the front of the shop. It greeted Marissa eagerly, the stub of a tail wagging, all three heads panting in excitement. Its barking riled up the other animals, and the shop became a rattling cacophony of activity.

Marissa yelped, stumbling backward, away from the overenthusiastic animal. She'd never spent much time around the large, hairy creatures, and her snake instincts caused her to recoil at the dog's friendly greeting.

"Aurora!" a voice snapped from the register. Arthur whistled, and the energetic dog trotted back toward its owner. "Sorry about that. We haven't had many visitors today, so she got a bit overexcited. She thinks she's a puppy even though she's over a hundred pounds."

Arthur strolled closer, and his eyes lit up with recognition, which made Marissa shiver.

"Well, look who it is," he greeted cheerily. "You were here yesterday, weren't you? You were the one looking at the snakes."

Marissa didn't respond, her reptilian blood chilling in her veins. She wasn't sure if Arthur would recognize her from the day before, but he seemed to remember her a little too well. Her eyes flicked to the far side of the shop, where she could see the snakes on the back wall beginning to congregate at the front of their tanks.

"They seemed to really like you. Would you be interested in holding one?"

Marissa's eyes widened as she pressed her scarf tighter against her nose and mouth. Her reptilian half longed to interact with the creatures that she felt such a deep connection to. And while she feared Arthur would become suspicious, she also wanted to decipher the strong emotions she'd felt emanating from them the day before.

"Yes." Her voice was soft as she tried to hide her anxiety.

"Excellent. Right this way." Arthur led her to the back of the shop. "While I currently own The Menagerie, I'm also a herpetologist. So while my shop carries all sorts of animals, reptiles are my real specialty. We have many species here; some are imports, and others are from local breeders."

As they approached the snake enclosures, strange, foreign emotions began to rattle in Marissa's mind. Every snake had its eyes locked on her; their faces were deeply focused, as if they were trying their hardest to communicate. The emotions were stronger than the day before, and this time, they all melded into one clear expression, a forewarning that something major was about to change. But with the limitations of snake emotion, Marissa wasn't sure what that meant.

"Unbelievable," Arthur remarked, his voice an astonished whisper. "They look like they're trying to communicate with you. Can you ... actually hear them?"

Marissa was quiet as she gazed, mesmerized, at the many pairs of reptilian eyes fixated on her. She didn't want to answer, as she knew Arthur would be in disbelief at her response. *He already knows I'm not normal. I can't give too much more away.*

"In fact, I'm curious about something," Arthur interrupted. "Come here for a moment."

Anxiety fluttered in Marissa's stomach. She was unsure of how to react, as she was wary of surprises. But her nerves melted as Arthur approached a large tank on the far-right side of the wall. Inside was a vibrantly colored snake, its scales in a swirling yellow-and-black pattern that reminded Marissa of a bumblebee. It sat unmoving at the front of its tank, its deep black eyes glittering like shining onyxes. Its forked tongue outstretched as they approached.

"It's a jungle carpet python," Arthur explained. "He just shipped in from the southern part of the valley, near Naga territory. Gorgeous little serpent, but the thing's got an attitude like a demon. Bites any hand that comes near it. But you seem to have a way with snakes that I've never seen before. Would you like to give it a try?"

Marissa hesitated for a moment, then nodded.

The heavy glass door slid sideways, and the snake descended from the tank. Its soft black eyes met Marissa's, and she felt as if they were windows to its soul. It gazed at

CHAPTER 4

Marissa knowingly, like an old friend, as it slithered up her outstretched arm and settled in a coil around her neck.

"Incredible," Arthur whispered in awe before shaking his head. "All of my years of study, learning all I could about reptiles ... and I am bested by a teenage snake whisperer."

"Excuse me," Marissa huffed. "I am eighteen years old. I am not a child."

"Really?" Arthur tilted his head back, his eyebrow raised. "You look awfully young. I would've guessed no more than fifteen."

Marissa shrugged and rubbed the snake's smooth head with her finger. A soothing shiver ran down her spine as its tongue flicked against her wrist. *Nothing in the world is more calming than holding a snake.* Their heartbeats seemed to meld into one, and they breathed in unison. They shared a bond without words, a kinship between two serpents of different worlds.

Yet, this snake was different from the others. The soft emotions that radiated from the scaled creature weren't an eerie warning; they were a powerful expression of happiness. This snake was thrilled to be in her presence, as if their meeting were fate. Marissa felt a deep tug of longing in her heart as the little python caused her emotions to spiral, unlike any other snake she'd ever met.

"If you don't mind me asking," Arthur remarked as he closed the python's tank. "Do you have any pets?"

Marissa shook her head.

"Interesting, considering the effect you have on them. Would you consider purchasing this carpet python? He'd make a lovely companion for someone as skilled with snakes as you are."

The idea set off a happy spark in Marissa's heart. With her years spent alone and away from humans, she had become terribly lonely. This shop, with its a-bit-too-friendly owner and variety of scaled creatures, was the most social interaction she'd had in a long time. *A snake companion would be delightful.*

She felt the copper coins in her pocket, or lack thereof, and grimaced with realization.

"How much is he?"

"For you, I'll do a discount," Arthur chuckled. "Most customers prefer that their snakes not be biters, so he's a hard sell. But he is quite a difficult species to acquire in the kingdom, so let's say ... two gold? I'll even throw in some fresh rats."

Gold!? Marissa's heart sank. She'd never even seen a gold coin.

"I appreciate the offer." Marissa sighed as she unwound the snake from her neck. "But I'm afraid he's a little out of my price range. He's lovely though."

"Very well." Arthur gestured for Marissa to place the snake back into the enclosure. There was an awkward stillness in the air as Arthur slid the tank's glass doors shut. He looked up, and his eyes met hers. They were a soft shade of green and reminded Marissa of a dense forest.

"Listen."" He scratched his head. "I haven't had much business tonight, so..." He paused. "What do you say I close a little early and we head to the nearby inn? They have a fantastic meatloaf, though I'm also quite a fan of their fried fish..."

He backtracked when he saw Marissa's eyes widen. "Look, I'm sorry if that was sudden... I just want the chance to talk, if you'd like. I've never seen the snakes so drawn to someone. I'd love to learn more about you. I'll even cover dinner."

Marissa took a step backward. She'd never felt such an intense mixture of fear and excitement. *Dinner with another human, one who wants to talk to me...*

Don't do it. If he finds out, you're dead.

"I... I can't." Marissa stumbled toward the door. "But I appreciate the offer. It was nice to see you again. I... I should go."

Marissa's foot lurched under her weight as she nearly tripped over Aurora. Her muscles quaked with sadness and fear as she watched Arthur's face fall. Without another word, she darted out the front door, the loud metallic doorbell clattering as she slipped away. She didn't want to wait around for Arthur's disappointed response.

MARISSA STOMPED HER WAY BACK TO THE ABANdoned storefront, her head down and her hands shoved deep in her cloak pockets. The sickening burn of regret surged through her body and threw her brain into despair.

This was a bad idea. I never should've gone back to that shop. I never should've held that snake. I never should've interacted with Arthur. I never should've...

Her mind pounded insult after insult into her body like a hammer hitting a nail and dumped the remainder of her meager self-esteem out of her subconscious. She tore open the back door of the storefront with such force that it bounced off the wall with a loud thud. Once it was firmly shut behind her, she bolted upstairs, tossed herself in the corner, and hugged her knees to her chest.

But she refused to cry. A lifetime as an outcast half-Naga had shriveled up that instinct.

She lifted her sorrowful head and peered around. The fireplace was still warm, but her dinner had been reduced to bones and she'd already read her book several times over. *What am I supposed to do with myself?*

Marissa had been stuck in a survival mentality since she'd left the orphanage. She slept in a filthy, abandoned storefront, scrounged up what sparse change she could, and hunted for rats in alleyways. She was determined to be content with her meager life, as she had no means to change it. But visiting The Menagerie awoke a deep longing inside her, one that she couldn't turn off. For the first time in her life, she began to wonder if this would be all she ever knew or if she'd ever have the opportunity to do more with her life than just struggle to exist.

CHAPTER 4

I want to do something with myself other than scrape by, hidden away from the world. I want...

The back door creaked open, and the sound of heavy boots against wood stomped across the downstairs. Marissa's blood ran icy in her veins. The building had been abandoned for quite some time, considering the height of the dust layer caking every surface in sight. *Why is someone here?*

"So, as you can see." A deep voice flowed up the stairs. Marissa shuddered as she recognized the sound of not one, but three pairs of shoes jostling up the old wooden steps. "It needs some work, but it's a prime location in Augustree. This street is quite busy in the daytime. I'm renting it out for a very fair rate, and..."

Marissa's head spun around the room in a frenzy. *I need to hide, somewhere, anywhere.*

She only had a few seconds before the strangers reached the top of the stairs. The room was bare and dusty, with no boxes or furniture to hide behind. She scrambled for a closet door but realized it was locked. She frantically shook the handle, her wild eyes locked on the staircase. *This is the only other room upstairs, and it's bolted shut. I'm trapped...*

Just as three figures peeked up from the stairs, Marissa dove behind the only object in the room; the giant cuckoo clock. It was too thin to fully shield her from view, so Marissa hugged her knees together and prayed they wouldn't look in her direction.

Her eyes snapped open. *Wait a minute, my belongin—*

"What is this?" A man in a dark brown suit plucked Marissa's yellowed book and rusted dagger off the dusty floor. The gray-haired landlord was in the opposite corner, speaking to a well-dressed lady with a fur scarf around her neck. As the man spoke, the landlord stopped prattling on about his property and spun around.

The three of them gathered around Marissa's meager belongings, which she had left exposed next to the fireplace. Marissa's body quaked as the man held his palm over the ashy remains of her fire. *He's realizing it's still warm...*

"SQUATTER!"

Marissa jolted as the woman's eyes fell on her half-exposed body, tucked away in a shadowy corner of the room. She didn't wait around for the others to notice—she scrambled down the stairs before anyone had time to react.

Hurried, thumping footsteps trailed after Marissa as she threw the back door open and made a hard turn down the street. She wove between city blocks, trying to throw the landlord and his guests off her trail. Once she felt she'd put enough distance between them, she tucked herself into an alleyway, took a few heaving breaths, and kept a sharp eye out for the angry trio.

They never appeared. Marissa heard faint shouts from around the corner, but it was well after dark, and the landlord was an older man. He likely didn't have the stamina or patience to go chasing after a flighty teenager. Marissa stepped out of the alleyway and into the inky black night.

Now what? The landlord is certainly going to lock the door behind him. I've lost my belongings, and I'll have to find another place to sleep...

She wandered aimlessly down the empty streets until she came across The Menagerie's familiar sign, though the shop's broad windows were dark and devoid of activity. Marissa slumped onto the stoop in front of the door, burying her face in her palms. *No money, no place to live, no one to talk to...*

"Oh, you again?"

The door creaked open, and Marissa's head spun around. Arthur stood in the doorway, appearing to be confused by the somber woman blocking his path.

"What're you doing out here? Bad night?" he asked.

Marissa's weary eyes lowered, but she did not respond.

"You're a mystery, I'll say that much." Arthur clicked the door shut behind him. "But my offer still stands. I'm headed to the inn for some food, and you're welcome to join. I imagine you don't want to stay out here on my front stoop all night."

Marissa locked eyes with him. The warm, longing spark that burst through her heart when he first asked her to dinner returned. She exhaled deeply and decided to put her hesitancies aside. *When I said no, all I felt was regret... what more do I have to lose?*

"You're right. I'll come with you if you don't mind."

"Excellent," Arthur's enthusiastic tone made Marissa smile. "Let me just lock the door and we'll be off."

Chapter 5

THE BLUE BIRCH INN WAS A SMALL, QUAINT establishment located on the edge of the merchant's district. It bordered a series of tall limestone buildings full of towering machinery that loomed like silent titans in the dark night air. The faint scent of metal and smoke filled Marissa's nostrils as they strolled down the quiet cobblestone streets.

"So, are you from Brennan?" Arthur asked.

Marissa was startled by his sudden question. He'd been quiet the entire walk, which was fine with Marissa. With her isolated upbringing, she'd never been a conversationalist, and while she longed for companionship, she feared revealing too much about herself.

"Not really," she responded. "I grew up in the outer villages. I only recently came to Brennan. I don't really know my way around."

"Well, the kingdom is made up of four districts—there's Augustree, the merchant's district, where The Menagerie is located. And right now, we're on the border of Everwind, the industrial district, where all the factories are. And to the south is Alistar, the church district, and to the west is Silverkeep, the residential district. And in the middle of it all is the royal palace."

"It's fascinating," Marissa remarked, as Arthur pulled the inn's front door open and ushered her inside. "Very different from where I grew up."

The dimly lit dining room was full of weary blacksmiths and carpenters looking to wash down a long day's work with a few bottles of mead. Marissa's nose was overwhelmed by the greasy, intoxicating smell of human food as they stepped into the inn. *It all smells so good... but I can't eat any of it without removing my scarf.*

"Feel free to seat yourself." The barkeep gestured toward a nearby dining table with a grayed cleaning rag. "The hostess will come by and take your order shortly."

As the pair sat in the corner of the dining room, away from the banter of the bar, Marissa studied the menu in front of her. It was printed on thick parchment in dark inky lettering, perhaps the work of one of the nearby printing presses.

This place is nice... a little too nice for a half-Naga street urchin.

She shook the self-deprecating thoughts out of her head and peered over at Arthur. He looked up from his menu and smiled.

"You can remove your cloak, you know. We're inside." He gestured to his own coat and scarf draped over the back of his chair.

Marissa's body stiffened in her seat. "I'm fine, thank you."

"Very well. It seems that the hostess is quite busy in the back, so I imagine it will take some time to order." He rested his elbows on the table and leaned forward. "So, tell me a bit more about yourself. Could we start with your name?"

Marissa's brain twisted over itself with worry. *It's just your name. You have a human name. It's harmless to tell him. But what if...*

"Marissa. My name is Marissa."

Arthur smiled. "Marissa. That is a lovely name. So where are you from?"

Marissa shifted in her seat. *Is this how the night is going to go? Him asking for every detail of my past? I'm bound to slip up. He'll realize something doesn't make sense, and...*

Arthur's forest green eyes gazed curiously into hers, waiting for a response.

You're so kind. I wish I could talk to you. I hate this. Why can't I just be normal for once in my life?

Marissa cleared her throat. "Well, Arthur, why don't we start with you? Aren't you the reptile expert? I want to hear more about your history."

He chuckled, the stem of his empty water glass twisting in his fingers. Marissa knew Arthur had caught on to her dodging his questions, but he didn't seem to take issue with talking about himself.

"Alrighty then. Well … I am twenty-three years old, grew up here in Brennan, and I've loved animals, especially reptiles, ever since I was a child. My father hated the beasts, but I spent much time around stables and local menageries. I will never forget the look on my father's face when I brought home a ball python."

Marissa smiled behind her scarf. "Your first pet was a snake?"

"It was entirely accidental," he continued. "His name was Oliver. He was for sale at a menagerie right here in Augustree, and he was discounted for having a kinked tail. I fell in love with him, and I was a rather impulsive child. It took my entire month's allowance, but I walked out of there with my newfound friend as the happiest kid in the world. But alas, my father made me return him the next day."

"So that started your reptile-keeping?"

"Indeed, much to my father's disdain. He wanted me to be a librarian like him. I do love books… but I wanted to travel. Explore. I wanted to traverse the entire Valley of Scales and become the greatest herpetologist in Brennan. I especially wanted to learn more about the reptilians. We know so little about their society. Maybe I'd even figure out a way to communicate with them."

The reptilians. Marissa's posture softened. The Valley of Scales was a mysterious and beautiful place, a tangled web of dense forest and swampland, and the reptilians were its original inhabitants. There were four species: the snakefolk, Naga, the lizardfolk, Varan, the gatorfolk, Gharian, and the tortoisefolk, Testudo. Their territories bordered the central kingdom of Brennan, which the humans had founded eight hundred years ago.

"So... did you do it? Did you travel and visit the reptilians?"

Before Arthur could answer, the hostess walked up to the table and asked what they'd like.

"Hmm ... actually, I'll have a mead. Your orange one, please. And for my meal I'll take the fried grouper," Arthur turned toward Marissa. "What would you like?"

Marissa's eyes flicked from Arthur up to the hostess.

"Um ... I'm fine, thank you."

"Are you sure?" Arthur seemed confused, gesturing to the hostess that they would need a moment. She nodded and returned to the kitchen.

"I... I already ate."

Not technically a lie.

"How about a drink, then? That orange mead I ordered is fantastic."

Marissa froze. Arthur's eyes widened with realization.

"I'm sorry ... I didn't mean that. Look ... if you don't want to drink, it's fine. I have no ill intentions, I swear. I'm just ... confused. You've given me your name, but you won't say another word about yourself, and you're still hiding behind that cloak and scarf."

Silence. Marissa's heart sank.

"You don't want to see what I look like."

She cursed herself as soon as the words escaped her mouth. *You idiot! Why would you say such a thing!? This is why you don't interact with humans, you fool!*

Arthur looked bewildered. "Look, is it scarring? Burns? I really don't care what you look like, Marissa. I just wished to chat and have a nice meal, but if..."

His words dulled, becoming blurred whispers in Marissa's reptilian ears. Beyond their table, near the bar, her suspicions roused. She had picked up on a faint conversation between two burly patrons who kept eyeing their table.

"That man over there ... that's him, isn't it? I say you go confront him!"

That man... they're pointing at Arthur. What do they want with him? This could be bad...

"But back to my point," Arthur continued as Marissa's attention snapped back to him. "I mean it when I say I won't judge. People find me a bit odd too. We're all human beings, deserving of respect and kindness."

Marissa frowned. *But I'm not human. Not entirely.*

A large hairy hand clasped the edge of the table. Marissa looked up and saw a sour face with a crooked nose and bushy beard. Sweat beaded across the man's forehead. *He's one of the patrons at the bar, the one who wanted to confront Arthur.* Marissa gulped.

"You... you're that pet swindler out in Augustree."

Arthur calmly lifted his head, refusing to be intimidated.

"I am the owner of The Menagerie, but I am certainly no swindler. In fact, I recognize you. Didn't I sell you one of my dear Aurora's pups a few weeks ago?"

"Indeed," the man grumbled. "Damn dog ran away last week. I thought those beasts were supposed to be loyal!"

"Well, how did it manage to run away?"

"I went outside and found an empty chain and a broken collar. Stupid mutt jumped the fence and everything. I want a refund, you crook."

Arthur gave a long, heaving sigh of exasperation. "Cerberus puppies are highly intelligent and very loyal to their owners. They generally don't take well to being chained in a yard. Dogs belong inside, good sir. Now, there will be no refunds given, and I politely ask that you leave me and my companion alone."

The man's voice lowered into a threatening tone. "I'm not going anywhere."

Marissa's snake-like reflexes took over, and she dove in front of the man just before he could land a punch to Arthur's face. His burly arms shoved her, and she collapsed to the ground, her fangs banging against the hardwood floor. The man's large, heavy boots stomped around near her head, making it difficult for her to stand up. She was partway underneath the table, and she could hear the man's irritated shouts, Arthur's calm defiance, and the angry barkeep yelling at them to cut it out.

Marissa placed a hand over her mouth and recoiled in horror as she felt her bare lips and nostrils. The man had yanked off her scarf when she dove for him, and it was now clasped in his angry fist.

"And you!!" That fist swiped under the table and grabbed Marissa by the collar of her cloak. As the large man pulled her above the table, her hood slid over her back, further revealing her half-Naga form.

"How dare you get in my way, little girl! Who do you think you—"

As soon as he locked eyes with her, they both froze in horror. Marissa's blood curdled like Naga venom, and the man tossed her cloak collar and scarf out of his fist like it was on fire.

"REPTILIAN!!!"

Marissa panicked as she once again fell to the floor. She lifted her head and saw Arthur's face above the table, staring at her in shock. The unruly man's panic alerted the rest of the bar patrons, and soon everyone stared in terror at the snake girl.

"REPTILIAN!!! MONSTER!!! GET IT OUT OF HERE!!!"

She was frozen in horror, with so much panic pounding through her veins that the frantic scene appeared surreal. Her worst nightmare was unfolding in front of her. An entire bar full of humans, petrified by the mere sight of her face, and the one person she was just beginning to trust, now knew what she really was.

What was I thinking? Venturing into the kingdom, thinking I could exist among normal humans... how long could it really have lasted? This was all inevitable... I don't belong here... I don't belong anywhere...

Marissa felt a sharp tug on her scaled bicep and nearly screamed. She jerked her arm back, fearing that some disgusted human was itching to punish the half-reptilian that dared to enter their society... until she looked up and realized it was Arthur. As he pulled her out from under the table, she could see the panic on his face, but no disgust. They locked eyes for a moment, and Marissa saw Arthur's forest green ones widen in a mixture of surprise and fascination.

The screams shook them both out of their stunned state. Marissa peered around and noticed that many of the patrons had retreated upstairs, while several others were stomping toward them. *We need to get out of here, now.*

Arthur tossed a few coins at the hostess before bolting out of the inn with his hand still clasped around Marissa's arm. He didn't let go until they were back at The Menagerie's door.

As soon as Arthur loosened his grip on her arm, Marissa bolted. She ran as fast as her scaled legs would take her, half-delirious with shock and fear, desperate to get as far away from Augustree as possible.

CHAPTER 5

It's okay, it's okay. I'll just leave Brennan. I'll go back to the outer villages, where I'll be far away from everyone, and...

"Wait!!!" a faint shout echoed after her.

Is ... Arthur following me?

"I'm not going to hurt you! Please stop running!"

Marissa heard his footsteps slow as he panted. She stopped, sighed, and turned around. Arthur was about ten feet behind her, his palms on his knees as he caught his breath.

"My goodness, you're fast." He looked up with an awkward grin. "You know, I was serious when I said I didn't care what you looked like. What exactly are you, anyway?"

Marissa lowered her scarf, revealing two serpentine slits where a human nose would be. "I am a snake. A half-Naga."

"A half-Naga," he remarked in amazement, standing up straight. "Well, that explains a lot. I certainly understand why you would be so nervous in an inn full of people. Come, let me bring you upstairs to my apartment. We can talk privately there."

Marissa huddled into her cloak as she followed Arthur through the cobblestone streets with a million frantic thoughts scattered through her head.

I mean, if he was going to hurt me, he would've done it by now. He's a herpetologist, right? A reptile expert. He means no harm... I hope.

She wanted to trust him. He was one of the few humans in her life that had offered her even a shred of kindness. And now he knew … and yet, he seemed fascinated by her existence.

They returned to The Menagerie. The shop was closed, the lights off, and most of the animals had settled into slumber. Including Aurora, who lifted a single head as they passed, her body guarding the front door. As they walked through the store, Marissa took a moment to watch the carpet python explore his tank as Arthur dug a brassy key out of his coat pocket.

"This way." He led Marissa into a back room, where they ventured up an ancient, creaky stairwell that smelled of old wood and must. Upstairs was a small, plain door with a coppery plate that had 201 stamped across it in bold black numbers. Arthur fumbled with the brass key in the lock, twisting and turning it until they heard a rather loud click.

"Sorry," Arthur apologized. "That damn lock is finicky."

The door squeaked open on its stiff hinges. The antiquated apartment was small, but Marissa was filled with wonder as she stepped inside. The first thing she noticed, which she'd seen in most buildings in Brennan, were the magical lamps that flickered on as soon as they stepped into the room. They illuminated the small apartment, their light shining much brighter than the oil lamps used in the outer villages. As she approached the lamps, she realized that instead of a flame, each lamp contained a single stony orb pulsing with soft white energy.

"These are glowstones, magical light sources from beyond the valley," Arthur remarked as he noticed

Marissa staring at the lights. "Incredible, aren't they? No need for those dirty oil lamps. I bought them recently— they're a brand-new discovery, and I hope they continue spreading through the rest of the kingdom and into the outer villages."

Marissa wandered farther into the apartment. Several large enclosures were embedded inside a wall in the living room, and one by one, her eyes locked with every reptile in the tanks. Within a few minutes, she had two boa constrictors, a green iguana, and three bearded dragons all gathered at the front of their tanks, gazing intently at her as if waiting for her command. Marissa felt the same unsettling forewarning radiate from them, and she quivered.

"They know." Marissa heard a voice whisper behind her. Arthur stared at the tanks in amazement. "It's like you share an unspoken bond with them."

Marissa turned away from the tanks, and she and Arthur stood face to face, alone in the dark stillness of his apartment. He took a step toward her.

"May I..." His voice was soft. "See you? Without your cloak and scarf?"

A shiver ran down Marissa's spine. Without taking her eyes off Arthur, she unbuttoned her cloak and unraveled the snaking scarf from her neck, placing both on a nearby couch. She was now barefoot, dressed in loose trousers and a long white blouse, with her half-reptilian face fully exposed.

Dark black-and-brown scales mixed with traces of human flesh. A serpentine nose, a white-gummed mouth full of sharp teeth, and a pink forked tongue. *At least my eyes are human, a soft shade of blue.* Marissa caught a glimpse of herself in a nearby mirror and squeezed her eyes shut in embarrassment. *Ugly.* Pain burned through her face. There were times when Marissa admired her shimmering scales and sharp fangs, but when interacting with humans, she was deeply ashamed of them. She knew that they had a strong disdain for reptilians. Her entire life, since her days as a child at the orphanage, she had been told that she was a monster. *Ugly.*

Marissa figured she was ugly in Arthur's eyes as well. *I look so reptilian, so unlike humans...*

He stepped closer, his footsteps gentle. He paced around her, studying her features.

"Incredible," he whispered. Marissa lifted her chin, her posture stiff. "I've never heard of a half-reptilian. I had no idea it was even possible... where did you come from? Do you know anything about your parents?"

My parents. They were rarely a thought in Marissa's mind. She had come to accept what she was a long time ago and didn't bother pondering over where she came from. Yet, her parents were still out there somewhere, one human and one Naga. Sometimes she still wondered where they were and why they abandoned her.

"I don't really know anything about them," she responded. "Except that my mother, who left me at an orphanage when I was a baby, was human. So, my father must be a Naga."

"Interesting." Arthur took a seat at the dining table and gestured for Marissa to do the same. "So, let me ask... where have you been living? If you're eighteen, I imagine they made you leave the orphanage."

Marissa gulped. "Just a few days ago. I've been ... uh..."

She couldn't bring herself to admit that she was a vagrant. *But how else am I supposed to survive? Is my half-snake self supposed to march up to the nearest inn and ask for a job?*

"I see." Arthur understood the meaning of her silence. "Well, Marissa, I have a proposal for you. You can stay with me, and I'll give you plenty of coin for your time, but in turn, I need your help."

Marissa raised a thin eyebrow, surprised. "My help?"

"Yes. You see, meeting you... it's almost like fate. I have an important mission I need to complete regarding the reptilians."

"What mission?"

"There's this Naga," Arthur continued. "It seems to be some sort of outcast. For the past few days, it's been terrorizing the outer villages, breaking into homes and scaring the villagers. We don't know why, and we need to find out before someone gets hurt."

Marissa's scales shivered at the thought of encountering a full-blooded Naga. She had never seen one before and had no idea how they would react to her half-snake self.

"So, why do you need my help?"

"I'm not sure if you're aware, but reptilians can't speak. In fact, we're not even exactly sure how they communicate, but they do it silently. But since you're half-reptilian... I'm curious if you might be able to talk to them."

Talk to them? Silently? Marissa knew surprisingly little about reptilians considering her heritage. She knew she had strong scales, heightened senses, and some semi-dangerous venom, but she didn't know the true extent of her abilities. But she did know that whenever she interacted with another reptile, especially snakes, she could sense their emotions like they were her own.

Maybe I can do this. And he said he'd pay me for my time. What else am I going to do, continue wandering the valley with no money and no home?

"Okay, I will help you. I take it we will need to travel to the outer villages?"

"Yes. It's about a day's journey to our destination. It's nearly eleven o'clock, so let us head for bed and we'll discuss further plans in the morning."

Arthur stood up and led Marissa down a short hallway. Through a cracked door at the end of the hall, she could see a large king-sized bed, with its intricate posts and silky embroidered comforter. *This place is so old and small, yet so elaborately furnished...*

"This is my guest bedroom." Arthur pushed open a nearby door. "You can rest here for the night."

Marissa walked inside and perched herself on the plush twin bed. Its sheets were patterned with delicate flowers, and its downy comforter was as puffy as a loaf of bread. Her heart was giddy with excitement. *I haven't slept in a real bed in days, and this is the nicest one I've ever laid in.*

A deep warmth washed over her as she sunk her body into the mattress, having never felt so cozy. She peered up and noticed an elaborate portrait of a massive, bizarre-looking reptile hung on the wall. It had the sturdy legs of a lizard, the leathery skin and tail of a crocodilian, the strong shell of a tortoise, and the slithering neck and head of a snake.

"That's the reptilian god of life and death," Arthur remarked as Marissa stared at the painting. "I don't know what its name is, but I learned about it through my research. Had that portrait modeled after some old reptilian artwork we unearthed years ago. Anyway, make yourself comfortable. Sleep well. Good night, Marissa. I'll see you in the morning."

Chapter 6

*R*AMSEY WASN'T SURE WHAT TO EXPECT. HIS fingers fiddled and curled around each other in his lap, and his right foot tapped the floor repeatedly like a hyperactive spring. He was on a plush bench in the hallway outside the throne room, and he couldn't figure out why he'd been summoned by the most powerful man in the kingdom at eight o'clock at night.

He had a few theories. The most prevalent one was that this had to do with his younger brother's antics. He couldn't believe that Arthur had had the nerve to interrupt his conversation with the king the day before, especially to discuss his pitiful concern for the beasts scouring through the outer villages.

CHAPTER 6

Dammit, Arthur ... everything that our family does for you, and you squander it on your pathetic optimism. What do you expect? That the humans and reptilians will just put centuries of feuding aside and make peace? I bet they'll join hands and do a jolly dance down the streets of Brennan.

Arthur had always been a wild one, full of his own ludicrous opinions and defying every bit of advice that the royal family tried to drill into his head. He had blatantly touted his love of reptiles around the palace throughout his childhood, much to the king's frustration, until he was stripped of his position as a herpetologist and kicked out of the palace a year ago.

What made Ramsey even angrier was that deep down, he was jealous of his younger brother. In his twenty-five years of life, Ramsey had been held to the highest standard by his parents, expected to be their golden child, simply because he never dared to act up. Arthur was given much more freedom because he knew how to push their parents over the edge.

His second theory was less obvious, but Ramsey couldn't ignore the signs. While he was a distant relative of the king, of noble bearing but royally insignificant, he couldn't help but notice that the king was always ... watching him. He'd engaged Ramsey in frequent conversation during family events, always smiling in approval at Ramsey's carefully crafted responses. He'd even lock eyes with Ramsey while he was out marching with the royal guard, always with a deep smile across his face.

"Sir." A guard paced forward and stopped briskly in front of Ramsey. "His Majesty will see you now. Please, follow me."

The hallway was dimly lit, and the sound of their footsteps clattered off the cavernous walls. The guard stopped in front of a pair of dark wooden doors, nearly ten feet high and laced in leafy gold trim. He twisted the glimmering handles with a gloved hand, swung the doors open slowly but firmly, and stepped aside, gesturing for Ramsey to enter.

The towering room was empty, except for a lone figure perched on an elaborate purple-and-gold throne. There were two other chairs on the raised platform, but Ramsey didn't dare let his eyes drift toward them. He already knew why they were empty.

It had been two years since the king's only child, Liam, caught pneumonia and passed away. It was a shock to the entire kingdom—Liam was in perfect health, an accomplished fencer and equestrian who was beloved by all who met him. He was the same age as Ramsey, and they had spent many family events together in their youth. Rumors swirled around the palace that they were trying for another child, but with the king nearing fifty and Queen Alexandra supposedly having fertility issues, it hadn't happened.

With his son gone and no heir to the throne, King Gabriel had thrown himself into his duties. Since his bloodline would end when he passed, he was determined to be the greatest king Brennan had ever known.

The queen, on the other hand, had succumbed to a deep state of grief; she so rarely appeared at public events that some civilians believed her dead. Even the royal family saw little of her, as she spent most of her time shut away in her private quarters.

But the question remained—even if the king and queen had no surviving heirs, someone needed to be next in line for the throne. King Gabriel needed to choose someone to surpass him, and every young royal in the palace was trying to gain his favor.

Ramsey took a deep breath as he stepped toward the king, a sharp-faced man with sleek brown hair and a thin mustache. A trailing cape with intricate designs stitched in glimmering gold thread covered most of his body and draped down onto the floor. Atop his head was a bulbous, heavy crown dotted with gemstones that flickered in the dim light. Ramsey assumed it wasn't very comfortable, as the king's head movements were subtle and stiff. King Gabriel kept his eyes locked on Ramsey, and a warmhearted smile stretched across his face and crinkled the corners of his eyes.

"Hello there, Ramsey." His smooth voice echoed across the vast room. Ramsey froze in place, about twenty feet from the throne, and pushed his chest forward in a deep bow.

"I am honored to be here, Your Majesty."

Ramsey's eyes shifted to the back wall of the room, where behind the throne, a lone guard stood tall and alert with her hand resting on the hilt of a sheathed sword. On her other hip was an elaborate flintlock pistol, trimmed in gold just like the powder horn slung over her shoulder. She was a small woman, wiry and petite, with thick auburn hair that trailed down her torso in frizzy waves. *That's odd. Everyone in the palace knows that the king doesn't like guards listening in on his private conversations, much less a woman who looks like she could be blown over by a strong gust of wind.*

"Don't mind her." The king's voice boomed as Ramsey's eyes flicked away from the guard. He stood stiff, pretending he hadn't been looking in the guard's direction. The king chuckled and pointed at his ear. "She's deaf. Can't hear a thing. But anyway, I imagine you're wondering why I've summoned you here today. Don't worry, you've done nothing wrong. In fact, I have a proposition for you."

Ramsey nodded, his mind spinning with anticipation about what the king would say next.

"As you know, I am getting up there in age, and eventually, someone will need to step up and take my place. I am aware that I have many sniveling young relatives who are pining for the throne, but none of them have impressed me. Except for you."

M-me? Ramsey's stomach dropped, his heart fluttering with excitement.

"Your parent's pride in you speaks for itself. You are an incredibly intelligent, well-spoken, assertive young man. Most importantly, you act as such because it's who you are, not because you want a chance at the throne. We shall make it official; you are next in line to be king."

Ramsey stiffened his whole body, trying his hardest not to tremble. His heart pounded in disbelief. *All these formalities, my highly structured upbringing, always feeling like I had to be perfect... it was all worth it. I promise, Your Majesty, I will devote myself wholly to the kingdom. I will be the great King Ramsey, ruler of Brennan.*

"However, in return, I have a request."

"Of course."

Anything, Your Majesty, just say the word.

The king lifted the hem of his robe, revealing a large but thin chunk of limestone perched in his lap. He lifted the heavy slab and held the flat side toward Ramsey. Across the gritty surface of the rock, a series of crude etchings had been carved out in deep gouges. To Ramsey's unknowing eye, it looked like nothing more than the rather forceful scribbles of a child.

"As you're aware, some of my soldiers unearthed this tablet in reptilian territory a year ago. It's written in ancient reptilian, a sort of hieroglyphic writing system, and my finest researchers believe they have finally deciphered it. It's a shame your brother couldn't assist. He is a fountain of knowledge, I will admit, it's just that his loyalty to the kingdom has always had a leak."

Ramsey exhaled sharply, refusing to engage in conversation about Arthur.

"So what does it say?"

"This is only a broken piece of the full tablet, but this section outlines directions to an ancient temple deep in Naga territory. My researchers believe that this confirms their theory about the Valley of Scales' past. As I'm sure you're aware, the humans and reptilians ended up on the brink of a major war not long after our ancestors founded Brennan."

Ramsey nodded. It had been eight hundred years since humans first settled in the valley, but with little technology and so much turmoil with the reptilians, most of their written records had been lost to time. The royal library's finest scholars had long attempted to piece together the events of the past, but much of it was still muddled in speculation and legend.

"We believe there's a secret that the reptilians have been hiding all this time. At the peak of the conflict, to wipe out the humans, they attempted to summon one of their gods with a magical idol. But they were unsuccessful, and the remnants of the idol are now hidden throughout the valley. My researchers theorize that this temple holds one of those remnants."

Ramsey's body stiffened as he tried to maintain a serious expression. *Magical idols? Hidden temples?* It sounded like nothing more than a folk tale. *The king can't possibly believe this... summoning a god... it's impossible...*

"I know you think I'm insane." The king's tone lowered, and Ramsey shuddered, his face burning with embarrassment. "But it's a chance that we need to take. If the idol really does exist, we must prevent the pieces from falling into the wrong hands. My deepest fear is that the Naga is acting strangely because it is trying to finally summon their god. This could mean the end for all of us."

Ramsey's mind spun in frantic horror at the possibility of the legend being true. *The king is right. The reptilians are acting strangely, and we must take every precaution possible.*

"I'm assuming you want me to track down the temple?" Ramsey asked.

"Yes. If the temple is real, find the idol piece and bring it here. We must keep it safe."

"I'm up to the task, Your Majesty. I'll do whatever I can to help the kingdom. But what about the Naga?"

"Once my guards find the Naga, they have been instructed to search its body for any idol pieces. But regardless, we must secure the one from the temple. The reptilians can't summon their god unless the idol is complete. We cannot let that happen."

Ramsey bit his lip. *Search its body* implied that the guards did not intend to let the Naga live. He thought back to his brother's futile pleas the night before and grimaced with realization.

"There's one more issue, Your Majesty. My brother ... as you know, he's incredibly stubborn. I imagine he's out there searching for the Naga right now, trying to beat us to it."

The king sighed. "I assumed the same. But do not worry, when my guards inevitably come across Arthur, they'll march his defiant self back to the palace. But if he does come face-to-face with that Naga, hopefully he'll come to his senses about the reptilians before they kill him."

Ramsey gulped at the king's last sentence but nodded firmly. "Yes, Your Majesty, I understand."

"Excellent. I knew I picked the right person for the job. Remember, someday you will be king, and these are the sorts of challenges you will face. Several of my finest soldiers will be accompanying you on the journey. Please, get plenty of rest tonight. We will have saddled horses ready for you at the stables tomorrow morning."

"Thank you very much for your time, Your Majesty."

As Ramsey turned to leave, King Gabriel stepped off his throne and clamped his large, hairy hands on Ramsey's shoulders. The look in the aging king's eyes reminded Ramsey of a father proudly admiring his son.

"Good luck, my noble heir. Please do not fail me."

Chapter 7

DESPITE THE COMFINESS OF HER BED, Marissa stayed up for a while after Arthur fell asleep. Being a half-Naga, she was a bit of a night reptile. She was curious about the apartment, but decided it wasn't best to be slinking around Arthur's home late at night. Instead, she lay quietly in her bed, admiring the milky white moon outside the window and pondering her current situation.

Am I really going to come face-to-face with a Naga? If he's breaking into villages, he's probably dangerous... am I up for this?

I could leave. Marissa heard soft snores coming from the master bedroom—she doubted that Arthur would notice her slipping out the front door. *But then what? I was unmasked in an entire inn full of people. I would have to leave Brennan, venture far away from the city, and I would never see Arthur or The Menagerie again. I would, once again, be completely alone.*

Eventually, her wandering mind managed to fall asleep, and she awoke early the next morning to a gentle sunrise ... and a sharp, bitter smell.

Marissa stumbled wearily out of the guest bedroom and down the hall. Arthur was wide awake, sitting at the kitchen table with a large parchment map in front of him. In one hand was a mug of some sort of steaming liquid.

He grinned. "I take it reptilians aren't morning people?"

Marissa grumbled and sat across from him.

He gestured toward his cup. "Coffee?"

Marissa cocked her head. *Coffee?* She realized that the bitter smell was coming from a boiling pot on the stove.

"What's that?"

"A slightly unpleasant liquid that helps those who are not fond of waking up at eight o'clock." He chuckled.

Her eyes flicked from Arthur's mug to the pot on the stove, then back again.

"I'm fine, thanks."

Arthur turned the map sideways so Marissa could see it. It was a detailed map of the Valley of Scales, including the kingdom of Brennan, the outer villages, and the reptilian territories.

"You see, we're here, in Augustree. We need to head this way, south toward Alistar, through the city gates and into the outer villages, until we're ... right here." Arthur pointed to a small dot on the map. "It's a town called Vale. That where the Naga was last spotted, just a few days ago."

Vale? My hometown, the orphanage... Marissa's mouth opened, then quickly snapped shut. She decided it was best not to say anything.

"There's another slight detail," Arthur remarked with weariness in his voice. "The Naga wasn't alone. According to the witnesses, he had two Varan with him."

"Lizardfolk? But why?"

"Like I said, we don't know. But that's why this is so concerning. The reptilian races don't generally interact with each other. It's important that we track them down and put a stop to this before it gets worse."

Face to face with three reptilians? Marissa knew that Naga were huge, with some standing eight feet tall. She was small even by human standards, barely five foot two. Her head came up to Arthur's shoulder. *I am no match for a full-blooded Naga, especially since they are immune to my venom.*

"Well." Arthur placed his mug in the sink. "I am packed and ready to go. I have an assistant that will be minding the shop while we are gone."

The two of them wandered downstairs. Out the shop window, the cobblestone streets were quiet, with the residents just beginning to wake. Arthur snapped his fingers, and all three of Aurora's heads lifted.

"Come here, girl. Let me put your leash on."

Aurora trotted over to her owner, and Arthur fastened a braided leather leash to his pet's stiff collar and plucked a short blade out of a locked drawer beneath the register. As Arthur fastened the weapon to his belt, Marissa gave him a sideways glance.

"Just a dagger? But the outer villages are littered with bandits. What if they have guns?"

Arthur sneered, "If they could afford guns, they wouldn't be bandits. I'm generally one for new technology, but when it comes to weapons, I prefer simplicity. Guns are a remarkable achievement, but to be honest, they're slow to load and fire, which is troublesome when you have a bandit in your face about to stab you. The blade is still the ultimate weapon; hence why the guards still strap bayonets to their muskets. And when the dagger isn't enough, I've got three sets of sharp teeth at my disposal—Aurora is a highly trained guard dog."

Marissa knew little about guns, only ever catching glimpses of the old ones locked away back at the orphanage. But she quickly realized another, more discreet reason for them not to carry the flashy weapons—the Naga would never trust a human with a gun.

"Do you have another dagger?" Marissa asked. "I ... lost mine yesterday. And I need a way to defend myself."

"Unfortunately, I do not. But..." Arthur gave her a funny look, "Aren't Naga venomous?"

Her eyelids narrowed. "I wouldn't dare use my venom on a human."

"Why not?"

She scoffed. "They already think I'm a monster. Besides, my venom isn't powerful enough to kill a human. And it won't work at all on that Naga, who sounds awfully dangerous."

Arthur sighed. He bit his lip, contemplating her request.

He clapped his hands together. "Alright, I have a solution."

Marissa perked up with realization as Arthur unlocked a large tank at the back of the shop. He waved his arms toward her.

"Come on now. You have to grab him. I'd rather not be bitten."

Her eyes glittered with joy as the curious little carpet python slithered out of his enclosure. He settled around her neck, just as he had done the night before. Marissa felt the python's deep happiness, and a joyful warmth trickled through her heart.

"There you go." Arthur slid the enclosure shut. "Consider it an additional payment for helping me. No one is going to harm a woman wearing an ornery snake as a necklace."

The python's head trailed up Marissa's face. She giggled as its tongue flicked against her cheek. She knew the little snake wouldn't be much help against a giant Naga, but at least he would keep bandits away.

"Thank you."

"You're very welcome." Arthur lifted a small satchel off the counter. "Alright, snake whisperer. We've got a long day's journey ahead of us. Let's get a move on. I'd like to be in Vale by dusk."

"Alright, it's just a few blocks this way to the nearest carriage house." Arthur pointed as they paced through the streets of Augustree. "About a three-hour ride to the southern gates, and then we'll rent a self-driven cart and reach Vale by evening."

The early morning air was cool and damp, and most of the shops had just opened. Every few feet was a new storefront, a new set of windows full of mysterious and exotic goods. It was a clear day, without a cloud in sight, and the sun, still low in the sky, cast deep, chilly shadows across the kingdom streets. Marissa huddled into her cloak.

Arthur eyed Marissa, straightening his jacket. "Are you cold?"

Marissa huffed, hunching her shoulders as a crisp breeze blew past them.

"I'm surprised," Arthur remarked. "It's a pleasant morning. Cool, not too chilly, but comfortable."

"Comfortable for you humans."

Arthur chuckled. "Ah, I see. Indeed, reptilians aren't fans of the cold. At least it doesn't snow in the Valley of Scales."

"Frozen water falling from the sky? Sounds horrible. Have *you* ever seen snow?"

"Indeed, I have." Arthur grinned. "I've been far beyond this valley, to lands where great winged dragons roam the skies and glittering fae wander in enchanted forests. There's a big world out there beyond those mountains. But to be honest ... the Valley of Scales is still my favorite place. Nothing beats the beautiful homeland of the reptilians."

As they turned the corner, a small stable with several stalled horses and rows of covered wooden carriages came into view. Arthur walked up to the cashier's window while Marissa paced toward the horses, in awe of their towering, muscular frames but too afraid to touch them. The stable smelled deeply of leather and hay, a homely scent that reminded her of the outer villages.

Marissa turned her head and watched as Arthur placed two silver in the cashier's gloved hand. Within a few seconds, a fully fitted carriage pulled by a grayish mare with a stringy yellow mane clip-clopped in front of them and came to a halt.

"After you." Arthur waved a hand toward the carriage. The vehicle lurched slightly as Marissa stepped inside. *I've never ridden in one of these before.* She decided it was best to sit with her back to the driver so he couldn't see her face. Arthur hopped into the opposite seat, facing Marissa, and the carriage wheeled down the cobblestone street to the thump of steady hoofbeats.

"It's difficult to believe that the massive kingdom of Brennan was built on swampland," Marissa remarked, her eyes gazing out at the streets as the kingdom swept past her. "Doesn't seem very structurally stable."

"It really isn't. The humans had to bring in tons of dirt and sand from other regions. I imagine the reptilians were not happy when our ancestors first set up camp hundreds of years ago."

"But why did they even come here?" Marissa asked.

"We're not exactly sure why. Our early ancestors weren't very good with written records, and much of our early history has been lost. But we have guesses. The land may be swamp but it's rich in resources. Also, humans are highly intelligent, capable of building great civilizations, but they're a bit physically weak compared to the bigger beings of the world. Some scholars theorize that our human settlers were driven out of their own homeland and ended up here."

"Fascinating." Marissa's attention was drawn away from Arthur as the carpet python around her neck stirred. His head was periscoped above her shoulders, staring off into the distance, his tongue flicking in long, slow motions. Marissa peered out the window and noticed a large rat scurry into a nearby alleyway.

Arthur shook his head. "Always hunting, those snakes. They have such an incredible sense of smell. I assume you do as well?"

"Yes. Sometimes I swear I can smell others' emotions. Like, people smell different when they are happy. Or angry. Or afraid."

"So, speaking of your snake." Arthur eyed the python. "Are you going to give him a name?"

Marissa hadn't thought about that yet. She racked her brain, trying to think of an appropriate name for such a majestic yet small creature.

"I am going to name him Nim."

"Nim? Never heard that one before."

"It's from a book," she explained. "One of my favorites. Nim is the name of a winged snake who befriends lone animals in a forest. His best friend is a wolf who was cast out of the pack by his own father."

"Sounds interesting. What book is this?"

"*Nim's Forest*. It's a children's book, only a few chapters long," Marissa explained, a bit embarrassed. "But it's one of my favorites. I still read it regularly. Or, rather ... I did. Until I lost it."

"Ah, I'm sorry to hear that."

Marissa's heart sank into her stomach at the reminder that she'd lost her belongings and would be unable to read her favorite book again. Thankfully, Arthur seemed to understand her melancholy and didn't press for answers. *Maybe I'll be able to find another copy someday.*

"It's disappointing, because it's so difficult to find any books about snakes." Marissa sighed.

"I have a few. Have you ever heard of *Crown of Fangs*?"

"I haven't."

"It's a great series, a modern variation of the legend of Medusa set right here in the Valley of Scales. I actually brought it with me." He gestured toward the satchel hanging from his shoulder. "But unfortunately, the serpent-headed woman is portrayed as evil. I've yet to find a novel where a snake is the hero. In fact, maybe I'll have to give *Nim's Forest* a try." Arthur chuckled.

"Could I borrow it sometime?" Marissa asked. Her heart perked up at the thought of a new book to read. "Even if Medusa is evil, I've never had the opportunity to read another book about snakes."

"Certainly. In fact, here you go." Arthur dug a small novel out of his satchel and handed it to Marissa. She ran her fingers across the shiny, embossed hardcover, amazed at its quality compared to the torn paperbacks that lined her childhood bookshelf.

"I've already finished it once. I was going to go back and re-read my favorite parts, but I'd rather you experience it first."

"T-thank you. That is very kind."

"Of course." Arthur craned his neck and tapped Marissa's shoulder. "Would you look at that. Talking really does pass the time. We're almost to the palace."

The royal palace looked even more majestic in the late morning sunlight. Marissa remembered when she first came across the palace and how she was too exhausted and hungry to appreciate the intricate architecture. *I'm still nervous about facing the reptilians, but at least my stomach is full and I slept in an actual bed last night.*

"All that space for one family," Marissa remarked as the carriage wheeled past.

"Well, sort of. There's the King and Queen, of course, but there are also many aunts, uncles, and cousins. And second cousins, and so forth. All of them live under one roof, in the hundreds of rooms throughout the palace. It's quite beautiful inside. They occasionally offer tours to those who have the coin."

Marissa felt like a tiny ant below the massive structure as the carriage passed through the outer palace grounds. The gardens were intricate and colorful, bursting with plant life but not a leaf out of place. It made Marissa think back to the gardens at Thorburn. When she was young, Beatrice had spent many hours behind the estate, tending to a variety of perfectly trimmed plants. But as children came and went and the estate fell into disrepair, so did the gardens. When Marissa had left just a few days ago, there were more weeds and dry twigs than actual flowers.

Once they passed through the palace grounds, they reached the southernmost district of Alistar. They saw many nuns and priests quietly stroll past the carriage, their heads down and their paces brisk. The churches weren't quite as majestic as the palace, but they were still beautiful. Marissa studied the massive stained-glass windows that decorated the front of each one as they passed.

"What sort of religion do people follow in Brennan?" she asked.

"All sorts," Arthur responded. "You'll find a shrine for every major deity, surprisingly even some of the reptilian ones, but the Church of Alistar tends to rule the roost here. It's an old-world religion that the settlers brought from far beyond the valley. It's certainly interesting, if a bit far-fetched."

A low rumble interrupted their conversation. Arthur craned his neck up to the sky. Eerie gray clouds blanketed the horizon, making the air dark and damp with an incoming storm.

"You've got to be kidding me," Arthur groaned. "The sky was perfectly clear when we left The Menagerie. Well, the self-driven carts at the gates aren't covered, and I won't be able to navigate through the outer villages in a downpour. I guess we can hop off here in Alistar and wait out the rain."

Chapter 8

MARISSA SIGHED WEARILY AS ARTHUR PLOPPED down with his arms crossed next to her, his face lined with an angry frown. They were huddled together under a tiny awning near the Riverview Inn; the rain pouring down a never-ending torrent of water and noise. Arthur was soaked from when he walked out of the inn, his shoes stomping the wet cobblestone.

It was now late afternoon, and it was still storming. The gray clouds blanketed the kingdom in a dark gloom and sparkling bits of lightning streaked across the sky and crackled through the air in deep, booming roars. They'd tucked into a nearby church when the rain first began to trickle down, but as the hours passed and the murky sky showed no traces of sunlight, Arthur reluctantly decided they'd have to stay overnight in Alistar and leave for the outer villages in the morning. He had instructed Marissa to wait outside the inn while he booked them a room for the night, but judging by the sour scowl across his face, he had been unsuccessful.

Marissa hugged her knees to her chest. She'd didn't like seeing Arthur so mad.

"I can't believe they said no," he grumbled. "We're not likely to have any luck at the other inns in Alistar, either. 'No unmarried couples allowed.' I could understand if they didn't want me bringing Aurora into the building, but no. They're perfectly pet friendly, just not human-friendly."

"But we're not ... together, just travelers. Besides, why won't they let unmarried couples stay in a room together?"

Arthur shot Marissa a *you-can't-be-serious* look before groaning and shaking his head. "Forget it. It's not important. Heh, imagine if they found out you were half-Naga. Some religious folks have a thing against snakes. All because of some fairy tale about an evil serpent that tricked a woman into eating a grape or something. Apparently, it doomed us all for eternity."

"We would've had to sneak Nim in."

"Nim can bite the receptionist for all I care. We still need to figure out where we're going to stay tonight." He flicked his finger through the thin waterfall cascading off the edge of the awning. "I swear, the weather has been insane lately. The Valley of Scales isn't usually known for having massive thunderstorms in October."

CHAPTER 8

Marissa stood up and braced herself before stepping into the heavy rain. It pelted against her cloak in tiny, watery punches. She shivered. The storm had significantly dropped the temperature, and she was now both freezing and wet. Nim hunched down and gripped her neck tighter as he, too, disliked the cold.

"Marissa!" Arthur exclaimed. "Come back under here! That's your only set of clothes. You'll get them soaked."

"We don't have a choice." She sighed and peered up at the sky. The clouds were still dark gray, without a hint of blue in sight. "We can't just stay out here. I'm freezing, and I'll embrace the storm for ten minutes if it means finding a warm place to sleep."

Arthur groaned. "Well, I guess I'm already wet. Let's go."

They wandered the district, not having much luck. The pelting rain was so loud that they could barely hear each other speak. The streets were empty due to the storm, and all that surrounded them were churches and shrines.

Finally, Marissa noticed an abandoned building between two churches. It seemed to be some sort of closed-down inn. *How ironic,* she snorted.

"Arthur, this way."

Incredibly, the door was unlocked. The building had been completely stripped of all furniture, and they found themselves in a large, dark, empty room with old musty floors. Aurora happily trotted into the room and shook herself off. Bits of water flew from her short gray fur and sprayed the hardwood.

"We should stay upstairs, in one of the old guestrooms," Marissa commented, walking toward the stairwell. "I don't want anyone to see me through a first-floor window."

The rooms were bare and a bit dusty, but at least they were warm and dry. Arthur had given Marissa a spare shirt and pair of trousers to change into, and relief washed over her as she closed herself into one of the rooms, stripped her soaked clothes off, and hung them from an empty curtain rod.

She raised her arms above her head and stretched, her bare scales quickly drying in the warm indoor air. She rubbed her hands over her legs, admiring their smooth, almost slippery texture, then the door burst open.

Marissa screeched. Arthur caught a brief glimpse of her naked, scaled body before slamming the door so hard that its hinges rattled.

"I am so sorry!!" he stammered. "I had no idea you were in here. There are so many rooms, and ... anyway, I've been scouring through the building for supplies, and I managed to find two old lamps and some oil in a closet. Be sure to check the closet in here, too. I'll ... leave you be."

Marissa heard soft footsteps outside the door as he stumbled away. Nim flicked his tongue for a long time, as if in disgust, before slithering off her neck and curling up in a dark corner.

The guestroom closet was empty. *I guess I should put some clothes on and join Arthur in searching the rest of the rooms.*

BY THE TIME NIGHT FELL, THEY HAD MANAGED TO scrounge up some old pillows and a single ratty blanket to go with the lamps. The lamp provided a bit of dim orange light for the pair to hover around as they lay on the bare floor in one of the guestrooms, Aurora and Nim at their feet.

"This is not how I expected to be spending the night," Arthur grumbled.

"What? Would you rather be at a cute little inn, eating fried grouper and sipping orange blossom mead?"

"Oh, hush," he hissed. His frustration softened. "You didn't answer my question yesterday when I asked where you lived. So let me guess ... it was a place like this?"

"Abandoned storefront, but yes. At least it was better than sleeping on the streets, which I have done several times."

Arthur rolled onto his back, staring up at the ceiling. "You've never fit in, have you? Not quite human and not quite Naga, living on the fringes of society?"

"I'm used to it. I lived in an old storehouse back at the orphanage."

"Well, I imagine once this is all over with, you'll need some coin. Why don't you come work for me at the Menagerie? There's plenty of reptile droppings to clean."

Marissa shot him a dirty look, and he grinned.

"I am serious, though. I'll make sure your salary is enough for your own place. In fact, the third-floor apartment above my shop is vacant. It's quite old, so the rent is very fair."

Marissa smiled warmly at him.

"That's a very generous offer. In turn, I promise that I will help you with whatever you need on this journey. And if that means having to face a huge angry Naga, then I will."

"At least you're immune to their venom." Arthur laughed. He peered out the window. "It's getting late, and we've still got a bit of a walk tomorrow to get to the gates."

"I'm actually going to stay up for a while." Marissa pulled *Crown of Fangs* out of the large pocket in front of her cloak. She loved the crisp, woody smell of the fresh paper as she opened the book. Its spine creaked, still new and stiff from the printer. "I've always been a fan of reading in the dark. I'll go in the corner and bring the lamp with me."

"You enjoy. I'm going to sleep." Arthur rolled over onto his back, crossing his arms above his head and using them as a pillow. "Don't stay up too late. And rest well. Aurora's got sharp ears—all six of them. She'll bark if anything happens while we sleep."

Chapter 9

DMIT IT, EZRINTH, WE'RE LOST.>
< *CA* The stubborn Naga ignored the gripes of the
two lizardfolk behind him, his slitted eyes focused on
the bits of snake shed in his palm. The group had been
stuck in the dense jungle for days, and as much as Ezrinth
refused to acknowledge the truth, he'd lost the girl's scent
a while ago.

<l knew that those two tiny pieces of shed wouldn't
be enough,> one of the Varan hissed. The two lizardfolk
trudged behind the slithering Naga, their paces slowing
as exhaustion and frustration took hold. <We should've
searched the grounds for the rest of her shed. I bet she
buried it somewhere.>

<And give that scared human enough time to call for reinforcements? Absolutely not.>

As much as Ezrinth feared staring down the barrel of one of their terrifying projectile weapons, he knew they probably could've spared a few moments to check the area around the storehouse. He shook his head. *My overconfidence is getting the better of me.*

<Look, Ezrinth, something's gotta give. It's been days, and we've been surrounded by endless forest, without a single human village in sight. I know you want to find her, but—>

<I have to,> Ezrinth growled, masking his fear and disappointment with anger. <And like I said, I'll search every human building in Squamata if I must.>

But, as desperate as Ezrinth was to find her, he knew the Varan were right. Not only had they been aimlessly wandering the forest for almost a week, unfamiliar with human territory, but Ezrinth's body decided to shed at the worst possible time. He had felt angry and pathetic as he spent three days hiding in the forest, his scales dull and his eyecaps clouded over with a bluish tint. The shedding process left him completely blind, and even with his sympathetic Varan companions as bodyguards, he spent every sightless moment in fear that a human would sneak up and shoot him.

But today, Ezrinth's eyes had cleared up, and he was determined to press onward. The trio crunched through the thick underbrush, pushing aside spindly twigs and crackling palm fronds, and they came across a clearing.

CHAPTER 9

A long path cut through the jungle, about twelve feet wide, and made up of sandy lumps of dirt. Ezrinth turned around and noticed the Varan's faces had lit up.

<Thank the gods. We found the main road again.> One of them sighed with relief. <Wait a second. What's that?>

The Varan pointed a scaly claw at a pair of figures off in the distance. They were moving at a rapid pace, and as they came closer and their features crept into view, Ezrinth's eyes flared in panic.

<Retreat!!!> he hissed, pulling his two companions into the brush. They crept backward into the dense green foliage, trying to make as little noise as possible, but every twig snapping under the lizardfolks' large feet made Ezrinth grimace.

The trio heard rustling behind them. As Ezrinth spun around, he caught brief flashes of purple and gold shining through the thick tangles of leaves. The guards had clearly spotted them coming down the road, and they had dismounted their horses to trudge through the forest on foot. But the reptilians were now too deep in the forest for the guards to find, and Ezrinth watched as they fumbled through the brush, stringy branches hitting them in the face as they aimlessly tore their way across the forest. The city folk were so disoriented by the maze of greenery that they ended up stumbling in the opposite direction of the reptilians.

Ezrinth shuddered as he recognized the horrifying weapons strapped to their belts, long mechanical devices that boomed like thunder and fired projectiles that could tear right through reptilian scales. As humans were much smaller and more vulnerable than reptilians, Ezrinth had never been intimidated by them alone. But he did fear what they could create, and as every year passed and their technology advanced further, the humans became a far greater threat.

One of the Varan pulled Ezrinth forward, and he quietly slithered through the brush until the humans were out of sight, and they reached a clearing carved out by a thick stream. He gazed at the stagnant water, its dark surface smooth and glossy, his mind still reeling from their near-encounter with the humans.

<Ezrinth, this is bad,> one of the Varan uttered in a worried tone. <We can't keep searching like this. The humans know we're here, and I imagine they're not happy.>

The Naga huffed, his face deeply lined with contemplation.

<I understand,> He sighed. <But I can't give up. Forget about being discreet—let's go back to Komodo and gather reinforcements. If we're going to be caught by humans wielding those dreadful weapons, we at least need to be able to put up a fight.>

<But Ezrinth, this is incredibly dangerous. We have other concerns to take care of, and—>

<Don't you understand?! If we want to take back Squamata, war is inevitable. And it must start somewhere. I refuse to be afraid any longer; I'll fight my way

through a whole army of humans to find her. And as the newly appointed leader of the Varan warriors, I expect you to follow my orders.>

The Varan didn't say a word, their solemn heads pointed at the ground.

<That's what I thought. Now let's head back to Komodo, and quickly, before any more humans catch sight of us.>

MARISSA MANAGED TO SLEEP PEACEFULLY through the night. Arthur did not.

"My damn back still hurts," he grumbled, gripping his side as they strolled through Alistar in the damp yet crisp air of the early morning.

Marissa smirked. "You could've used a pillow. I did."

"I still don't understand how you touched those repulsive things. They'd clearly spent the past few months being consumed by moths."

Marissa shook her head and strolled a few paces past him. Arthur may have been intelligent, kind, and perhaps even charming, but he was also acting a bit haughty.

"Hey, now." Arthur raised an eyebrow. "I see that look in your eye. There's nothing wrong with enjoying normal human comforts, like a bed. Like I said last night, I'll make sure you're not sleeping in abandoned buildings once this is all over."

Marissa nodded, hopeful but uncertain about Arthur's promise.

"Anyway, how did you enjoy *Crown of Fangs*? Your nose was still buried in the book when I fell asleep."

Marissa gave an awkward smile. As much as she enjoyed books, she was embarrassed by her elementary-level reading skills. As a half-Naga, she wasn't allowed to attend school like the other orphans, and her mind would get hung up on some of the more complex words in the novel.

"I did get a bit sucked into it. I'm on chapter three, at the part where Medusa is cursed with her head full of snakes."

"Ah, well, I won't spoil anything. I'm glad you're enjoying it."

"I am, even though the snake lady is the villain. But I like how they describe her as both beautiful and terrifying. As if you don't have to be one or the other."

"That's true of a lot of things," Arthur remarked. "There's beauty in even the scariest of places. But most people can't get past their initial fear to see it."

Marissa pointed. "Right there. I see stables."

They had made it to the southern gates of Brennan. The massive, interwoven iron structures loomed over the other buildings, their pointed tips casting eerie shadows over the cobblestone. They were magnificent pieces of architecture, yet they also served as a sinister warning to any lurking invaders—especially reptilians.

Even though it was early in the morning, a line had formed outside the stable office. Marissa assumed that people who had business in the outer villages wanted to start their journeys early in the day. Within the hour, they had reached the front of the line, signed some paperwork, and paid the two-silver rental fee for a cart and horse. Marissa couldn't help but notice the large amount of gold coin tucked away in Arthur's satchel as he paid the stable master.

The self-driven carts, meant for travel through the outer villages, were simple wooden structures with thick wheels for traversing over sandy dirt roads. She sat next to Arthur as he firmly took the reins in his hands. He had clearly done this many times. Aurora sat in the back of the cart, curled up and ready to take a nap. The slight rattle of the wooden wheels combined with the firm clip-clop of hooves against cobblestone as their cart rolled toward the gates.

The royal guardsmen gave them a nod as they passed, the massive iron gates heaving open with a loud metallic groan. Beyond them lay a dusty road cutting between a familiar tangled forest of massive oak trees. Clusters of wispy gray moss drooped from the branches, and the slight breeze made them resemble wandering spirits, welcoming them to the true wilderness of the Valley of Scales.

"At least we'll have plenty of shade," Arthur remarked as their cart trotted through the forest. "Beautiful old trees. They must be ancient."

The next several hours were quiet as their cart rolled through the dense, almost primordial forest. The canopy became thicker and thicker, and wiry vines twisted across the trunks of the knotty old trees. Every twenty minutes or so, the wide dirt road would fork into a new path cut between the dense growth. The winding trails led to small towns or clusters of farms off in the distance.

"We're keeping a mighty fine pace." Arthur clicked his tongue at the chestnut mare pulling the cart. Its long neck, flaxen mane, and flicking ears bobbed in front of them. "We'll arrive in Vale in no time."

Thud.

Suddenly, they weren't moving anymore. Marissa was nearly knocked out of her seat from the jolt. The mare, startled by the sudden stop, stomped nervously in place.

"What the hell..." Arthur jumped off the cart, and Marissa followed. A wide, sloping pothole underneath a mound of dead brush had snagged the front left wheel. Arthur attempted to push the cart forward, but it wouldn't budge.

He stood up and groaned, gesturing for Marissa to help him. As she did, the mare noticed Nim out of the corner of her bulbous brown eye. Horses had a reputation for reacting horribly to snakes, and this mare was no exception. It whinnied harshly, its nervous stomps turning into frenzied gallops as it lurched forward.

"This may actually help us!" Arthur shouted as Marissa used the scarf around her neck to cover up Nim. "Come here!"

The mare reared, her panicked neighs becoming even more shrill. But the horse was pulling forward, away from them, and Arthur and Marissa pushed their shoulders into the back of the cart with all their strength.

Wait a moment...

Marissa stopped pushing and stood up, her attention drawn to the right side of the forest. Her reptilian ears could hear the rustling cracks of footfalls against the underbrush, but she couldn't tell if they were human or animal.

"What are you doing!?" Arthur hissed, exasperated by her lack of help. "Push!!"

Before Marissa could respond, two figures popped out of the brush. They were dressed in ragged pants and gray tunics, and both held daggers in their fists. The hair on Aurora's back pricked up as she growled, ready to lunge.

Bandits. This was an ambush. They dug this pothole on purpose.

"Ey, what do we have here?" The larger man's wormy yellow smile made Marissa grimace. "A little lady and 'er gentleman, with 'er cart stuck in a ditch. How unfortunate."

A loud leather snap cracked through the air like a bullwhip. Marissa's stomach dropped as the mare broke its leads in fear and galloped away down the road.

"Looks like yer stuck, pretties," the smaller man remarked, eyeing the snarling three-headed dog in front of him. "We ain't lookin' for a fight. Just drop yer coin and take off. We won't harm ya. Nearest town's up the hill past the stream."

Marissa could tell by the look in Arthur's eyes that he didn't plan to run. His fingers slowly paced toward his dagger. He gave a sharp whistle, and Aurora lunged.

The smaller man screeched as one set of Aurora's jaws sank into his forearm. He collapsed on the ground, but not before jabbing his dagger into Aurora's shoulder. One of the other heads yelped, but Aurora refused to release her bite.

The larger man grabbed Marissa's arm and pulled her against his stocky chest. The sour stench of stale beer and body odor overpowered her reptilian nostrils.

"I bet yer a pretty one behind that lil' cloak, my girl. What d'ya say we—"

The man hadn't noticed Nim, still hiding underneath her scarf. The snake darted out in an instant, and like he was an extension of Marissa's own body, she commanded him to strike.

"Gaaaahhhhh!!!" the man screeched and released Marissa, grasping for his neck. Pain seared through the puncture wounds as dark, slimy blood oozed down his throat.

Arthur froze, watching the scene in amazement. He whistled again, and Aurora released her grip on the other man. The two dazed bandits stumbled off into the brush, crying and yelping in pain. A trail of blood speckled the dirt behind them.

CHAPTER 9

Marissa took a deep breath, still shuddering from the disgusting bandit's touch. She looked over at Arthur's bewildered face. Peering down at her neck, she noticed a small drop of clear yellowish liquid drip from Nim's open mouth.

"Is that ... venom?" Arthur remarked. "I don't understand."

"What do you mean?"

"I happen to be an expert on reptiles. Carpet pythons aren't venomous. Is there something you're not telling me?"

Marissa tilted her gaze down at Nim. He had closed his mouth and was huddled around her neck, completely unfazed by what had just occurred. "I... I don't know what happened. But that's not important right now." Marissa gazed back at the cart. The horse's leads were crumpled in a pile, still attached to the lopsided vehicle. "We need to get to the nearest town before any other idiots decide to ambush us."

Chapter 10

*I*T TOOK OVER AN HOUR OF PLODDING ALONG THE dirt road, with Arthur worriedly reassuring his limping dog that everything would be okay, before he and Marissa noticed a few small buildings peek out between the dense trees.

"Finally," Arthur groaned, examining Aurora's shoulder for the dozenth time. Cerberus dogs had tough skin, and the wound wasn't more than an inch deep, but she still had several thin streaks of blood oozing down her fur. She was limping, but Marissa could tell by the deep gaze in Aurora's three pairs of eyes that she knew she had to struggle through the pain to get help.

Marissa's thoughts flashed back to the disgusting bandit's grasp, Nim striking his neck, and the man screaming in pain as snake fangs punctured his skin. The road was too dangerous to travel on foot. It was early evening, and travel was even riskier after dark. Their skittish mare was long gone, and they needed to find a place to stay—and a cart to take them to Vale in the morning.

The little town, Orchid, was nothing more than some dark storefronts with a few farms scattered in the distance. Arthur and Marissa sighed with relief when they noticed an old wooden Orchid Inn sign on the only lit building in town.

A raucous mixture of chatter and music filled Marissa's ears as soon as Arthur hurled open the heavy wooden doors. It was packed—it seemed like every villager in Orchid was spending the night. A jubilant band played old folksongs while a single waitress hurriedly bustled through the rows of crowded tables like a rat in a maze.

Marissa covered Nim with her scarf as they wandered inside. He seemed to understand that he needed to stay hidden. The bar was standing room only, but Arthur managed to shout loud enough for the overwhelmed bartender to hear, "An orange mead, please!"

Arthur peered down at Aurora's shoulder again. "So many people inside the only lit building in town, and only a single bartender and waitress. Something isn't right here."

Before Arthur could ponder further, the barkeep slid a mug of frothy orange liquid in front of them. The mead sloshed from side to side, with some foam spilling off the edge and settling on the sticky counter. Arthur grabbed some napkins off the table and dabbed some of the mead onto Aurora's shoulder.

"Oranges have healing properties," Arthur explained as he caught notice of Marissa's bewildered face. "The reptilians have used them as medicine for centuries. And since the whole village seems to be closed except for this bar, this mead will have to do for first aid. Plus, alcohol helps stave off infection. The wound should be mostly closed by morning."

"Sir?" Marissa looked up from Arthur and Aurora and caught the bartender's attention. "If you don't mind me asking, why is the inn so crowded tonight?"

The bartender, a grisly old man with graying black hair and a puffy beard, gawked at Marissa as if she had two heads. "Y'all clearly ain't from 'round here. And yer clearly insane to be travelin' through the outer villages. Ya haven't heard 'bout the reptilians?"

"And how they're invading villages? Yes, we have." Marissa gulped, shaking off her worry. The eerie look in his eyes was a stern warning. "We need some help. Is there any way for us to get a ride to Vale in the morning?"

The bartender groaned and heaved his elbow onto the counter, his eyes locked with Marissa's. "We 'ere invaded less than a week ago by those monsters. Broke right into my house while I was away workin', scared my wife half to death. Now everyone in Orchid is beggin' for a room here, too scared to stay in their own homes. We're the only ones who've got guns, but the bloody inn owner has skipped town, and now Marjorie and I are stuck holdin' down the place. If y'all can find a soul in 'ere brave enough to leave this inn and take ya to Vale, I'll eat my damn apron."

Marissa's shoulders fell. *This is impossible. We can't possibly travel there on foot. We'll be an even bigger target for bandits.*

"MAAARRRCUS!" a voice shouted over the crowd. The bartender grunted and turned around. The waitress stood at the opposite end of the bar, strands of wispy hair coming loose from her bun. "Tiny escaped."

"WHAT!?" the bartender roared, slapping his palm on the counter. "I've got a whole bar to manage by myself, and that damn thing got out *again*? That's the second time this week!"

"Is Tiny your dog?" Arthur asked, his attention now away from Aurora.

"Y-yes," the bartender muttered in an unconvincing manner. He turned back to the waitress. "Listen, Marjie, I can't deal with Callum's pet right now. Will you go find him, please?"

The waitress gave an exasperated sigh and gestured toward the dining tables. "Does it look like I can step away right now? I swear, Marcus, if you—"

While the two of them bickered over the mysterious missing animal, Marissa slipped away from the bar and out the front door. Arthur gave her a strange look as she left, but she just nodded, signaling that she would be right back.

It was dusk, and the eerie indigo darkness had almost fully settled in. But Marissa had excellent night vision and had no difficulty creeping around the back of the inn and into the nearby forest. It only took a few moments of crunching through the dense brush to find it. It was impossible to miss—even Marissa shuddered a bit as the massive snake, nearly fifteen feet long, rose from the ground until its eyes nearly met hers. Its head was almost the size of a dog's, and its large, forked tongue seemed to flick in slow motion as it studied the half-Naga girl.

Marissa's posture softened. In the dim twilight, the snake's slitted eyes seemed to sparkle. It had a calm, gentle demeanor for such a large creature, and Marissa could sense that it was happy to see her. She took a deep breath and lowered her scarf, revealing both Nim and her reptilian face. She stuck her forked tongue out and could smell a hint of sadness. The creature's sorrowful emotions seemed to say, "Help me."

"Tiny!!!"

Marissa heard a voice echo behind her. She threw her scarf back over her nose and mouth and turned around. The bartender was jogging toward the forest with Arthur in tow.

Arthur looked bewildered as they approached. "You mean Tiny is not a dog ... but a giant reticulated python? You keep one of the valley's largest species of snake in your inn, and it escapes regularly?!"

"It's not my damn animal," the bartender grumbled. "The owner has a ... peculiar taste in pets. I say it's 'cause he likes to show off, orderin' these creatures from every fancy shop in Brennan." He turned toward the massive snake and grimaced. "I'm not a fan of those slithery beasts. I dunno how I'm gonna get him back in the bin."

"Her."

"Excuse me?"

"Tiny is female," Marissa stated bluntly, not breaking eye contact with the snake.

The bartender opened his mouth, but Arthur cut him off before he could stutter in confusion.

"This is Marissa," Arthur explained. "She's one of Brennan's leading experts on snakes. In fact..." He grinned slyly. "I bet she would happily bring Tiny back to her home in exchange for, I don't know ... a ride to Vale in the morning?"

The bartender glowered angrily at Arthur, but realization set in as he stared at the colossal creature, and his shoulders heaved.

"Alright, fine. But make sure that beast can't escape again."

Marissa grinned beneath her scarf as she gestured for the snake to follow her. Tiny did for a few paces, but then stopped. Marissa turned around, and Tiny gave her a sad but firm look of refusal.

"Marcus, is it?" Marissa stepped toward the bartender. "Do you mind showing me this snake's enclosure?"

Marcus shrugged. "Sure, I guess. It's in the back storeroom, near the owner's quarters. Come with me."

They ventured around the back of the inn. As they entered the back storeroom, Marcus lit a nearby lamp. Its soft orange glow illuminated piles of elaborate paintings and sets of fine pottery shoved into haphazard boxes.

"Why does the owner keep so many luxury goods crammed into the back of his inn?" Arthur asked.

"He doesn't have room for it all. Callum's from old money up in Brennan and treats the inn like his personal vacation home. He refers to himself as a collector. Bah. Hoarder, more like it. Has more money than he knows what to do with," Marcus grumbled as he wandered into the back of the storeroom. "'Ere's the beast's enclosure."

"Uh..." Arthur eyed the structure warily.

Marcus stood in front of a large shelving unit about eight feet long and three feet wide. He pulled open one of the drawers, which was barely a foot tall.

"Sir..." Marissa piped in. "We asked you to show us Tiny's enclosure. That is a drawer."

"It's a snake rack," Arthur corrected, stepping toward the structure. "Some keepers and breeders use these. They're not bad, but this one is far too small for such a large snake, and you need more enrichment than just some mulch and a water dish. Tell the owner that if he constructs a proper enclosure for Tiny, she'll probably stop escaping. I bet the poor thing is horribly bored."

Marcus raised an eyebrow. "I'll be damned. Looks like Callum's gonna have'ta take responsibility for his pets. Don't worry, I'll see to it that the snake gets a proper habitat. I sure as hell ain't huntin' that beast down again if it escapes."

With the issue solved, Marissa was able to guide Tiny out of the forest and into the storeroom. She felt a pang of sadness radiate through her heart as the snake slithered into her drawer and Marcus pushed it closed. Marissa kept repeating in her head that Tiny would receive a new home soon, and she just needed to be good and not escape for the next few days. Thankfully, despite the limitations of snake communication, she seemed to understand. The snake gave a final friendly tongue flick as the drawer clicked shut.

"Alright, you two." Marcus turned toward them. "Go see Marjorie and she'll get ya a room for the night. Six o'clock wake-up time—I've gotta get ya to Vale and back before the inn opens. I'm a man of my word." He stepped toward the door. "Now let's go back out there, have a pleasant night, and forget any of this ever happened."

Marissa took a long last look at the snake drawer, shoved pitifully in the corner of the old storeroom, before following Marcus and Arthur back into the jolly dining room.

She swore she felt the snake say, "Thank you."

MARISSA LET NIM SLEEP ON HER CHEST THAT night. She patted his smooth, scaled head as she lay awake reading *Crown of Fangs*.

He's such a gentle, intelligent snake. But I still don't understand how he became venomous. Arthur is a reptile expert; he couldn't possibly be wrong...

Nim lifted his head, staring directly into Marissa's eyes.

Who are you really? she asked in her head, setting her book on the bedside table. Nim simply flicked his tongue and settled back down on her chest.

She couldn't sense any change in his emotions, but Marissa was certain that Nim was no ordinary snake. But she had no way to prove it, and if he was special, he probably wanted people to assume he wasn't. Either way, she was grateful for his company.

"You know." Arthur suddenly rolled over in the twin bed next to Marissa's. She was startled, as she hadn't realized he was still awake, especially since he'd had two mugs of mead. "The little guy is pretty cute when he isn't trying to bite."

"I mean, he did get taken from his home in the forest to sit in a pet shop."

Arthur chuckled. "I know. It's generally not good practice to purchase wild-caught reptiles, but I sold some of his siblings to an experienced breeder. Once we get carpet pythons started in captivity, we don't have to field-collect animals anymore. Plus, captive-bred babies are friendlier and hardier."

Marissa tilted her head to the side, toward Arthur's bed. He smiled at her.

"Hey, Arthur?"

"Yes?"

"Do you think Nim is ... not normal? Like, there's something different about him?"

"None of us are normal," he chuckled. "We're all weird and wonderful in our own ways. He is a bit of an odd snake, I will say. But keep in mind, he's a rare species, not seen very often in the valley. As far as the venom goes... I guess there's a lot we still don't know about snakes. I'll have to do more research. Also ... you really can hear them, can't you?"

"Somewhat. Snakes are simple creatures. They don't have a language like humans; they act on instinct and emotion. I don't really hear them, I feel them."

"That's incredible. I wonder if the reptilians communicate in a similar way. But I must say—that snake certainly likes you. More than I've ever seen a snake like a human."

"I'm not fully human," Marissa remarked.

"Of course. About that ... you really don't know anything about your parents?"

"Not really. My mother dropped me off at an orphanage shortly after I was born. She was human, so my father must be a Naga."

"If you don't mind me asking, do you ever wonder where they are?"

Marissa snorted. "Why would I care? They abandoned me. Clearly, they thought I was a freak, just like the rest of society."

"Marissa..." Arthur's voice was soft.

"It's true, though. I try to pretend like it doesn't bother me, but it does. Hiding behind a cloak and scarf, afraid to get too close to anyone... it's a painful way to live. My whole life, I've felt like a monster, not fitting in... I always thought I was destined to be alone."

"You're not a monster," Arthur stated firmly. It seemed to make him upset to hear Marissa call herself one. "The world can be very cold to outsiders. I may not be half-reptilian, but the truth is ... I never fit in either. In my family, my older brother Ramsey was the favored child. He'd be playing piano and reciting ancient poetry while I was out digging in the garden. I was hyper, stubborn, impulsive... everything my parents hated. It wasn't until I became an adult that I accepted who I was, regardless of my parents' opinions. Once I did that, I was free."

Marissa felt a calm warmth settle over her as Arthur openly spoke about his past. It was incredible to feel an emotional connection with another being—something she'd never experienced before.

"Anyway," Arthur continued. "There are outcasts in every society, regardless of species. You're not a monster, Marissa. You're special. I know it sounds corny, but I genuinely believe that you exist for a reason."

"Thank you, Arthur..." Marissa whispered, still stunned by the sudden warmth in her chest. "For being my friend."

"Of course. I hope you don't feel like I'm using you to communicate with the Naga. I hope our friendship endures long after this journey. And remember, I still need help back at the Menagerie." He smiled and rolled onto his back so that he faced the ceiling. "Well, as much as I enjoy our chats, we do have to be up very early, so I recommend we get some sleep."

Chapter 11

A HARD KNOCK ON THE DOOR INTERRUPTED Marissa's sleep far too early.

"Good mornin'!" Marcus's loud, haughty voice echoed on the other side of the door. "Get yer sleepy butts movin'. I've already got the cart hitched."

Marissa grumbled as she rose out of bed. Arthur was already awake, sitting at the foot of the bed and fastening his shoes. He grinned at Marissa.

"Sleepy?" he teased. "You sure you don't want to try coffee?"

Marissa grimaced. Nim crawled off the sheets and settled around her neck, giving Arthur a defiant tongue flick.

They followed Marcus downstairs, where the once bustling dining room was now completely empty.

Marjorie, the waitress, was sweeping the floors as they entered.

"Breakfast doesn't start until 8 o'clock, but I set something aside for your journey." She smiled and gestured toward the bar, where a small basket of muffins sat on the counter.

"Thank you very much!" Arthur grabbed the basket as they walked out the door.

"You're welcome! You three be safe out there!"

The first thirty minutes of the ride were quiet. Marissa stayed at the far end of the cart while Arthur and Marcus engaged in small talk. *Marcus seems friendly enough, but he and the rest of the town certainly dislike reptilians.* Marissa warily eyed the shiny brown-and-silver gun that Marcus had insisted on taking with him for protection. *One slip of my scarf and I could be dead.*

She focused on the vivid scenery that swirled around them as they clip-clopped down the dusty road. The thick foliage was a pseudo-jungle, a place where giant, looming oak trees mixed with tangled green vines and palmetto shrubs to form a dense, primordial canopy that blocked out the sunlight. Every mile or so, the twisted forest would thin, and bits of swampland peeked out between the trees. While the forest was rugged and wild, the swampland was quiet and serene, a place of dark mucky beauty where spindly legged birds dove for wild fish and the eyes of alligators peeked up between dense reeds.

To her reptilian half, it felt inviting and cozy, and she experienced a deep longing emotion, almost like nostalgia. Her whole life, she had been torn between her human practicalities and the desire to roam wild and free in the swamplands. She was half human and half reptilian, yet she felt that she would never fully fit in with either society.

As they got closer to Vale, memories flooded her mind. She thought about her childhood at the orphanage. Beatrice made her wear long clothing and a mask while around the other children to hide her snake identity. There was one boy, Jack, who was very fond of teasing her. He told the other children that she was full of diseases and that's why she had to wear a mask.

She snapped one day while out playing in the garden. Jack wanted the toy she was using, so he shoved her to the ground. As he did, her mask slipped, and the children could see part of her reptilian face. While the other children screamed, Jack pointed and laughed. He called her all sorts of names. *Ugly, monster, gross.*

See, I told you she had diseases.

So Marissa did what any angry seven-year-old reptilian would do; she bit him. He survived, as her half-Naga venom wasn't powerful enough to kill a human. But Beatrice was infuriated and sent her to live in the storeroom not long after.

Marissa's thoughts were interrupted by a hand on her shoulder. Arthur had noticed her quietly brooding next to him, and his gesture offered a subtle bit of comfort. She wasn't used to being touched by others and found the sensation both calming and perplexing.

"Your snake-loving friend is awfully quiet," Marcus remarked as he fiddled with the reins. "I imagine wearing that little creature around your neck keeps people at bay."

Arthur squeezed Marissa's shoulder, requesting that she not react. She resisted the urge to hiss at the comment.

"My apologies," Marcus grumbled when he realized that Marissa was offended. "I shouldn't judge. Admittedly, I'm not a fan of snakes. But we're all different, I guess. And I am grateful that you wrangled Callum's monster of a pet back into its enclosure."

"Anyway," Arthur interjected, changing the topic. "Could you tell us more about the reptilians who invaded Orchid? We're on a mission to figure out what they want and how we can get them to go back home."

"Brave souls," Marcus chuckled. "I mean, I have no idea what they wanted. I wasn't home when they broke in. My wife said that two Varan and a Naga burst through the door, scurried around inside, and left with disappointed looks on their faces. They didn't hurt anyone, but they weren't exactly friendly either."

"So clearly, they're looking for something," Arthur remarked. "Interesting."

"I heard that they reached Vale not long after. So, you're headin' there to investigate?"

"Indeed. I have a friend there who might be able to help us."

"Well, I reckon they're headin' in a circle," Marcus remarked. "All around the outer villages, searchin' every town 'til they find what they're lookin' for. Then

I hope they scurry back off to whatever muck hole they came from."

Arthur squeezed Marissa's shoulder again as she huffed.

"Well, thank you for the information," he said. "We've really appreciated your hospitality."

"Yer very welcome." Marcus pointed up ahead. "Road's splittin'. Lucky for you two, that means we're almost to Vale."

A QUEASY FEELING SETTLED LIKE A ROCK IN Marissa's stomach as they approached her hometown, the one she had left only a few days earlier. It looked no different than most of the other towns in the outer villages—just a small square bordered by a few houses and farms. *It feels so familiar, yet so foreign...* Marissa shuddered as she caught a glance of the Thorburn Estate tucked away in the distance.

"If you don't mind dropping us off at the apothecary's home," Arthur requested. "We have some business to attend to there."

"Not a problem. Be safe, you two. Don't be gettin' torn apart by angry reptilians."

As Marcus let them off the cart and wheeled off into the distance, Arthur gave Marissa a knowing look.

"C'mon, you know humans and reptilians have never gotten along. Besides, Marcus was kind enough to give us a ride."

Marissa grumbled as they approached the cottage, making sure her scarf was wrapped tightly around her lower face. Arthur raised a fist and tapped his knuckles a few times on the front door. "Sienna! It's me!"

A petite redhead cracked open the door and poked her head out. She wore a headscarf over her thick, glossy hair and a simple tan dress with a long white apron. Her small hands were stained with various colors from flowers and berry juice.

"Ah, Arthur!" Sienna gave him a brief hug. "I was worried about you. You were supposed to be here two days ago!"

"We ... had some mishaps, to put it lightly," Arthur grumbled. He gestured toward Marissa. "Anyway, this is my friend Marissa. She's especially gifted with snakes, and I was hoping she'd be able to help me find the reptilians. And Marissa, this is Sienna. She's the local apothecary here in Vale, and an old friend of mine from university."

"Pleased to meet you." The redhead smiled warmly. "Come on inside. I just put on some tea."

Sienna's home is fascinating, Marissa thought in awe as her gaze flicked around the cottage. Her walls were covered in framed specimens of insects, animal skeletons, and dried flowers. She led them into her laboratory at the back of the cottage, which was well lit by the multitude of open windows. The entire room was lined with chest-height tables that contained dozens of beakers, test tubes, and potion vials. On one of the tables was a large pile of freshly picked flowers and herbs, and on another were several yellowed jars of preserved reptiles, including two snakes.

"My apologies. It's a bit messy in here. I have so many orders to keep up with lately." Sienna ushered them into a small sitting area. "I'll be right back with that tea."

Arthur smiled at Marissa, but she resisted making eye contact. The nauseous feeling in the pit of her stomach had grown. Except this time, it wasn't just from being in her old hometown. Something about meeting the beautiful, bubbly redhead made it worse, especially when she hugged Arthur at the front door...

Is this ... jealousy? Ugh. Marissa shuddered, disgusted by the distasteful emotion.

"I hope you like it!" Sienna cheerfully exclaimed as she set a small tray on the table next to them.

"It's ... blue," Marissa remarked.

"It's made from butterfly pea flowers. That's what gives it such a bright blue tint. I managed to order some from far beyond the valley. Please do try it. It's delicious."

Marissa held the small teacup in her hands, enjoying the steaming warmth of the liquid. She had never been one for human drinks, but she figured she could give it a try. She pressed her palm against the soft skeins of cloth wrapped around her nose and mouth, remembering the always-present hindrance to her eating and drinking around others.

An idea sprung into her head. *Drinking isn't as messy as eating. If I just part the fabric a little bit, I should be able to take a sip...*

Marissa felt a bit of the hot blue liquid seep into the very edge of her scarf as she drank, but Sienna didn't seem concerned by her abnormal behavior. *She's too polite to say anything, but I bet she's wondering why my face is covered.*

"I feel different," Marissa remarked as she set the sweet blue drink on the table. "More relaxed. It's like a fuzzy, happy feeling."

"Exactly!" Sienna exclaimed, a wide grin on her face. "You see, I'm always investigating the healing powers of new plants. I'm hoping to ship more of this flower to the valley. It certainly seems to cure melancholy."

"So Sienna," Arthur piped in. "I hear you've been very busy lately?"

"Indeed, I have been. Ever since the reptilians started invading homes, I've gotten requests from all over the valley for antivenom. Personally, I think people are a bit paranoid since the Naga hasn't harmed anyone, but I'm always happy to supply medicine just in case. In fact, while we're talking, let me finish up this last dose."

Sienna wandered over to one of the high tables, where a small glass vial was held upright by metal prongs. Inside the small tube-shaped container was a translucent mixture tinged with a faint yellow the color of dandelions. Sienna leaned forward and plucked a dropper and another vial, barely larger than a pinky finger, off a wooden rack. A single clear drop, containing the last bit of liquid in the near-empty vial, plopped into the larger vial, and the entire yellowish mixture gave off a faint, almost snake-like hiss.

"Back when the Valley of Scales was first founded, antivenom was difficult to make," Sienna explained as she swirled the yellow liquid with a thin metal spatula. The hissing sound dissipated. "We used to inject small amounts of venom into horses until they built up a tolerance, then separate out the antibodies from their blood. Not only was this a lengthy, expensive, and difficult process, but fresh venom is very hard to come by, especially from Nagas. But over the past few decades, a group of pioneering apothecaries has simplified the process. Now, all it takes is one drop of venom mixed into a special herbal remedy. Then bam—instant antivenom, which is important when you live in a valley full of snakes."

Marissa had always wondered how antivenom was made, and she didn't realize that apothecaries needed actual snake venom for the process. Her eyes were fixated on the swirling yellow vial as Sienna carefully packed it away in a wooden box.

"There, all finished." Sienna returned to her seat. "I'll need to make a trip to the courier to have that delivered."

"So, speaking of Nagas." Arthur sipped his tea. "That's why we came to visit you today. We're trying to track down the one invading the outer villages. We were able to speak to a bartender in Orchid, which was also invaded by the reptilians. He said that it seems the Naga is searching for something. We just don't know what."

"Well, the Naga was here about a week ago, right after it went through Orchid. The Naga and its two Varan companions ransacked all the houses in the village, including mine." Sienna frowned, gesturing toward some cracked glass vials. "But I do know that the first place they visited was the orphanage."

Marissa's scales went cold at the mention of her old home. Arthur still didn't know that she was from Vale, but he'd probably find out quickly if they needed to question the headmistress.

"I wish we'd gotten to Vale sooner; they could be long gone by now." Arthur sighed. "And they haven't been seen in any villages since?"

"Not that I'm aware of," Sienna replied. "There have been rumors of the guards spotting them creeping through the forest near the main road, but nothing concrete."

"Well, while we're here, let's head to the orphanage and ask some questions," Arthur declared, much to Marissa's dismay. She pulled her cloak farther down her forehead and huddled into her scarf. Nim poked his bright yellow head out, extending his neck toward Sienna and flicking his tongue.

"Oh my goodness." Sienna's face lit up. "What a beautiful carpet python. I'm quite a fan of reptiles myself... may I pet him?"

"Uh ... that might not be a good idea," Arthur's tone was wary. "He's, uh..."

Marissa realized that he was concerned about Nim's newfound venom. *He probably doesn't want to explain how a harmless carpet python is suddenly a threat.*

"He won't hurt her." Marissa locked eyes with Arthur. She tried to mentally relay to him that she understood her pet snake's intentions. *He's protective. He won't bite unless someone tries to hurt me.*

"Uh, alright then," Sienna replied, confused. "Just a quick pet."

Marissa's nerves shook as Sienna stepped toward her, and her neck stiffened as Sienna extended a slender hand toward Nim. He reached forward, tickling Sienna's palm with his forked tongue. Marissa smiled. *She is the only human I've met besides Arthur that appreciates reptiles.*

A deep sadness washed over her. Despite Marissa's initial jealousy, Sienna seemed like a good person. Marissa's loneliness and desire for human connection flooded her body and made her face burn.

"Are you some sort of expert on snakes?" Sienna asked. "Your little python just seems so comfortable around you."

Marissa's stomach churned with worry, and she curtly nodded, hoping Sienna wouldn't ask more questions. As appreciative of reptiles as Sienna seemed, Marissa couldn't let the kindly apothecary know her secret, and her innocent comment had crept a little too close to the truth. Paranoia engulfed Marissa's mind, but in the chair next to her, Arthur's grin sent a warm feeling through her heart. Her nerves slowly melted away.

"Indeed, she is," Arthur praised, although Marissa noticed a tinge of concern in his eyes. "That's why I need her help. In fact, we should probably leave for the orphanage soon."

"Of course," Sienna agreed, still not taking her eyes off Marissa. "And be sure to come back later. You're welcome to stay the night. I want to help you however I can. I respect the reptilians, and I really want to see this resolved without bloodshed. I imagine you've heard about the king, and…"

"Yes," Arthur sighed, his brows furrowed. "That's why it's important that we hurry. Thank you again for your hospitality. Marissa, let's get going."

WITH EVERY STEP TOWARD THE ORPHANAGE, Marissa's heart beat louder and faster in her chest. Once they were just a few hundred feet away, blood pounded in Marissa's ears. Even the sky was an eerie shade of gray, signaling an incoming storm.

"Arthur?"

"Yes?" He stopped and peered back at me.

"Before we go up to the orphanage… I have a question. What was Sienna talking about with the royal family? I heard her mention bloodshed."

Arthur sighed, his gaze dropping to the ground. "I'm sorry. I didn't want to bring this up. But there's a reason why I wanted to get to Vale as quickly as possible. The truth is, while I want this resolved peacefully, the king of Brennan does not. He's sent his guards on the hunt, and I must find that Naga before they do. I don't want to see it killed."

The horrifying thought echoed through Marissa's mind. She shuddered at the mounting tensions between the humans and the reptilians. *So much anger and hatred, all because they can't understand each other.* Marissa had never met this Naga, or any Naga, but her reptilian half sympathized with them. They still didn't know why it was in the outer villages or what it was searching for, but the Naga hadn't harmed anyone.

"I will do whatever I can to ensure the Naga lives," Marissa declared. "I will find a way to settle this. I refuse to be afraid of my own kind."

"I'm glad I have your help. To be honest, I don't know if I could do this on my own."

"Well." Marissa gazed toward the large, disheveled mansion in front of them. She could hear the faint shouts of young children rise from the gardens behind the home. "In order to save that Naga, let's meet with the headmistress. But if you don't mind, could you be the one to do the talking?"

Arthur nodded in understanding. Side by side, step by step, they approached the haunting place Marissa had left only a week earlier. On the large, wooden front door was an elaborate but very old brass knocker in the shape of a lion, which Arthur tapped a few times.

It took almost a full minute for the door to be answered. On the other side, Marissa could hear the scrabbling of curious children and a familiar voice telling them to shoo and go tidy up their rooms. A middle-aged woman with heavy eyelids and graying almond hair pulled back in a tight bun greeted them at the door. Beatrice looked confused—the orphanage rarely received visitors. When Marissa was a child, every time the doorbell rang, the frazzled headmistress worried that it would be another abandoned baby for her to raise.

"May I help you?" Her voice was coarse.

"Yes." Arthur stepped forward. "My name is Arthur, and I am a researcher from Brennan. Me and my companion are trying to track down the Naga that has been invading the outer villages, and we heard that they came through here about a week ago."

As Arthur spoke, Marissa's body stiffened. Beatrice wasn't paying attention to Arthur; instead, her eyes were locked on Marissa. She may have been covered by her cloak and scarf, but her distinctive dark bangs and bright blue eyes were still visible.

"Marissa!?" Beatrice exclaimed in a crude manner. "Is that you?"

Marissa bolted behind Arthur, who tilted his head at Beatrice. "Wait, you two know each other?"

Beatrice exhaled sharply. "Eighteen years I raised you, you little half-snake mongrel, and now those creatures come busting down my door. I've had enough of reptilians, in any way, shape, or form. I demand that you leave this property at once."

Arthur stared at Marissa, wide-eyed. "This is the orphanage you were raised in? Why didn't you tell me?"

"Enough chatter," Beatrice growled, her voice sharp. "Leave. Now."

Arthur hesitated, but Marissa stomped down the estate steps and back toward the village square without a second thought.

"Marissa, wait!"

She refused to slow down. She had no idea where she was going or what she would do next, but she knew that she wanted to be as far away from the orphanage as possible.

"Marissa!!!"

"You see that!?" Marissa hissed, swiveling around toward Arthur. "I told you, I am a monster—hated by the very woman who raised me!"

"You're not a monst—"

"Stop it!" Marissa cried out as thunder boomed from the dark clouds overhead. "Stop telling me I'm not a monster! That I'm special. Look, I get it. You like the reptilians. But most people hate them! Did you just say the guards would kill that Naga if they found it? They'd do the exact same thing to me! I have no home, no family, and no society to belong to. That has always been my fate. Stop pretending like it isn't."

"Marissa..."

His soft voice made Marissa even more upset, and she bolted away from the orphanage, past the main village square, and back toward the main road as the rain began to trickle from the sky. By the time she slowed down and slumped against a large tree trunk, it was downpouring. There was nothing in sight except a long, empty road surrounded by dense forest. She sat with her knees against her chest and huddled into her wet cloak, watching heavy raindrops pelt the soft dirt.

For most of Marissa's life, she had forced herself to never cry. The orphanage had toughened up her emotions, and her reptilian half reasoned that crying wouldn't fix anything. But with no sign of Arthur and no one else around, she howled long mournful sobs into the stormy air, letting out years of pent-up anger and frustration. Tears poured from her blue eyes and mixed with the rainwater that splashed her face, dripping down her cheeks and soaking her scarf. She tore away the long black cloth, tossed it on the ground in frustration, and buried her ugly reptilian face in her knees.

Why did I do this to myself? Why did I push away the one person who cares about me? He was only trying to help, and I yelled at him.

Now no longer concealed by the scarf, Nim's head hovered toward Marissa's ear, his tongue flicking her cheek. She felt a deep, comforting emotion radiate from the little snake, and she patted his head in appreciation. They sat listening to the rain, Marissa's emotions numbed and her eyes itchy and swollen from crying. As much as she wanted to run back to Vale and apologize to Arthur for her outburst, she needed a moment alone.

But a sudden rustle in the forest caused her to jolt. She relaxed when she noticed a flash of muddy green and realized it was just a lizard. But her reptilian intuition made her do a double-take. The creature was half-hidden by the thick underbrush, but she could make out bits of its broken silhouette. It was vastly different from any other reptile she'd seen, with huge black eyes and a row of white spines trailing down its dragon-like body. At first, Marissa assumed it was just a rare species, but as her reptilian senses deepened, she realized this was no ordinary lizard. It emanated a deep, primitive, almost mythical aura that sent Marissa's mind spiraling.

She took a deep breath, breaking away from the creature's gaze. The rain had quieted, but there was now a faint rumbling noise coming down the road. Unfortunately, the sound startled the strange lizard, and it bolted farther into the brush and out of sight. Marissa shook her head, reassuring herself that the encounter was nothing to worry about, and caught a glimpse of a distant carriage galloping down the road. Within a few seconds, she could make out a frazzled-looking woman holding the reins, begging her horse to run as fast as he could.

"Ma'am!" she shouted at Marissa as she stood up. Marissa quickly threw her scarf back on, covering up both her face and Nim as the woman pulled the small rickety cart to a halt.

"Please," the woman panted. Her face was as red as Marissa's, and her frizzy hair stood on end like it was full of electricity. "How much farther is Vale?"

"Um." Marissa was startled by the urgency in her voice. "Not far, maybe a quarter mile. You seem like you're in a hurry."

She nodded. "Yes, we need to get to the apothecary right away."

"The apothecary? I know exactly where it is."

Marissa heard a groan coming from a blanketed figure in the back of the cart. The woman grimaced at the sound of it.

"Please, can you guide us there? It's urgent."

Marissa froze. She was wary of interacting with strangers, as there was always the risk of them discovering her secret. But she could feel the desperation in the woman's eyes, and despite Marissa's fears, she knew her conscience wouldn't let her turn them down.

"Okay," she reluctantly agreed. "I'll come with you. But what happened?"

"Here, quickly." The woman hopped down and lifted the blanket. A large, burly man with wavy auburn hair and a thick mustache was slumped in the back of the cart. His face contorted as deep waves of pain shot through his body. The woman rubbed the ailing man's arm and uttered soft reassurances that everything would be fine. As she unbuttoned his shirt, Marissa's reptilian blood ran cold.

On his exposed chest was a large snakebite.

Chapter 12

"**M**ARISSA!!!"

Arthur still couldn't find her. He plodded solemnly down the dirt road, his clothes still damp from the earlier rain; the odd chirps and screeches from the primordial forest his only source of company.

He wished that Marissa wasn't so hard on herself. He didn't mean to sound insensitive—of course, a half-Naga hiding among humans would live a difficult life. But while other humans saw her as a monster, he saw her as miraculous. He enjoyed her company; she was intelligent, curious, and incredibly brave. But most importantly, she viewed him, a strange reptilian-loving geek who never lived up to his family's expectations, as a friend. He thought back on their misadventures over the past few days, particularly the night they stayed at the abandoned inn and the brief glimpse of her bare scales shining in the soft light...

Stop it, he hissed at himself, shaking away the strange, foreign feelings that crept through his body. *I need to find her; no more distracting thoughts.*

He turned his head as a low rumble echoed from farther down the road.

"Marissa?"

His shoulders dropped when he realized it was just a traveling cart. But as he continued strolling down the road, he noticed that the cart was going very fast. *Too fast.*

"Arthur!" a faint voice called from the cart.

As the cart came closer, Arthur saw Marissa next to the driver, standing upright as she frantically waved him down.

"There you are!" he exclaimed as the cart pulled to a sudden halt. "I'm glad you're alright, but what is—"

"No time to explain." Marissa grabbed his arm and pulled him into the cart. "We need to get to Sienna's house. Now."

"Wait," Arthur stuttered in confusion as the driver shook the reins. Her face was splotchy and red, and her eyes were damp with worry. Even with her old horse at a full gallop, she begged him to run faster. The cart was traveling at a dangerous speed, and its creaky old wheels rattled with every hoofbeat. "What's going on here?"

"This man, her husband," Marissa pointed at a blanketed lump in the back of the cart, "He has a large snakebite on his chest. She said a Naga bit him." She turned toward the driver. "Where exactly did this happen?"

"We're from Copperton, a mining town east of here," she explained in a rushed tone, as if out of breath. "I need to focus on driving. I promise I will explain everything once we arrive at the apothecary. You said she has antivenom, correct?"

"Yes," Marissa responded. "We were just there, and I know she's been filling orders for it the past few weeks."

"Excellent." The woman snapped the reins again. Sweat stained her horse's neck, and his wheezing breaths echoed through the forest. She peered back at her aching husband.

"Don't worry, dear. We'll get you help soon."

MARISSA SAW SIENNA'S EYES WIDEN IN ALARM AS their cart came storming up to the apothecary. Sienna barely had time to ask questions as Arthur helped unload the ailing man from the back of the cart, but one glimpse of his chest told the apothecary all she needed to know.

Her panicked green eyes flicked toward Marissa, whose throat locked up in horrid realization. Marissa knew what was wrong. Just a few hours earlier, she'd watched the apothecary carefully squeeze the last drop of snake venom out of a glass vial to be shipped off to a waiting customer. It had never occurred to Marissa that the vial may have been the last of Sienna's supply. *Good gods... I hope I'm wrong...*

Marissa watched as Sienna took a deep breath, managing to emanate a false sense of composure. She calmly escorted the injured man and his wife into her infirmary before curtly pulling Marissa and Arthur away from the closed door. Her calm demeanor was gone, and the wild flash of panic had returned to her eyes.

"We have a serious problem." Sienna's voice was eerily low.

Marissa gulped. *I was right... this is bad...*

"That vial you saw me make earlier ... that was the last of my venom supply. I already brought that last dosage to the courier. I'm not supposed to get another shipment of Naga venom until tomorrow. The wife said they're from Copperton, correct?"

Marissa and Arthur nodded in unison.

"Dammit, that's over an hour away. The venom is already well into his system. We don't have much time..."

"Well, what options do we have?" Arthur asked. "Are there any other apothecaries nearby who would have antivenom?"

"The closest one is two hours from here." Sienna bit her lip, her worried eyes full of dread. "Not all apothecaries make antivenom. The patient won't survive long enough for us to travel there. Good gods, this is horrible, I never should've shipped off that vial..."

As Sienna continued contemplating solutions, the alarm in her voice rising with every sentence, a deep, conflicting realization crept over Marissa. She noticed Arthur peering at her out of the corner of his eye. He was silent, but his facial expression conveyed what she already knew: *Do it. I promise Sienna won't harm you.*

Marissa, with her half-Naga heritage, was the solution—she could produce venom. *It's not as potent as a full Naga's, but if all Sienna needs is one drop, certainly, I can supply enough to save this man's life.*

But that means revealing myself. She struggled to swallow as anxiety mounted in her throat. Her reveal to Arthur had been an unfortunate accident, out of her control... but now she'd have to do it willingly. She remembered Sienna's glee when she interacted with Nim, and as much as Marissa feared for her safety, she wanted to believe that Sienna wouldn't harm her.

Marissa stepped forward.

"Sienna..."

"Yes?" The apothecary raised her head. Marissa noticed that her worried face was now just as frazzled as the wife's.

"I can save him."

"You can? But how-"

"First, you must promise me that you won't freak out or try to harm me. Please."

Sienna seemed taken aback by the seriousness of Marissa's tone, but nodded. "Of course. You have my word."

"Okay." Marissa took a deep breath. "Here, let me show you..."

Marissa's fingers trembled as she removed the hood of her cloak and pulled her long black scarf away from her face. She squeezed her eyes shut, preparing for the worst.

"W-what?" Sienna stuttered. Marissa opened her eyes and saw Sienna step forward, cupping a hand over her mouth. "Are you really ... a reptilian?"

"I am," Marissa whispered. "I am a half-Naga."

"Unbelievable." Sienna's voice was soft with shock. "What an amazing coincidence that you two found each other. I had no idea half-reptilians were even possible."

"Indeed. I'm only half-Naga," Marissa replied. "But my venom should be able to save him, correct?"

"It should." Sienna rushed them toward the table where she'd prepared antivenom earlier. She handed Marissa a small glass cup with a rubbery substance stretched across the top. "Here. Bite down and try to produce as much venom as you can. We may need to use several vials since you're not a full Naga."

Marissa gently took the cup and slipped away toward the kitchen. She didn't want to perform such an activity in front of others.

"And Marissa?"

Her head spun around just before she exited the room. "Yes?"

"Thank you so much. You revealed yourself to save someone's life, and I deeply admire you for that. I know you don't know me well, but I swear I'll keep your secret. I don't want any harm to come to you." A tinge of apprehension returned to the apothecary's eyes. "Anyway, enough chatter from me. Please hurry. I fear he's running out of time."

IT TOOK A TENSE ETERNITY FOR SIENNA TO EMERGE from the infirmary. Marissa, Arthur, and the man's wife had been instructed to wait in the laboratory. The room was eerily silent, as the wife was too anxious for conversation. Marissa and Arthur decided that it was best to ask questions after her husband had recovered.

As the woman sat in a wicker chair, her back hunched and her jittery hands wringing with worry, Marissa noticed the true extent of her condition. In addition to her sunken-eyed, tear-streaked face, she was frighteningly thin, with odd bumps and bruises lining her emaciated arms. She couldn't have been over thirty, but her feeble appearance made her look much older. This wasn't just stress from her husband's injury; she'd clearly been unwell for a long time.

Marissa then peered over at Arthur. He gave her a subtle, comforting grin, silently reassuring her that, despite the risks, she did the right thing. But they both knew that Marissa's heroic act had to be kept a secret—unlike Sienna, the injured man and his wife were strangers, and they doubted that the couple would tolerate Marissa's presence if they knew her true heritage.

Especially after this ordeal. I may have saved his life, but that was after one of my kind nearly ended it.

The infirmary door creaked open, and the three of them bolted upright.

Sienna clasped her hands together but gave a small smile. "It took several vials ... but he's pulling through."

His wife exhaled deeply and bent forward, wiping her hands over her frazzled face. "Oh, thank the gods! I was so afraid. I don't know what I would've done if ... never mind. I don't want to think about it. Please, may I see him?"

"Certainly." Sienna stepped aside so she could walk through the door.

"Hey, sweetie." Her voice was gentle as she stepped into the infirmary. "How're you feeling?"

Through the open door, Marissa could see her husband lift his head from his pillow and smile. He nodded. "Much better. Naga venom is no joke."

"Then why did you fight it, you idiot!?" Her voice rose alarmingly fast. "You should've just let that damn snake through! Risking your life over a ransacked house. You've always been too stubborn for your own good..."

Marissa and Arthur stared at each other in bewilderment. *Five minutes ago, she was a nervous wreck, begging the gods to let him live, and now she's yelling at him?*

Sienna chewed her lip and slowly closed the door. She turned toward Marissa and Arthur, a deep, twisted frown of confusion on her face. "Whelp, better give them a moment. I'm going to finish washing the teacups. I'll be in the kitchen."

Marissa and Arthur were left alone in the laboratory, with the muffled arguing of the bite victim and his disgruntled wife echoing through the wall. Arthur sighed loudly, attempting to ignore the shouts. "So, you were raised here in Vale?"

Marissa huffed. *Why do we have to come back to this?* "Yes."

"Why didn't you say something?"

"Because it doesn't matter," Marissa grumbled. "Beatrice hates me. That horrid old estate can go to hell, and the reptilians clearly didn't find what they were looking for there."

Arthur's face fell. "You're right. Beatrice may be an old hag, but if the Naga continued traveling to Copperton and bit our deeply troubled friend in there, then we didn't need her help. What we really need to do is talk to the bite victim." Arthur's eyes flicked toward the infirmary door. "Once he's done being chewed out by his wife."

Sienna returned to the laboratory. Upon realizing that the couple was still arguing, she groaned and tapped her fist against the door. "Could you two please stop? It's important that we talk to you. We need still need to know what happened."

The angry chatter ceased, and the door creaked open. The wife appeared in the doorway, a polite fake smile plastered across her face as she ushered them into the room. Marissa, Arthur, and Sienna gathered around the husband's infirmary bed. He was still in his miner's uniform, weary-eyed and his face drained of color, but he was alert and no longer in pain. Marissa noticed a chalky white material smeared across his hands and arms.

"Hello," the man greeted solemnly, grunting as he shifted upright in his bed. His chest was wrapped in gauzy bandages that were spotted with fresh blood. Even though he was no longer in danger, his face was still sour and grim.

"We're glad to see you've recovered. My name is Arthur, and this is Marissa. We're from Brennan, and we're currently investigating the Naga who has been terrorizing the outer villages. We were wondering if we could ask you some questions. Could we start with your names?"

The man grumbled, "Thomas. And this is my wife, Marian. I work in the mines, and we were all at home for lunch when I noticed that damn Naga everyone has been talkin' 'bout slitherin' toward my house."

"And like an idiot, he wouldn't let the Naga in," Marian interjected. "Stood his ground right in front of the door. Stabbed the giant angry snake with a dagger, like that'd do any good. All the other workers wisely fled, but not my oh-so-brave husband."

"Hush," he hissed. "I wasn't lettin' that monster into my house. Plus, if I let one in, the other dozen or so would've been followin'."

"Dozen?!" Marissa and Arthur exclaimed in unison.

"Yeah. Not snakes, though, those spiny lizard-things. The beast had a small army of 'em, and they ransacked every house in town."

"Including ours, once the Naga chomped down on my husband," Marian grumbled. "We were forced to flee town to get antivenom." She glared at Thomas. "Whole lotta good defending the house did."

Arthur's shocked gaze fell onto his lap. "This is bad. The Naga only had two Varan with it when it was in Vale. It's getting a lot bolder to be attacking homes in broad daylight with a small army. Whatever it's looking for, it's becoming desperate to find it."

"Listen, I'll be honest with ya," Thomas muttered. "I don't want anythin' more t'do with those monsters. I say let the royal guard put some bullets through 'em and let that be the end of it. I just wanna go home."

Thomas's words sent a bolt of frustration through Marissa's heart, and she stood silently with her jaw locked in a tense frown. *He was nearly killed by a Naga. No wonder he hates them. And he can never know that another one saved his life.*

"Well, we appreciate your help," Arthur replied. "Sienna, are you still alright with us staying the night?"

"Of course," Sienna responded. "And Thomas, we'll get you on your way soon but it's important that you res—"

"No," he grunted. "That damn venom is outta my system, and I feel fine. I don't need rest. What I need is to get back to Copperton."

Marian bit her lip but didn't object. Sienna sighed.

"Very well, let me help you out to your cart."

As Marian and Thomas prepared to leave, Arthur ushered Marissa outside. The back garden was smaller than the one at Thorburn Estate, but there were far fewer dead branches and wilted leaves. Sienna's garden was teeming with life—an array of medicinal plants overflowed the flowerbeds, sprawling in every direction and looking plump and shiny in the sun. A few orange trees formed a small circle of shade, their leaves rustling in the gentle breeze. Within the shade, Marissa and Arthur settled into an intricate but rusted wrought-iron bench.

Marissa took a deep breath, pushing the violence and hatred out of her mind and instead focusing on the serenity of the wild garden. Its unkempt beauty reminded her of the nearby forest and swamplands. She loved how the foliage always remained green in the Valley of Scales, even as winter approached.

"Hey, Arthur?"

"Yes?"

"Do you really think that the royal guard will kill the Naga if we fail?"

Arthur sighed. "I don't know. I certainly hope not. Listen, Marissa, about that..." His voice grew soft and weary. "I also have a secret. This is something I should've told you a while ago. I really needed you to trust me, but now I realize for that to happen, I can't lie to you."

"What is it?"

"Well, I haven't been upfront about who I am. The truth is, my name is Arthur Brennan. My father is the king's cousin."

"Wait, *what*? You're royalty?"

"Sort of. I'm a rather distant royal, but my parents and brother live in the palace. I promise, no one else knows your secret. I would never endanger your life. As I've told you before, I'm not exactly favored by my family. That's why I live in a ruddy old apartment above my shop and not in some fancy palace quarters."

Marissa sank lower in her seat. Her mind swirled with a million questions. *He's a distant cousin. He doesn't even live in the royal palace... but can I trust him?*

"I see that look on your face," Arthur remarked. "I'm tracking down the Naga because I truly do care about the reptilians. I certainly don't want the Naga being found by some snooty guard that will shoot it as soon as it looks at them funny. The rest of my family may be willing to resort to violence, but I am not. So please, I want you to still trust me. Don't be upset."

Marissa looked at the long black scarf still cupped in her hands and appreciated that she was currently able to go without it. *Because I trust him.*

When I first met Arthur, I also had a secret to hide. I can never forget that he accepted me as I am from the moment he found out I am half-Naga.

"It's okay," Marissa responded after a brief silence. "I'm not mad. I still trust you."

"Thank you. I appreciate it." Arthur sighed with relief. "Now that I've come clean ... there's another concern related to my family that I haven't told you about."

"What is it?"

"After I graduated from university, I worked as a herpetologist at the royal palace, studying the reptilians. It was my dream job, and I threw myself into my work ... until I realized the cost it came with. As I dove deeper into my research, I realized I wasn't doing this for the sake of understanding the reptilians, but to give Brennan an advantage over them. It all came to a head about a year ago."

"Is that what caused you to leave the palace?"

"Yes. It all started when part of an old stone tablet was unearthed near Naga territory. It was the greatest archeological find in Brennan history, written in ancient reptilian hieroglyphs. But by that time, tensions had grown between me and the king. He hated my sympathies for the reptilians, and the ancient tablet was the final straw. He knew its contents would be a massive trove of information, larger than anything we'd ever had, and he didn't want my disloyal eyes deciphering it. So I was kicked off the team before the tablet even made it to their lab."

"What happened to the tablet?"

"I don't know. But that was a year ago, and I imagine the team has made at least some progress decoding it. That's the part that worries me. I fear that the king knows something we don't, and that's why he's so adamant about hunting down the Naga."

Marissa lowered her head, her mind deep in thought. There was too much apprehension and mystery surrounding the situation, and it made her tense.

"I think you're right. Arthur, I never told you this, but back at The Menagerie, when the snakes were staring at me... their emotions felt like a warning. They know something is about to happen, but I don't know what it is. What are we supposed to do?"

"Find the Naga," Arthur stated definitively. "That's all we can do. Ultimately, we are two people amid a valley-wide feud that goes back eight hundred years. We must take this one step at a time."

As Marissa went to speak, Sienna stepped outside and joined them. Marissa quickly closed her mouth, deciding it was best not to frighten her with talk of rising tensions and impending conflict.

"You know." Sienna's voice carried over the breeze as she approached. Marissa could hear the faint clip-clop of hoofbeats in the distance as Marian and Thomas disappeared down the main road. "For what it's worth, I don't think that the reptilians are monsters. After all, one of them saved a human's life today. I'd say that's pretty heroic."

"But everyone else doesn't see it that way," Marissa grumbled.

"I mean, the reptilians think we're monsters, too. Remember, Brennan was only founded eight hundred years ago. The reptilians were here first, whether we like it or not. And as we all know, tensions would be a lot lighter if we could communicate. But that's what makes *you* special." Sienna gestured toward Marissa and grinned. "I bet you're the first person in history who can talk to both humans and reptilians."

"I told you." Arthur grinned at Marissa, lounging back on the bench. "You won't listen to me when I say you're not a monster. You're the key to ending all of this."

Maybe I am. But I'm still afraid. Arthur and Sienna were her allies, but the venom-filled words of those Marissa had interacted with over the past few days still rattled through her mind.

I hope they scurry back off to whatever muck hole they came from.

Eighteen years I raised you, you little half-snake mongrel, and now those creatures come busting down my door.

I say let the royal guard put some bullets through 'em and let that be the end of it.

A single teardrop slithered out of her eye and down her cheek before splashing into a tiny puddle at her feet. It seeped through the dirt and disappeared.

"What I really want is to find peace." Marissa's voice was choked with emotion. "I want to live in a world where reptilians and humans can coexist, not one where they're always on the brink of war and killing those who cross their borders. But it feels impossible. I'm just one person, and most of the valley believes I shouldn't even exist."

"Well, like I mentioned earlier, tracking down the Naga and his army of Varan will be a good start," Arthur responded. "I say it's time for dinner, and later this evening, we can pull out that map and discuss our plans."

Sienna clapped her hands together. "Sounds wonderful. I do quite enjoy having guests over. I make an excellent chicken stew."

"MARISSA!"

Her eyes shot open, and the fear and anxiety that clasped her chest faded away. Moments ago, she had been surrounded by dozens of haunting faces, gawking and screeching and mocking, but now it was silent, and she instead stared at an empty ceiling.

"Are you alright?" Arthur asked.

Marissa sat up and rubbed her aching head. Arthur was in the corner of the room, seated at an old writing desk with a large parchment map spilling off the edges. Relief washed over Marissa as her nerves settled. She wasn't in Brennan. Or the orphanage. She was in Sienna's guest bedroom, where only an hour earlier, she had decided to take a nap.

"You seemed to be having a bad dream," Arthur remarked.

"Ugh." Marissa shook her head and buried her face in her palms. She had been so tired after dinner—*maybe the pressure and stress are getting to me.* But she never would've laid down if she'd known the sort of horrible nightmares her mind would conjure up.

It started in Augustree, where she stood unmasked and uncloaked in the city square. She huddled inwards, desperately trying to cover up her reptilian face and exposed scales. She heard callous laughter and looked up. A crowd of about a dozen people gawked at her like she was a street performer. But their curiosity quickly twisted into shock and disgust. Some were horrified; others sneered and called her ugly. Monster! You're an ugly monster!

The crowd thickened, nearly a hundred ridiculing faces leering toward her. They seemed to congeal into a multi-headed behemoth, their faces blurring and twisting. Suddenly, a bright light flashed, and she was now a young child standing in the gardens outside the orphanage, barefoot in a thin robe, being bullied by the other children. They surrounded her in every direction, their faces pinched in disgust, and she felt an overwhelming urge to bite every single one of them.

That was when Arthur's shout pulled her back to reality.

"So, now that you're up." Arthur hunched over the desk, adjusting the map in front of him. He traced the thick parchment with his finger. "I say we head north to Copperton. Maybe the other miners in the town will be more willing to talk with us."

"We'll fall further behind," Marissa remarked as she stood up, stretching her arms and rubbing her bare scales. She couldn't help but notice Arthur staring, but his gaze quickly darted back down toward the map as she spun around. "We need to go past Copperton and face the

Naga and Varan head-on. They're probably on their way to the next town."

"That's the problem." Arthur gestured for Marissa to join him. She peered over his shoulder at the map. "Right there." Arthur pointed. "There are three possible villages that they could go to next. We have no way of knowing which direction they're headed without talking to the witnesses in Copperton."

"Actually," Marissa paused, "I have an idea. I'm a reptilian and therefore have a highly developed sense of smell."

"Indeed. I never thought of that. You want to try and sniff out the Naga?"

"We should still go to Copperton, like you suggested. I may be able to pick up a scent trail. Maybe they even left some articles behind."

"That sounds like an excellent plan." Arthur rolled the map up. "Unfortunately, we'll have to wait until morning to set off. But it will still be less than twenty-four hours since the reptilians were in Copperton. Hopefully, that will be enough time."

Chapter 13

"THIS IS BULLSHIT," DEVON GRUMBLED AS their horses trudged through the dense reeds, their hooves making soft sucking sounds as they stomped the muck. The Naga built their communities deep in the swampland, a perfect habitat for snakes but a difficult, dangerous, and messy expedition for humans. "The whole magical idol thing is just a fairy tale. I guarantee you we're wading into a snake pit for no damn reason."

The group of four men, clad in royal purple-and-gold armor, had been traveling through the swamp for hours, with the forest getting denser and the water getting deeper. Devon was a guard captain, considered one of the best in Brennan, but he'd clearly never spent much time outside the safety of the kingdom. He had complained the entire trip, but Ramsey wanted to remain optimistic. *The king has evidence that it's true, and if it is, the entire kingdom is in grave danger.*

But there was still the problem of following vague directions from an 800-year-old tablet through dense swampland to find a half-buried, forgotten temple that may or may not exist. It felt like they were going in circles, as every bit of the mucky terrain appeared dizzyingly like the next. With no landmarks in sight, the dreadful sense of being hopelessly lost crept into the pit of Ramsey's stomach. *At least we haven't come across any Naga villages. They'd likely put arrows through our heads on sight.*

"I swear, the valley is far too wet and humid, even in October," Devon continued grumbling as his horse paced along in front of Ramsey's. The beast's stomping hoofbeats splashed Devon's ankles as it plodded through the foot-deep water. "How long are we supposed to be searching for this temple, anyway? Is there a point where we admit it's not real and—"

"Shhh! Devon, hush. Get back."

Ramsey pulled his horse to a firm halt and hunched his body into the foliage around him. A few hundred feet away, half-hidden by thick tangles of reeds, was a Naga village. The humble thatched huts, which were perched on stilts just a few feet above the water, were devoid of activity, but Ramsey had caught a glimpse of a juvenile sitting at the water's edge. Ramsey swallowed, praying the child wouldn't look in their direction. He watched as the scaly creature sat with its body coiled on the mucky shoreline, braiding bits of reeds in its clawed fingers.

Devon's horse grew impatient and began snorting and stomping in place, churning up the water around it. Ramsey froze in horror as the little Naga's slitted eyes locked curiously onto the half-hidden band of soldiers in the distance. Ramsey's breath slowed as he waited for the Naga's reaction. He noticed it wasn't panicked or angry... but curious. *It has likely never seen a human before.*

The Naga looked away, slithered back up the shoreline, and disappeared behind a thick cluster of trees. *It's going to tell the adults.*

"Run, now!" Ramsey whisper-yelled, digging his heels into his horse's belly and taking off at a fumbling trot. The soldiers' horses churned up the water around their legs like a swirling storm, but all subtlety was gone as soon as the little Naga realized they were there. They needed to escape as quickly as possible.

"Ramsey, where are you going!?" Devon shouted frantically. "Brennan's back this way!"

"What are you talking about? The tablet says the temple is farther south."

"To hell with the imaginary temple! We need to escape—the Naga know we're here!"

Ramsey brought his horse to a halt.

"King Gabriel put me in charge," he stated firmly. "And I say we push forward."

The remaining two guards were silent, their eyes flickering warily between Devon and Ramsey. Eventually, they nudged their horse's bellies and trudged forward, heading south toward the open swampland.

That's what I thought.

As they urged their horses onward through the ankle-high water, Ramsey noticed that the village, now a faint silhouette in the distance, was massive. The few thatched homes had sprawled into hundreds, clustered in groups and lining the edge of the forested peninsula. Ramsey feared more Naga had seen them, but even if they hadn't, he knew it wouldn't be long before that child told the others about the strange creatures wading through the swamp.

"The capital..." he whispered, pulling a small journal out of his satchel. In it, the researchers had written the roughly translated directions to the temple. *Follow the swamp south past the capital until reaching the edge of a...*

His thoughts trailed off as he caught a glimpse of white limestone in front of him. The structure was half-buried in the swamp and covered in such a thick layer of foliage that it looked more like a simple rock formation than a temple. *Does that Naga village even know that this is here?*

"Is ... that it?" Devon eyed the structure warily.

Ramsey circled his horse around the submerged structure. It was tilted sideways as if it was once on solid ground that eroded unevenly with time. He pulled back on the reins when he came to a watery entrance on the far side of the structure. The inside of the rugged triangular opening led into a cavern of darkness that echoed the sounds of trickling water.

Ramsey pulled a lantern and a single glowstone out of a pack strapped to his horse's saddle and dismounted. His boots splashed the waterlogged marsh, and he was thankful that the king had supplied them with waterproof ones. He crept up to the entrance, placing a hand on the cool limestone, and held his glowing white lantern into the darkness with a wary hand.

"We're really going in there, aren't we?" Devon grumbled.

More splashing sounds followed as the rest of the men slid off their horses. They followed Ramsey single file into the cavern, stepping slowly and keeping back several paces. Ramsey peered over his shoulder and sneered. *Cowards.*

Ramsey waved his lantern around the murky structure, and its soft white light illuminated a series of crude wall etchings, illegible to humans and half-eroded by the persistent drips of water that streamed down the limestone walls. The cavernous structure was eerily silent, as if all noise had been sucked out of the thick, damp air, and Ramsey found it deeply unsettling as he plodded onward, inky black water churning at his feet.

Drip, drip, drip. The single, penetrating sound was torturous on his eardrums.

The single drips melded into a smooth trickle as the four guardsmen reached the far side of the temple. Below them, a smooth, streaming waterfall cascaded down a series of steps that led into an underground abyss.

"You've gotta be kidding me," Devon grumbled. "What if this thing collapses?"

Ramsey sighed, ignoring his complaining colleague, and trod carefully down the stairs. The limestone steps were coated in slick moss, and the soles of his shoes skidded across the slippery, wet surface. He shoved his weight deep into his boots as he strode down one step at a time, making sure he had a steady foothold on each step before descending farther.

His companions weren't as careful. As Ramsey approached the bottom of the stairs, he felt a hard shove on his back as Devon slipped on the slimy moss and tumbled forward, knocking both another guard and Ramsey to the ground in a domino effect.

Ramsey threw his arms out in front of him, landing with his face just a few inches from the ground. Water had seeped into his uniform, and the thick clothing felt damp and clammy against his skin. He scrambled to his feet, struggling to balance on the slick, mucky ground, and brushed himself off in a vain attempt to regain composure.

Farther up the stairs, Devon grimaced. "Sorry."

Ramsey shook his head and plucked his lantern off the ground, wiping a layer of thick brown mud off one side. He peered around as the underground cavern flickered into view. As it did, a chorus of soft hisses made Ramsey jerk backward, his eyes bulging as he fought to hold in his screams.

"Gahhhh!! Cottonmouths!!" Devon shrieked as he caught sight of them. Dozens of mottled black-and-brown snakes appeared in the darkness, their thick, s-shaped bodies wriggling toward them. Devon pulled a small blunderbuss from his waist, his shaky fingers attempting to pour gunpowder into the smooth circular barrel, when Ramsey hurriedly intervened.

"Are you insane!?" he hissed, yanking Devon's powder horn out of his jittery hands. "Put the gun away! If you fire that thing down here, they'll panic, and this whole tunnel could collapse."

"Then what are we supposed to do?" one of the other guards shouted in panic. "We're in the middle of reptilian swampland with no apothecary for miles. One bite and we're dead."

Ramsey took a deep breath, fumbling through his supply pack. *It's unlike the king to forget essential supplies such as antivenom. Maybe the servants forgot to pack it.* With no solution to a possible snake bite, he scoured his mind for ideas about how to get around the scaly creatures. Arthur's usually irritating knowledge of reptiles popped into his head, and for once, Ramsey was grateful that he had listened to his brother's prattling. He lifted his lantern and narrowed his eyes, studying the hissing snakes' features in the soft light.

"These aren't cottonmouths," Ramsey remarked. "Their pupils are round, not slits—they're banded water snakes, which aren't venomous."

CHAPTER 13

Even with the news that the snakes were harmless, the guards' wary gazes didn't fade. Ramsey peered over at his nervous companions and sighed.

"Look, I know you all don't like snakes, but they're bluffing." He stepped forward, waving the fiery lantern in the serpents' faces. They hissed sharply, but slithered backward in retreat. "They're skittish animals, and they know we can kill them with a single swipe of our swords. I bet they're meant to scare away intruders, and we must prove that we won't be intimidated by a bunch of limbless animals. Let's go."

Ramsey strode forward. Most of the snakes quickly scrambled out of his way, and he swayed his flickering lantern in the faces of those that wouldn't. His companions stayed several feet behind him, only daring to step forward once Ramsey had cleared the path.

"We have to hurry." Ramsey's voice was wary as he stomped forward. "We don't have much time. Those Naga are probably already hunting us down."

The trail of snakes abruptly ended as Ramsey reached the end of the tunnel, where recessed into a wall was an ancient limestone tomb. Its surface was dimpled and cracked, with small pieces chipped off around the corners. Ramsey noticed that its heavy lid didn't sit on straight, as if it had once formed a perfect seal, but time had crumbled it away.

Or ... someone was here recently.

It took both Ramsey's and Devon's strength to haul away the hefty lid. Ramsey gulped and took a deep breath.

Moment of truth. He peered inside the ancient tomb, shining his lantern into the pit, and ... nothing. The tomb was empty, except for a trio of prongs just the right size to nestle an ancient artifact.

Ramsey's mind flashed back in horror as he realized he'd completely missed the signs. The entrance to the temple was jagged and crumbling as if it had been sealed, but someone burst it open. The snakes had to get in somehow, and the mucky walls of the underground tunnel appeared freshly dug out.

The temple ... idol ... it's all real. But someone was here first.

That Naga...

A fast *whoosh* echoed through the air, followed by a horrifying scream. Ramsey turned around and found himself staring at Devon's dazed, wide-eyed face, a single arrow protruding from his forehead as his lifeless body splashed to the ground with a sickeningly hard *thud*.

Ramsey held his lantern up, and two shadowy, humanoid figures with the slithering bodies of snakes appeared at the top of the stairs. They raised their scaled arms, and a pair of arrows whizzed past Ramsey's head, one striking a guard in the chest and the other one clattering against the limestone tomb.

Two bodies lay at their feet. The only other remaining guardsmen whimpered, his face a grotesquely pale white.

"Fire!" Ramsey shouted, pulling his gun from his waist.

As Ramsey fumbled with his powder horn, frantically trying to load his weapon, another pair of arrows soared past them. As Ramsey bolted out of the way, he heard another thud, and he turned around to see his last living companion face down in the mucky water, the back of an arrow protruding from his head. The white fletching wobbled in the damp air like a grotesque flag. His gun had clattered to the ground, gritty black gunpowder from the half-loaded weapon spilling into the watery muck.

They're all dead... I'm the last one left...

The Naga readied another set of arrows, and Ramsey's trembling fingers could barely hold his blunderbuss upright. He managed to finish loading his gun just as the Naga released their arrows. He ducked, and his clumsy shot was far off target. The buckshot exploded out of the barrel with a loud crack. It mostly sprayed the edge of the tunnel, but a few bits of lead punctured the edge of the larger Naga's shoulder, ripping through its scales and causing it to stumble backward.

Ramsey had to force his stomach contents back down his throat as he stepped toward the two Naga with his gun still pointed at them. He paced slowly, not wanting to slip on the wet ground or startle the creatures into firing off more arrows. *They don't understand how guns work. I must pretend it's still loaded, that I'm still a threat.* The larger Naga collapsed on the stairs in pain, its pouring blood creating slick red streams down its scales, and the smaller one rushed to its aid in panic.

As Ramsey stepped closer, his gun barrel firmly locked on the smaller Naga, it stopped tending to its companion and looked up. Ramsey was finally close enough to see its features. He saw an animalistic, reptilian beast, just as monstrous as in his childhood stories, but the panic and fear that spread across its serpentine face was eerily human.

Ramsey stopped. The smaller Naga's gaze was fixated on him, its slitted eyes recoiling in horror. He slowly lowered his gun, his heart racing and his breathing coming in rapid, panting gulps.

The smaller Naga huffed grievously, as if to admit defeat. Ramsey knew by the glower in its eyes that it wanted to tear him apart for invading its land and barging into its temple, but the larger Naga was profusely bleeding and needed urgent help. The smaller Naga turned its gaze away from Ramsey and wrapped a scaly arm around its injured companion, slithering back up the stairs and out of the temple.

Ramsey turned back to his three dead companions; each slumped face down on the mucky ground with bloody arrows protruding from their bodies. He felt terrible for leaving them behind, but he needed to bolt out of Naga territory as fast as possible and pray that he wouldn't meet the same fate. He couldn't stand another second in the damp, watery confines of the temple.

He had a long journey home, and he was uncertain if he'd make it back alive.

I must, he huffed in determination. He stepped up the watery stairs, his shaky legs unsteady under his weight. *Someone must tell the king before that idol-wielding Naga destroys us all.*

Chapter 14

IT WAS ANOTHER EARLY MORNING, AND THEY needed to reach Copperton quickly. Even with Sienna's brand-new cart and strong draft mare, it took over an hour to reach the mining town. Marissa could see and smell it from several miles away. Large sooty plumes wafted above the tree line and into the clear blue sky. She pressed her scarf against her nose to block out the smell. It reeked of old ash, smoke, and various nostril-burning chemicals.

"I give the miners a lot of credit," Sienna remarked as the cart wheeled closer to the grimy smog hovering in the distance. "It's not an easy life."

"What would make someone want to be a miner?" Marissa asked. "I can't even stand the smell."

"Quite frankly, it's a last resort for many people," Arthur responded. "It comes with dirty, unsafe working conditions and terrible pay. Personally, I think the mine owners are crooks, making their fortunes off the backs of near-slave labor. If I could—"

"Arthur, wait." Marissa perked up. "Do you hear that?"

As Marissa pointed, Aurora stood up, the hair on her back raised and her sharp warning barks echoing through the forest. Arthur and Sienna spun around. In the distance, at the edge of the long dirt road, was a tiny, dark silhouette moving rapidly toward them.

"It's just another cart." Arthur shrugged. "We'll let them pass us if they're in such a hurry."

"No." Marissa's voice was wary. "Look closer."

Arthur squinted as the faint figures approached. It wasn't a cart—it was two horses trotting side by side, each topped with a rider in bright purple-and-gold regalia. As soon as they got close enough for Arthur to make out their stern faces, their horses picked up speed to a steady canter.

"Guards!" Arthur's eyes went wild with panic. "We need to get off this road now!"

Sienna clicked to her mare, who picked up the pace to a fast trot. "I can't outrun them! Any faster and this cart could tip. And there's no side roads to pull onto!"

Marissa's eyes flicked fiercely around them. On all sides of the main road were tangles of green jungle, too dense for a cart to pass through without becoming horribly stuck. Marissa desperately tried to spot a clearing or side road, but they were still several miles from Copperton, and the guards were gaining ground quickly.

"They're catching up," Arthur remarked nervously as the guards cantered closer. They were now less than fifty feet from the cart. Aurora's irate barks grew louder and more frenzied.

Forty feet ... thirty feet ... Marissa's ears rang as the three-headed dog's bellows mixed with the inevitable dread creeping over her body. She knew that they were after Arthur, but the worst that could happen was he'd be marched back to the palace for a time-out. But for her, being caught by the guards could mean death.

Her heart jolted as a flash of a black, s-shape flickered past them. It was within sight for just a moment, but it was just long enough for the cottonmouth to notice Marissa's presence. It flicked its tongue, and Marissa could feel its startled emotions creep over her. As the cart wheeled shakily down the road, Marissa kept her eyes locked on the snake's location even as it faded from sight.

She lowered her head and forced her panic through its mind. *Somehow ... I have to get it to understand we're in danger.*

Please ... help us.

A sharp whinny echoed through the air, as startling as a human scream. Marissa looked up and saw the cottonmouth coiled in the middle of the dirt road, its body hunkered down and its white-gummed mouth flashing a deadly warning. The horses wanted nothing to do with the creature, and they continued their shrill cries as Sienna's cart wheeled away. The guards were stuck; their horses refused to step past the hissing snake.

Marissa watched the guards scowl in defeat as they once again became faint silhouettes in the distance. Within a few minutes, they disappeared from sight.

Arthur took a deep sigh of relief, then turned toward Marissa. "That couldn't have been a coincidence."

Marissa shrugged, but a triumphant grin was hidden behind her scarf.

"You really can communicate with snakes," Arthur remarked in awe. "I'm incredibly thankful that we came across that cottonmouth. The last thing I want is to be hauled back to the palace. And I certainly don't want you being captured, either."

"I must say, I didn't realize your relationship with your family had degraded so severely," Sienna remarked. "They really don't want you interfering with the Naga, do they?"

"They do not. And it concerns me greatly. As I was telling Marissa, I think they know something we don't."

They continued down the road for several miles, eventually passing a tiny, run-down village just before they reached Copperton. Marissa was relieved to see the cluster of worn buildings and hoped that the little town would be a distraction for the guards.

"Well, despite the earlier excitement, we've made it." Sienna pulled her horse to a halt just outside Copperton. She seemed hesitant to get any closer to the ashy town. "Looks like I'll be taking the long way home to avoid those guards. As for you two, please be careful. I pray they don't come skulking around the camp."

"We'll be alright," Marissa reassured, trying to hide the uncertainty in her voice. "We passed by another village after the guards got stuck. That will throw them off our trail for a while."

"I hope so. Oh, and before I forget." She dug through her satchel and pulled out a small drawstring bag. It contained several potions and dried herbs, including some orange paste. At the bottom of the bag was a small vial of antivenom, left over from the batch Sienna had made from Marissa's venom.

"Like I said, I want to help any way I can." She smiled as Arthur took the bag and he and Marissa hopped off the cart. "I'll be rooting for you two. Stay safe."

Sienna's cart disappeared into the forest as Marissa and Arthur trudged toward the mining camp. Several weary-eyed men and women covered in chalky white dust stumbled past them, their heads down and their faces heavily lined with fatigue. Marissa didn't pay much attention to them; she was in a sharp state of alert, her eyes flicking around for any sign of the guards. She peered over at Arthur and noticed his demeanor was just as stiff. But as the pair wandered deeper into the mining camp and farther from the main road, Marissa's tension loosened. *We should be safe, at least for a while.*

"So, do they actually mine copper here?" she asked, hoping conversation would help alleviate their anxiety.

"Nope. There isn't any copper in the Valley of Scales," Arthur replied. "Or gold and silver, for that matter—it's all imported. It's called Copperton because they pay miners with copper coin. I think they mostly mine limestone here, which is used as a building material. Most of Brennan is made of the stuff."

A few hundred yards beyond them was a massive white pit, tiered in layers like a cake. A hundred feet down, the miners scurried around the bottom like ants. The area was surrounded by massive iron machinery, some of it several stories high. Powdery white dust rose from the pit and settled around the edges.

Marissa stayed back and observed the scene as Arthur tried to grab the attention of the miners as they passed. They brushed past him, sour-faced and uninterested in conversation. To the side of the large mining pit was a row of shack-like houses that seemed to slump at odd angles. A tired miner stumbled toward one of them, and as he got closer, Marissa realized it was Thomas. He heaved the flimsy door open on the shack closest to her and slammed it behind him with a rattling thud.

While Arthur was busy, Marissa decided to do her own investigating. She crept up to Thomas's house and knocked on the door. It swung open a few seconds later with a loud creak.

"Yes?" Thomas grumbled. His eyes narrowed. "Ain't ya the girl who led us to the apothecary yesterday? What do ya want now?"

His mood was even more sour than the day before. Past him, Marissa could see the interior of the filthy one-room shack. The furniture was almost unrecognizable underneath heaps of dirty clothes and slimy old dishes, and the gritty, cheap floors were coated in patches of white dust. *The house is empty. No sign of Marian.*

"I... I just want to talk." Marissa shuddered as the ill-tempered man hulked over her. "About the Naga, and—"

Marissa jolted as Thomas grabbed the doorframe with a loud slam of his palm. "I told ya, I don't want anythin' more t'do with those damn beasts!"

Marissa tried to peer inside again, but this made Thomas even angrier. He shifted his body to block her view. Her eyes narrowed.

"You weren't fighting the Naga to be brave," she accused. "You were hiding something. You didn't want the reptilians to enter your home."

His face wrinkled into an even deeper scowl, but Marissa could see a hint of worry in his eyes. She stepped closer, and he shifted back.

"I bet they took it, didn't they? After the Naga bit you and you were forced to flee?"

Thomas pointed a large finger at her. "Ya better shut up right now before I beat that little masked face in."

Marissa huffed, loosening the scarf around her neck. Nim popped out like a stalking weasel, neck coiled into an s-shape and ready to strike.

Thomas's eyes widened in horror. He stumbled backward, nearly tripping over the doorframe. "Snake!!! Get that damn beast out of my face! Good gods, is that thing poisonous?"

"Venomous, not poisonous. Tell me what you're hiding, or you'll find out." Marissa leered toward Thomas as he fell and crab-walked backward, scrabbling over the dirty floors.

"What in the world is going on he—"

Marissa thrust an arm out in front of Arthur as he approached, blocking his path.

"He's hiding something," Marissa blurted out before Arthur could open his mouth. "He didn't want the Naga entering his home for a reason."

Behind Arthur, Aurora's body stiffened, all three heads growling.

Thomas stared in horror at both Aurora and Nim before covering his face with his arms. "Alright! Damn animals! I never thought it would come to this ... we have so little ... poor Marian's gettin' worse every day ... I couldn't resist. They offered me too much money..."

"Wait, slow down." Marissa stood up straight and patted Nim, who settled back into her scarf. "What happened? What were you hiding?"

"The hide," Thomas whimpered.

Hide?

A deep horrid emotion trickled through Marissa's stomach, and she was so sickened that she feared she would vomit.

"Wait..." Arthur's eyes grew wide. "You're not a *poacher*, are you?"

"C-come inside. I'll tell ya what's been goin' on. As long as ya promise not to kill me."

Arthur shot Marissa a stern look, and she sighed.

"We won't harm you," Marissa swore. "You have our word. But we need to know everything."

Thomas moved aside, and Marissa and Arthur entered the cluttered home. Neither of them had any interest in sitting on the grimy furniture, so they chose to stand in the center of the room.

Thomas stood up, his chest heaving. He walked a few paces before plopping onto a couch. As he did, several dirty dishes slid off the cushion and onto the floor with a hollow ceramic thud.

"Okay, okay... so it all started many years ago, shortly after Marian and I got married. She kept gettin' sick, couldn't keep weight on, and she'd get bruises as soon as ya touched 'er. We kept takin' 'er to apothecaries all over the valley. Some sort of issue with 'er blood, they said, but they didn't have much medicine for it. She'd be alright for a year or two, but the disease kept rearin' its ugly head, and this year's been the worst. But then I heard the news; some apothecary in a village west of 'ere found a cure. Problem is, the medicine costs a fortune, and we're barely makin' ends meet. She's my wife ... I'll do anythin' to save 'er, and she's runnin' out of time. That's where the hide came in. Since money is so tight, I often go huntin' with my bow." He gestured toward the weapon, which hung on a hook next to a shelf stacked with piles of arrows. "A few months ago, I came across some shed skin.

I mentioned it that night at the tavern, and the miners told me that 'ere were merchants in Brennan that would pay a decent price for it. Sells well on the black market, they say—rich folks believe it's magic or some baloney. So next time I went out, I collected some. I couldn't believe it—a few pieces of the stuff sold for more than what I make in a week. So I kept collectin' more and more of it, venturin' farther east into Varan territory. Then they made me an offer I couldn't refuse."

"You killed one, didn't you?" Arthur's tone was solemn.

"Ya gotta understand how tight money is 'round here. Us miners don't get paid much, and if I don't do somethin' soon, I could lose my wife. My contact, that black market man—he offered me enough money to pay for her cure ... in exchange for the full hide of a Varan. So I went out with my bow ... it was just'a small one, not quite grown, out playin' in the woods. I had planned on makin' a trip into Brennan to sell it, but we've been pullin' double shifts in the mine and I ain't able to leave. I finally had some time off planned for tomorrow... but then those reptilians came burstin' in and stole the hide back. It was gone when I came back from the apothecary."

Arthur lowered his head, his face grim. Marissa's scales trembled with anger. She swallowed, trying to calm the horrible nausea in her stomach.

"How?" she muttered. "How could you be so greedy as to take a life for money? I can't believe I saved—"

Marissa's mouth snapped shut as realization singed through her face. She felt betrayed, saving the life of someone who killed her kind. And in her anger, she'd nearly let the truth slip. *A poacher... finding out I'm half-Naga...* the thought sickened her stomach.

Thankfully, Thomas barely noticed her slip-up. He was confused by the sudden halt in her sentence, but he was too deeply engulfed in his own emotions to prod further.

"Look, I did what I had to do." Thomas sighed, his sorrowful, frustrated face buried in his palms. "My wife is dyin', for heaven's sake! I know killin' is wrong, but I needed the money ... I did what I had t'do to save her. Ain't ya got family, girl? Wouldn't ya do the same for 'em?"

Marissa's throat shook as she forced down a hard swallow. *No, I couldn't, because I have no family.*

"What's wrong with ya?" Thomas scowled, now angered by Marissa's condemnation. "Puttin' those monster's lives above my wife's. Ya really are a reptilian-lover, ain't ya? Yer wasting yer breath. They're beasts, more animal than human."

Marissa lunged for him. She was a lot smaller than Thomas, but since she caught him by surprise, she managed to tackle him to the floor. He wrestled under her grasp, eventually slipping out from under her and backing into a corner of the room. Tears blinding her eyes, Marissa bolted after him, releasing an angry Nim from her scarf. *I risked my own safety to save you... you worthless, vile reptilian killer...* She was so overwhelmed with anger, so determined to make him pay... that she didn't notice him grab an arrow off the shelf.

She howled as he plunged it into her upper thigh, having never felt such intense pain. She crumpled to the ground just as Nim managed to strike Thomas's neck. She crouched with her knees touching the floor, about to collapse, as Thomas's screams mixed with the sound of blood pounding in her ears until she was almost deafened.

A firm hand pulled her upward. Marissa shifted and almost fell over, barely able to put weight on her left leg. Arthur lifted her arm around his shoulder and dragged her out of the shack. Thomas remained on the floor, screaming and grasping his throat.

"Murderer!!!" Marissa shouted behind her as Arthur slammed the front door, leaving Thomas completely helpless and alone.

Chapter 15

EZRINTH'S HEART POUNDED AS HE STOOD IN front of the Komodo temple. He had dreaded this moment since they first came across the Varan hide in that miner's rat's nest of a home.

He didn't know what had drawn him to the chest in the far corner of the room back when they were in the mining camp. Two of the Varan were busy tossing clothes over their shoulders as they scrabbled through the messy room. The bastard miner and his frantic mate were gone, their cart rattling down the road at full speed. The stubborn man was bolder than the rest, but one bite to the chest took care of that. Ezrinth was determined to search every corner of the valley—no human would stand in his way.

The chest wasn't part of their mission—it was unlikely that a living being would pop out of the musty old container. But Ezrinth was especially determined to search every corner of the home. The man stood his ground against an angry Naga—he was either stupid or hiding something.

The metal locks popped open with a loud click. Ezrinth lifted the lid, expecting to find gold or jewelry or some other insignificant human trinket. But his body ran cold as he caught a glimpse of the dusty brown-and-gray scales, speckled with the unmistakable pattern of a Varan.

He slithered backward, barely holding in a scream. He'd heard tales of poachers since he was a juvenile—horrible, malevolent humans that would murder reptilians for money. Yet it happened so infrequently that the young Naga thought of them as nothing more than tall tales. But decades later, poaching was now a very real horror, and the Varan chieftain's loss of his only child had shaken the entire community.

The hide was small, the scales tiny and uniform. *This must be her.* Horrid shivers ran down his tail. The Varan crept up behind him, their eyes wide and their claws shaking.

<Is ... is that her?> The smaller one's voice trembled.

Ezrinth nodded, his words quivering with anger. <I need to make sure he dies. I'll make him suffer, then burn his bones to the ground until there's nothing left.>

He bolted for the door, but the two Varan pulled the angry snake back.

\<Ezrinth, leave it. You already bit him. Let the venom run its course. We need to get this to Rathi right away.\>

Ezrinth clutched the Varan hide in his fist, tracing a claw over the tiny scales. \<You're right; as much as I'd like to see him die in person. Let's get out of this filthy human town.\>

It was now a day later, and they had arrived in Varan territory. The village elders went to fetch Rathi, leaving Ezrinth alone in front of the temple with the child's hide folded in his palms. His Varan companions surrounded him in a semicircle.

Rathi emerged, clutching his sobbing mate's hand. Pain radiated from the chieftain's eyes as his body shook and he struggled to maintain composure.

It was too late for his mate. She dove for Ezrinth before he had a chance to present them with their slain daughter's remains. She grabbed the hide from his outstretched palms and buried her howling face, hugging it as if it were still her living daughter. The elders quietly stepped forward and led the distraught mother away so she could grieve in private.

Rathi stepped forward. He took a deep breath to settle his shaking body and brushed streaks of silent tears from his face.

\<I can't believe you found it. I thought it was long gone, lost beyond those wretched city gates. Where was it?\>

\<In an old camp on the outskirts of human territory. It was locked away in a chest. The killer clearly intended to sell it.\>

<Did you encounter him?>

<Yes. I bit him, and he and his mate fled before I discovered your daughter's remains. I am so sorry, Rathi. If I had known, I wouldn't have let him leave alive. But my venom has likely finished him off by now.>

Rathi nodded, his face grim. <It's definitely Mikara's hide. In addition, several of my guards went missing, and today we came across their remains, once again stripped of their scales. I've received word from the other Varan villages that they're having the same issue. It seems that poaching is increasing. But there is some good news. The Gharian have become aware of your mission, and they reached out to me. It seems that a few of their own have also disappeared. Their chieftain said that if we can prove that we have what it takes to overpower the humans, they will join our cause.>

Ezrinth perked up. So much grief hung in the air, yet this news brought a spark of hope to the Naga's heart. *Mikara, if any good comes from your death, let it be this. I will put an end to the humans' reign of terror and reclaim Squamata for the reptilians.*

<But Ezrinth,> Rathi continued. <This plan will only succeed if we persuade all four reptilian races. What are we going to do about the Testudo?>

<Give it time,>Ezrinth grumbled. The valley's tortoisefolk race were highly seclusive pacifists, living deep in underground burrows and avoiding any sort of conflict. The Varan and Gharian wanted revenge against the humans, and persuading the Testudo to go to war

would be Ezrinth's biggest hurdle. <But for now, let's put aside our plans. If we want to persuade the Gharian and Testudo to join our cause, we must prove our strength, and now is the time to act.>

<What do you propose?>

<We show the humans what we're capable of. We avenge your daughter and every other reptilian slain by those filthy poachers.> Ezrinth turned toward the semi-circle of Varan warriors. <My companions, let us plan a return trip to where we found Mikara's hide. We have work to do.>

MARISSA KNEW SHE'D BE GETTING A LECTURE FROM Arthur, but right now, he was desperate to get them both as far away from Copperton as possible. Marissa struggled to hobble as Arthur supported her weight. She repeatedly hopped on her right foot as blood oozed down her left thigh, staining her cloak. Arthur panted, sweat streaked across his forehead, as they approached the main road.

He set Marissa down next to a large oak tree and took a moment to catch his breath, hands on his knees. Marissa leaned her head against the trunk, trying to block out the stabbing pain radiating up her body. She was too afraid to remove her cloak—she didn't want to see how bad it was.

In the still air, she heard a faint splashing noise. She peered around the wide tree trunk and noticed a small, stagnant river parallel to the road.

She crawled over to the water, dead vines and fallen leaves bristling under her palms. She hunched down, cupping the dark water in her hands and splashing it over her face. Nim slithered off her neck and dipped his nose in the water, his throat bobbing as he took in deep gulps. Marissa heard the crunching of footsteps, and Arthur kneeled next to her.

"Here." He dug through his satchel and pulled out Sienna's medicine bag. "Thankfully, we have the supplies to heal you."

Arthur untwisted the cap on the vial of orange paste and handed it to her. She peeled her cloak off her shoulders and placed it next to the river, then pulled her blood-stained trousers down several inches, exposing her underwear. She shuddered as the cloth slid over her wound, exposing her bare, scaled thighs. The gash wasn't very large or deep, thanks to the strength of her reptilian scales, but it still hurt. Dark, slimy blood oozed from within like jelly.

Marissa grimaced and turned her head away from the gruesome sight. Despite being an outcast half-Naga, she had lived a relatively safe life. The worst injuries she'd ever received were trivial cuts and bruises from playing outside in the garden as a child. She'd never been stabbed before, and looking into the grisly abyss of her own wound sent a deep, distressing nausea through her stomach.

Arthur seemed to notice her unease. "Here, want me to help?"

Marissa sighed. *Just let him do it. The sooner this wound closes up, the better.* She reluctantly handed the vial to Arthur and closed her eyes, her scales tensing under his touch as he applied the paste. His hands were just inches from her hip bone, and the unfamiliar sensation made Marissa shudder.

"I'm sorry," Arthur whispered softly, trying to ease her discomfort. "I know this is kind of awkward. I actually took some apothecary classes at university, though that's far from making me a healer. There," Arthur finished rubbing the paste around the wound, "give it about five minutes, and it'll close up."

The salve worked quickly, but even with the physical pain gone, disgust and anger still spewed through Marissa's veins like venom.

"How can humans be so cruel?" she hissed.

"It's complicated, Marissa." Arthur sighed, sympathizing with her frustration. "Murder is wrong, I agree with you, but people are willing to do desperate things to save the ones they love. Unfortunately, that can mean doing something as awful as killing another being. Most humans view the reptilians as little more than animals; Thomas doesn't understand the gravity of what he's done."

But as hard as Marissa tried, she couldn't comprehend it. She had no concept of love, and her young heart still saw the world as black and white, good and evil. All she could see Thomas as was a murderer, regardless of the reason.

"Sometimes emotions blind us, whether it be love or hatred," Arthur continued. "You're susceptible to it, too, you know. You swore to Thomas that you wouldn't hurt him if he told you the truth. And if Nim did inject him with the bizarre venom that snake isn't supposed to have, his blood is on your hands."

"Fine by me," Marissa grumbled, but a sudden deep sadness panged her stomach.

If he dies, can I really live with it? I did save his life just yesterday...

She quietly stewed next to the river, pouring handfuls of water over her closing wound. As it was mid-autumn, the water was slightly chilly. She noticed Arthur hang his coat on a tree branch and scrub his dirt-lined hands in the water. She rolled up her sleeves and dipped her whole arm in the river. A gentle, cozy sensation rippled down her spine as the cool water slid across her scales, and her mounting anger and frustration began to subside.

"Hey, Arthur? Naga live deep in the swampland, right?"

"Uh, yes," he responded.

"They must really love the water," she remarked. At that moment, she wanted to forget about the turmoil of the past several days. She wanted to put her stresses aside and focus on the water, just for a few minutes. *I spend so much time being human; right now, I want to be a Naga.* Suddenly, she pulled off her blouse and trousers, leaving her in only undergarments, and dove into the river.

CHAPTER 15

"Marissa!"

The water was only a few feet deep, and she quickly surfaced, her long black hair floating around her in tendrils. She wiped her face, brushing her thick bangs out of the way, and grinned at Arthur. *This is strange.* She never smiled with her teeth, even around Arthur—she feared she would scare him with her fangs. She did a slow backstroke through the water, admiring the dense canopy overhead as her body melted into the calm river.

Marissa had never been swimming before. She had rarely even seen a body of water. Yet it came so naturally to her. She dove back under the water and realized she could hold her breath for several minutes at a time. Naga truly were water snakes. *All my life, humans fearing me, calling me a monster...* For once, she felt completely at home, wild, and free to be her reptilian self.

"Arthur!" Marissa shouted as she surfaced. He stared at her from the shoreline, dumbfounded. "Jump in! It feels great!"

"It's October! You're insane!"

"Please?" She splashed some water in his direction. Some of it hit Nim, who recoiled before cautiously slithering into the river.

"Alright, fine. I'm covered in that white dust from the mining camp, anyway. And we should probably wash the blood off your clothes."

Marissa's face flushed red as Arthur lifted his shirt over his shoulders. She sank into the water, embarrassed by her sudden, strange emotions. She hadn't expected a bookish reptile expert to be ... muscular. He rolled up his trousers and turned toward her. She noticed the dense, triangular patch of hair on his chest and sank even lower into the water.

Get ahold of yourself. He's a human, and you're a...

Her thoughts were interrupted by a sudden torrential splash. Water sprayed in every direction, causing small waves to crash against the sandy shoreline. Arthur surfaced and stood up, the river coming to his waist, and shook the water out of his tangled chestnut hair. They locked eyes, and Arthur joyfully laughed.

"I won't lie; this feels great." Arthur sank back under the water, floating with his body stretched out in a star shape. He drifted past Marissa and flicked water into her face.

"Hey!" she responded by pushing a small wave toward his head. They swam in circles, laughing and splashing each other. Marissa stood up and went to push a torrent of water at Arthur, signaling her victory, but she ended up falling right into him.

"Hey now, be careful," he teased as she looked up. Marissa's blue eyes met Arthur's green ones, their faces just inches from each other. Unfamiliar emotions swirled through Marissa's body, making her head spin. She was terrified, yet she couldn't break away from his gaze.

Until she noticed it, just a few feet from the shoreline.

"Wait, where are you going?" Arthur asked as Marissa strode out of the water.

It smells strange, yet oddly familiar...

Draped across the brush was a long strand of reptile shed, several feet long and about a foot wide. Marissa picked it up and brought it toward her face, sticking out her long, forked tongue.

"Is that Naga shed?" Arthur asked as he emerged from the water.

"I believe so. There's a scent trail coming from it. The Naga was here not too long ago."

"Can you track it?"

"Well, yes, but... uh, look away."

"Wait, why?"

Marissa grimaced. "I need to use my sense of smell, and ... people find my snake tongue weird."

Arthur's bewildered expression morphed into laughter. "I've spent more time around reptiles than I have around people. In fact, most days I prefer them. I promise I'm not going to judge."

"Fine," Marissa grumbled, still embarrassed. She continued flicking her forked tongue in multiple directions until she finally locked onto the scent trail.

"It's headed that way." She pointed.

Arthur sighed. "That's back toward Varan territory."

"They're leaving the outer villages," Marissa remarked. "I guess the Varan hide was what they were looking for, after all."

"Maybe I was wrong," Arthur remarked in amazement. "Maybe I was just being paranoid, and this really was all just over a poaching incident. In that case, let's head back to Brennan. I need to explain the situation to the king and pray he doesn't escalate this any further."

Marissa frowned, the Naga shed still clutched in her fingers. "We're not done here."

"Wait, what?"

"This isn't over. We need to track down the black market and put an end to this."

"Marissa." Arthur's voice was heavy and stern as he slid his shirt back over his head. "No. Absolutely not. You know I want to help the reptilians, but going up against some of the most powerful crime lords in Brennan is not an option. It's far too dangerous, especially for a half-Naga that isn't even supposed to be in the kingdom."

"I don't care. I must try. You can report this to the king all you want, but you know that won't stop the poaching."

Arthur stared at the ground; his hands balled into fists. His brows were furrowed, and Marissa could see the painful indecisiveness on his face.

"Can you come up with a halfway decent plan?" he asked. "One that won't get us killed?"

Now that Marissa was out of the water, the crisp autumn air crept under her skin and made her damp scales shiver. She rubbed her arms, wishing she had a towel.

"We need to go back to Thomas's house."

Arthur tilted his head back and grumbled, "That was not what I had in mind."

"It's our only chance. Thomas said he had contacts in the black market. We need his help."

"Thomas is currently near death for the second time, courtesy of your pet snake. Even if he is still alive once we march back to Copperton, he'll put arrows through our chests the second we go near his front door. There is no chance that man is willing to help you after you tried to kill him."

"He stabbed me with an arrow! Besides, I didn't *tell* Nim to bite him."

Arthur gave Marissa a disapproving frown, his arms crossed, and she sighed.

"Okay, okay. This is my fault. So, let's go back to Copperton to save him. Didn't Sienna give you antivenom?"

"Well, yes, but..."

"I was wrong. Revenge is wrong. Killing Thomas isn't going to bring that Varan back. I caused this, and now I need to fix it."

"Alright, fine. Heal him all you want, but don't expect him to help you track down the black market. As long as you can accept that."

"I can." Marissa stared up at the smooth blue sky peeking out between the lacy canopy of leaves. "Now, let's go."

THE HOUSE WAS QUIET. IN FACT, THE WHOLE TOWN was. It was noon, and most of the dusty miners were in their shacks on their lunch break. Marissa gulped as she stood in front of Thomas's home, having no idea what awaited her on the other side of the door.

"We'll pull it open and stand behind it. Don't step into the doorway," Arthur instructed. "We'll see how he reacts."

They braced themselves. Marissa pressed her shoulder into the door, and in one smooth, quick motion, she yanked it open, shielding herself behind the flimsy wood. She expected to hear a shout or to see an arrow whiz out the door and skid across the dusty ground, but instead, they were met with silence.

Marissa and Arthur grimaced. This was not good. No reaction meant that they'd have no idea what awaited them on the other side.

Finally, a faint voice grumbled, "Who is it?"

"It's Arthur and Marissa," Marissa responded from behind the door as Arthur shook his head. She ignored him and continued, "Look, I know you don't trust us after what I did to you. But we have antivenom. May we come in and heal you?"

There was a long silence on the other side of the door. "Thomas?"

"Marissa, don't!" Arthur yelped and lunged for Marissa's arm as she crept around the other side of the door. She brushed Arthur off and locked eyes with a dazed man whose weary body hung partway off a decrepit couch. She watched his chest rise and fall with every staggered, painful breath. He didn't look angry or vengeful; his body remained still even as Marissa appeared in the doorway.

Thomas tilted his head toward her, and in his eyes, she saw a deep mixture of pain and remorse.

"Why?" he croaked. "Why did you come back?"

"Because I was wrong. I never should've attacked you. I still think you're a murderer, but letting you die would make me one, too."

Arthur crept up behind her, and she took the medicine bag from his hands.

"Come in." Thomas sighed. "Please."

Marissa cautiously stepped through the doorframe and kneeled next to him. His sad, grim smile made her conflicted emotions boil. It it had been clear during his time at Sienna's that Thomas was a troubled man, and sitting on a couch with venom coursing through his veins seemed to bring all those dark emotions to the surface.

"From the moment I fired my arrow, I knew we were wrong." Thomas's voice was soft as Marissa administered the antivenom. Following Sienna's instructions, she poured the vial over the puncture wounds on his neck. It disappeared into his skin, seeping into his bloodstream like magic. "Everythin' us humans think of 'em, everythin' that the kingdom made us believe ... it was all wrong. It was just a young one, playin', runnin' through the tall grass and chasin' those little brown lizards. I couldn't communicate with 'em, but I bet they had a lovin' family and hope for the future, just like my own daughter. And I ended their life. That's why I'm not mad at ya. Once y'all left, I sat here alone and decided that if this venom is gonna do me in, so be it. I've done enough harm."

"There we go." Marissa patted Thomas's arm. "You're going to be okay. You're going to live."

When Marissa had decided to return to Thomas's home, she was willing to put herself in danger if he wanted revenge. She had expected anger, violence ... not remorse. His regret didn't soften Marissa's anger and disgust, but she hated the fact that Arthur was right—Thomas just wanted to save his wife, and he didn't understand the seriousness of what he'd done.

Within a few minutes, Thomas was able to sit upright. "I wasn't expectin' to survive this. So, I've decided, if I'm gonna live, I'm gonna set things right. I'm in your debt for guidin' us to the apothecary when the Naga bit me, but I need to know the truth."

Marissa's reptilian blood ran cold. "What do you mean?"

Thomas locked eyes with Marissa. "Earlier, when ya stopped mid-sentence, ya said 'saved.' Between that, yer freaky pet snake, and that scarf around yer face, I wanna know what's really goin' on. Yer hidin' somethin', ain't ya?"

Marissa gulped and pressed a hand against her scarf, the few layers of fabric that hid her dangerous secret. She knew people always noticed it and probably wondered what she was hiding ... but no one had ever dared to ask for the truth. Realization overtook her as she stood up, and she nodded solemnly.

If this is what it takes to get his help... so be it.

"Thomas." Her voice was soft as her hands trembled. "There's something I need to show you."

CHAPTER 15

"Marissa, no!" Arthur cried from the doorway as he realized what she was doing.

Before Arthur could reach her, Marissa pulled her cloak and scarf off in one smooth motion, like ripping off a bandage. She wanted to do it quickly, before she changed her mind.

"I want to help the reptilians not only because I care about them, but because I am one. I am a half-Naga." She swallowed down her nerves. Thomas's eyes were wide, but his expression was gentle—he didn't show any disgust or horror. "I know what it's like to be feared, to be hated, to be misunderstood. I want to find a path to peace between the humans and reptilians."

"I'll be damned," Thomas remarked, his voice soft with amazement. "I shoulda known. Yer one of 'em."

"Indeed, I am. And before you judge me for being a reptilian, I'm the one that saved your life yesterday. Sienna was out of antivenom when you showed up. I had to supply venom so she could heal you."

Thomas shook his head, chuckling softly in disbelief. "I guess I really am in yer debt, then. Well, peace is certainly a lofty undertakin'. In the past, I woulda called ya a fool. I really want to aid ya, but with Marian bein' sick and all..."

"We know. You're worried about her. But we really need your help," Arthur interjected. "And if you come with us, I'll give you the money for her cure."

Marissa and Thomas's heads quickly spun in Arthur's direction, surprised by his generous offer.

"Good gods, you'd do that for me? You've got that sort'a money?"

"Yes," Arthur responded in a curt manner, not wanting to explain his wealth further.

"I ... I'll never be able to thank y'all enough." Thomas's voice shook with emotion. "Our lives have been rough, and we ain't always gettin' along... but she's my whole world. Whatever ya need me to do to save 'er, I'll do it."

Arthur nodded, a small smile on his face. "In that case, will you come with us back to Vale? We need your help."

"I s'pose I could. To be honest, Marian and I had a big argument after we returned home yesterday. She said she 'needed a break' and scurried off to her parents' home in Orchid. So she should be safe with 'em for a few days. But the bad news is, she took the cart."

"We need to hurry, then." Marissa peered out the single musty window. "Sienna wasn't expecting us to head back to Vale, so we don't have a ride. We'll have to walk. If we leave now, we can get to Sienna's before sundown. I certainly don't want to travel in the dark."

Chapter 16

NATHARA REMEMBERED THE FIRST TIME HER mother, Chumana, had brought her to the hidden Temple of Vaipera when she was a child. The structure was in near-ruin, covered in dense tangles of vines and half-buried in the murky swampland, and, most importantly, the entrance to the temple, marked with a solid slab of limestone, was sealed off from the outside world. It had been that way for nearly eight hundred years, ever since her ancestors had buried the wretched artifact in its watery tomb.

As the years passed, their visits to the temple became less frequent, nearly ceasing completely after Chumana passed away. Her family didn't want to arouse suspicion by making constant trips into the deep swampland several miles from the Naga capital of Nerodia. Nathara wished her ancestors had hidden the artifact within Nerodia so her family could keep a closer eye on it, but Orami reasoned that the artifact was best kept away from civilization, hidden deep underground and sealed in thick limestone.

At the time, Nathara had reluctantly agreed with his reasoning. After all, it had been eight hundred years, and the artifact had remained untouched.

Until now.

Nathara stood outside the temple in the late evening with her injured father, Orami, inspecting the jagged, gaping hole in the once impenetrable limestone. Earlier that day, they'd tracked down a band of humans intent on stealing the artifact. They'd managed to put arrows through the skulls of the obstinate intruders ... except for one. *One managed to escape.*

Nathara bit back her fury as Orami slithered around the structure, his wounded shoulder tightly wrapped in thick bandaging. She worried he'd damaged it further when he hauled the bodies of the humans' deceased horses into the temple, trying to keep the remains out of sight. They now lay deep inside the watery pit, doomed to decay in the dark confines not far from their ill-fated owners. *I wish we hadn't shot them,* Nathara grumbled to herself. *They were innocent animals.* When the pair had first discovered the humans invading the temple, Orami insisted that their method of a quick escape needed to be disposed of.

Nathara had insisted on investigating herself, telling her father that he needed to rest and not strain himself after his injury, but Orami had gruffly refused. He was silent, and Nathara knew he was just as enraged as she was. Nathara had been certain she'd be able to kill them all ... until the surviving human had pulled out the long metallic weapon that every Naga feared. They were incredibly lucky that the projectiles only pierced her father's shoulder. As desperate as Nathara was to prevent the human from leaving with the idol piece, she knew that further engaging the human would result in both of their deaths. They had tried to keep news of the humans' appearance from spreading; they didn't want to reveal the temple's existence or see their companions pursue the human and be killed by its deadly weapon. She'd even bandaged her father's wounds herself. By now, the human was likely long gone, back in its own territory, and out of the Naga's reach.

She couldn't stop blaming herself. *You coward,* she hissed. *This is all your fault.* But the Naga were no match for the humans' technology. Rumors of the humans inventing powerful weapons that could fire projectiles fast enough to blow through a Naga's tough scales started when she was a child, and ever since then, they'd become a far deadlier threat.

What further worried Nathara was that the humans had even come across the temple in the first place. It seemed unlikely that they'd stumbled across it by accident. Humans had little reason to venture into Naga territory that didn't involve conflict. *Somehow, they knew. But how?*

The idol pieces were a deeply guarded secret, known only by the reptilian leaders and their families. The humans had no use for the ancient artifact—the great serpent goddess Vaipera could only be summoned by reptilians. The legends described the idol as a divine gift, but Chumana had always told Nathara that it was evil, an indestructible curse that could destroy Squamata if the pieces ever fell into the wrong hands. Even if the humans couldn't summon Vaipera themselves, Nathara feared what sort of nefarious plans would cause them to steal an artifact they couldn't even use.

<Let's go,> Orami interrupted his daughter's thoughts with a scaled hand on her shoulder. He waved a lit torch toward the temple. <There's always a chance the human dropped it, or it was left on one of the others' bodies. We must not give up hope.>

The pair ducked their heads, creeping into the dark murkiness of the temple's interior, and slithered cautiously around the hefty bodies of the deceased horses. Nathara took a moment to wave her torch in front of the worn hieroglyphs and paintings that lined the limestone walls, her serpentine eyes scanning each remnant of her ancestors' past. It had been many generations since the idol had first appeared, and much of its history was muddled in myth and legend. Nathara froze, her gaze locked on a crude painting of a giant snake beast, several stories tall and crackling with an electricity-like power. Scrabbling at the base of its serpentine body, ant-like humans shrieked in fear, running in all directions.

All that we know for certain is that the great goddess can never be allowed to enter this world, no matter how tempting her presence may be.

She shook her head, pulling her attention away from the temple walls as her father ushered her downstairs. The damp, mucky cavern showed signs of being freshly dug out; Nathara knew the simple dirt passageway couldn't have held up for eight hundred years. But what caught her attention was the soft symphony of hisses that echoed from the darkness. She raised her torch and illuminated the copper-colored eyes of dozens of banded water snakes, their scaled heads raised. When they realized the visitors were just a pair of Naga and not more wretched humans, their tense postures relaxed into submission.

<Do you feel that?> Orami asked.

Nathara did. She lowered her eyes and concentrated on the snakes, attempting to meld her mind with theirs.

<They've been here a while,> Nathara remarked, her voice wary as she pieced together the truth. <At least a week, or maybe even several... which means...>

<The humans didn't burst open the temple,> Orami concluded. <Someone else was here first.>

Nathara's scales felt numb as horrid realization crept down her throat and wound through her serpentine body. She was already in despair over the humans stealing the artifact, but the truth was far graver.

<Ezrinth.> Her brother's name was barely a whisper. <Do you really think...?>

<He knows the temple is here. And the storm is coming; we can all feel it. If there was ever a time for him to attempt to summon Vaipera, it would be now.>

Nathara forced a swallow down her shaky throat. All her life, ever since her mother had told her about the temple, she had felt burdened with a devastating secret. But she reasoned that as long as the idol was sealed away, buried deep in the swamp, and hidden from the rest of the world, she would be safe. Between Ezrinth and the humans, the truth was spreading into the rest of Squamata, bursting open like the jagged entrance to the once-secured temple. They wouldn't be able to keep the idol's existence hidden for much longer.

The humans and reptilians had been in an unsteady truce for centuries. There was plenty of rising tension and isolated skirmishes, including humans and reptilians killing those who crossed into the others' territory, but there had been no major bloodshed. But now, the humans knew about the idol, and Nathara knew her angry, ostracized brother would stop at nothing to summon the goddess. War was inevitable, and the lives of everyone in Squamata, human and reptilian alike, would be thrown into turmoil.

<We must stop him,> Nathara declared, her reptilian nostrils flared. <We must find my brother, or he is going to be the end of us all.>

CHAPTER 16

It was an exhausting three-hour walk back to Vale. Marissa grumbled in her head the entire trip about how much she wished they had a cart. Her nerves were on edge, and she jolted every time a little brown lizard rattled the brush or scurried up a tree trunk. It was late afternoon, and the sun crept slowly down the clear blue sky.

I swear, if I see a bandit pop out of the brush, I'm biting them myself.

All three of them were quiet. They were tired, hungry, and not in the right mindset for conversation. Marissa hung back next to Arthur while Thomas walked up ahead. He whistled softly to himself as he strolled down the road, poking the dirt with a long stick that he'd found a few miles back. Even without a cart to ride in or gun to defend himself with, he seemed at peace in the eerily still forest.

How is he so calm? He's a killer. A murderer. A...

She let out a deep breath. Her anger was running out of steam—it was exhausting fuming about the quiet, whistling man in front of her for hours on end. *At least he didn't freak out that I'm half-Naga. I still can't believe I took off my cloak and scarf. I don't know what came over me.*

She didn't regret healing him, but that was partially because she didn't want any more blood on her hands.

Marissa shuddered at the thought of the bandits they had encountered in the forest just a few days earlier.

Regardless of his wife's illness, Thomas still killed someone, she thought angrily. *You can't fix murder just by saying you're sorry.*

A malevolent voice crept into her head, whispering for her to use Thomas to get what she and Arthur needed, then dump him off in Varan territory and let them decide his fate.

No. A soft voice of reason beat back the vengeful thoughts. *Don't take this out on a remorseful man trying to save his wife. Focus on the black market. Track down the real villains, the ones who prey on poverty-stricken villagers and dangle murder in front of their faces like a toy.*

"'Ere we are." Thomas stopped where the road split and curved through the trees. "If I recall, this is the path to Vale?"

"Indeed," Arthur replied. "Excellent timing. The sun is just starting to set."

Sienna was outside, tending to her garden as they approached. Loose strands of red hair poked out of her headscarf and glowed like fire under the setting sun.

"You're back? I thought you were headed north after Copperton?" she exclaimed. Her cheery but confused greeting morphed into surprise when she saw Thomas. "And you brought—"

"We need his help," Marissa explained. "We're going to infiltrate the black market and put an end to the poaching."

"Wait, what?!" Thomas's voice rose.

Marissa grimaced as she realized that they'd never actually told Thomas about their plan.

"Do ya have any idea what yer goin' against, girl?" he exclaimed. "The richest criminals in Brennan will squash ya like a bug the second ya step on their turf."

"I'm willing to risk it," Marissa grumbled. "Besides, we just need you to tell us where the black market is located. You can leave the rest to us."

"Sienna, may we come inside?" Arthur asked.

"Y-yes," she responded, her expression wary from overhearing their plans. "I just put on some stew."

The four of them settled at a round table in the kitchen. A small pot gurgled on the stove, hissing as it released warm steam that wafted through the room.

"So, what the hell happened?" Sienna exclaimed. "I dropped you off this morning, expecting you to continue traveling north, only to have you come plodding back here hours later with no cart and the snakebite victim in tow. And now you're going to infiltrate the black market? And how does he know where it is?" She pointed at Thomas.

Marissa sighed and turned toward Thomas. He softly but firmly shook his head.

"I have some contacts there. I'm sorry to say. I've done a few things I regret. But all that aside, I dunno exactly where the black market is. I just drop the goods off with my contact at the gates in Alistar. I could prob'ly persuade 'em to bring ya to the market, but we'd need a good reason."

"Marissa and I will disguise ourselves as wealthy patrons and pretend that we're looking to buy goods."

Everyone's heads swiveled toward Arthur, surprised by his bold plan. He exhaled sharply and turned toward Marissa. "Look, I know that probably doesn't sit well with you, but it's our only chance."

"No, it's okay." She sighed, her gaze on her lap. "I understand."

"So, Marissa," Thomas piped in. "What are ya lookin' to do there? Ya can't exactly sneak dynamite into their stalls or smuggle out boxes of hides. If they catch ya, yer dead, even more so for bein' a reptilian."

Marissa's shoulders fell. *I really have no idea what I'm doing. Is this hopeless?*

"I actually have some information that may be of use," Sienna spoke up. "I had two rather grisly visitors come in today. One of them needed treatment for a stab wound. I didn't ask questions, but I went into the other room to check on some vials while waiting for the orange salve to do its work. These walls are deceptively thin—as we all heard yesterday." Sienna shot a stern look at Thomas. "And I overheard their conversation. They mentioned that black market prices have shot through the roof. I guess some big buyer is paying top dollar for full reptilian hides."

"Really?" Thomas raised an eyebrow. "I hadn't heard 'bout that."

"Apparently, it just started a few days ago. They said that the black market has been swarming ever since."

Even more poaching? Marissa shuddered as her mind came up with horrid guesses as to what rich humans would need so many reptilian hides for.

"That's what I'll do," Marissa declared. "I'll find out who is buying all of those hides."

"And then what?" Thomas grumbled. "Ya can't just stop 'em. The black market is a monstrosity, with its ugly roots diggin' deep into the core of Brennan. A couple'a commoners will never be able to bring it down."

"Maybe we can," Marissa replied hopefully, but the expressions on her companions' faces were grim. "We must at least try. Arthur, you said to come up with a halfway decent plan. And we did. We'll disguise ourselves and sneak in. If we play the part, no one will suspect a thing. We just need to find out who is buying all those hides."

"At least the sneakin' in part ain't as far-fetched as it seems," Thomas remarked. "The rich bastards at the market wear cloaks and scarves to conceal their identities. So that means our bold little hero can hide 'er snake half."

"My sister's a seamstress in Brennan," Sienna noted. "She can help you out. I'll give you her address."

"It looks like this is really possible," Marissa remarked. "What does everyone else think?"

"I'm in," Arthur sighed. "I think it's insanity, and we're risking our lives, but personally, I cannot stand Brennan's wealthy criminals, and I'd love to see them knocked down a peg."

Marissa thought about Arthur's royal background and wondered what his family would think of him sneaking around the black market. As much as he had ostracized himself from them, Marissa didn't want to see him face even more scorn. *I have little to lose, and he's risking so much to help the reptilians...*

"Like I said, I'll do whatever ya need me t'do to save my wife," Thomas replied. "I'm in, too."

"I will be staying here," Sienna stated firmly. "But I do want to assist. Feel free to stay the night, and I can give you a ride tomorrow. I only have one guest room, but the couch is comfortable enough. We can head off to the gates in the morning."

The three of them turned to Marissa. She buried her fear deep in her stomach and let a small, righteous grin emerge on her face.

"Let's take down those murderous bastards."

Chapter 17

It was well past midnight, and Marissa still couldn't sleep. She was stuck in the eerie darkness, barely able to see a hand in front of her face. Nighttime usually calmed Marissa, but in her recent times of stress, it brought out all her worst fears. It was like the anxiety in her head fed off the darkness. She could hear its subtle, sinister voice trickle through the air. *Two people going against an entire underground crime ring. They'll kill you. If they catch one glimpse of your reptilian face, you're dead.*

A few days earlier, she wouldn't have been so fearful of death. Stealing petty change, hiding in an abandoned storefront, eating rats from the alleyway... she was barely surviving, just a rejected soul in a giant, heartless kingdom.

She peered over at Arthur. His dark form was still, his chest rising and falling in soft waves. As terrified as she was, their grand quest to find the Naga and uncover the secrets of the reptilians had given her a sense of purpose. *And Arthur...* her stomach twisted in nervous knots. Their newfound friendship made her tattered heart feel emotions she had never felt before. She stroked Nim as he slept on her chest, his shiny unblinking eyes devoid of movement. *He's such a beautiful creature.* Between Nim and Arthur, Marissa finally felt warmth and companionship, and she was determined not to lose them.

"Am I insane?" Marissa whispered to Nim. His head shifted, and he flicked his tongue. She felt guilty for waking him up.

"Yes," a voice muttered from the twin bed next to her.

She jolted. "You're still awake?"

"Well, trying not to be. I imagine I'm up for the same reason you are."

"I'm scared," Marissa admitted, her voice quivering. "I act like I'm so brave, trying to pummel through every obstacle to help the reptilians. I'm not stupid. I know the danger we're putting ourselves in. And you, with your family..."

"Outside of the Naga incident, my family barely acknowledges my existence these days," Arthur grumbled, rolling over onto his back. "It'll be fine. And Thomas is right. If we can disguise ourselves in cloaks and scarves, I doubt anyone will suspect a thing."

"I'm still surprised you said yes to this crazy plan."

Arthur shrugged. "Don't forget. I'm a herpetologist. I've dedicated my life to studying reptiles of all kinds. The reptilians never let me get close to their societies, but the glimpses I was able to catch taught me enough. They are intelligent beings, capable of love, kindness, and understanding, just like humans."

"You know," he continued. "I'm still shocked that you revealed yourself to Thomas. You do realize how dangerous that was, right?"

Marissa's face flushed like a child being scolded. "I needed to fix my mistake so that Thomas would help us. And I believe that to do so, I can't keep secrets."

"You're braver than I am, Marissa," he remarked.

"I know it's absurd, but I dream of a day when I can wander the streets of Brennan without covering my face. A world where I am not seen as an ugly monster."

"Hey, we talked about you not calling yourself a monster."

"To be fair, that's just what people think of me. I don't have to believe it myself."

"Good. Plus, now you have Sienna and Thomas on your side." Arthur stretched his arms over his head and yawned. "I've always doubted that one person can change this whole valley. But if there is one person that can, it's you."

"That's wishful thinking." Marissa chuckled, settling into her pillow. "We really should try and get some sleep. Thomas doesn't seem to be having a problem with it."

She gestured toward the cracked guest room door, where loud snores could be heard from the living room couch. Arthur smiled and shook his head.

"You're right. Sleep well. We've got a long day ahead of us."

SIENNA WOKE THEM UP THE NEXT MORNING FAR too early. Marissa grumbled as soon as the cheery redhead knocked on their door. As usual, Marissa wasn't a morning person, but in addition, she'd barely gotten any sleep. It took another hour after her conversation with Arthur to finally drift off.

Once again, Arthur offered Marissa coffee as they sat in the kitchen.

"Will it calm my nerves?" Marissa asked, warily eyeing the brown liquid.

"Well, no." Arthur gazed deeply into the steaming mug curled in his palms. "Quite the opposite. In fact, I probably shouldn't be drinking it, either. I'm just as tense as you are. Hey Sienna?"

"Yes?"

"Would it be possible to purchase some of those blue flowers?"

"The butterfly pea flowers? That's a great idea. Here." Sienna handed Arthur a small packet. "Just take some. Steep them for several minutes in boiling water and drink it right before you head to the black market. It'll keep your anxiety down."

"I've never been a tea drinker," Thomas remarked. "But maybe I'll have to try some. Seems like a better solution for nerves than alcohol."

They scarfed down a quick breakfast and wandered outside to the shed.

"Now remember," Sienna instructed as they helped her hitch the cart. "You're just two patrons looking to buy scarves and cloaks for the upcoming winter. Autumn won't ask questions, but don't let her find out you're royalty, and," Sienna turned toward Marissa, "definitely don't let her find out you're reptilian. She's terrified of them."

The four of them settled into the cart, with Sienna, Arthur, and Marissa sitting up front and Thomas sprawling out in the back, with Aurora at his feet. Sienna grabbed her horse's reins, signaling the large, stocky mare to trot forward. Within ten minutes, they were on the main road back to Brennan.

"I'll drop you off at the southern gates in Alistar," Sienna declared. "Are you comfortable getting a carriage to Augustree on your own?"

"Yes," Arthur replied. "It shouldn't be too far of a journey. Now I'm going to settle in and take a nap. Wake me when we're in Alistar."

Sienna chuckled and shook her head, but she seemed to understand that he hadn't slept well. Neither had Marissa, and the soft clip-clopping motion of the cart quickly put her to sleep.

"WAKE UP, SLEEPYHEADS." THOMAS GRINNED, elbowing Marissa in the back.

She opened her eyes, oblivious about where they were or how long they had been traveling. The soothing roll of the cart had overridden her anxiety, and she had been able to catch up on some sleep. *I even had a soft place to rest my head...*

Wait.

Marissa felt a smooth brown vest underneath her head and bolted upright. Thomas cackled in the backseat, his raucous laughter like the caws of an amused crow. Marissa smoothed the tangles out of her long black hair and brushed her bangs aside, her face flushed red with embarrassment.

Arthur was still asleep, his head tilted sideways and resting on his shoulder. And until a moment ago, Marissa's head had been resting on his chest.

How did that happen!?

She shot an accusatory look at Sienna, who shrugged and pretended to be focused on the road, a wry smile across her face. "What? You two looked comfortable. And unlike the chortling fool in the backseat, I don't judge."

Sienna flicked Thomas on the top of his head, and he snorted. "Alright, fine. I'm done laughin'. Are we there yet?"

"Almost," Sienna replied. "I can see the southern gates up ahead. That's why I told you to wake those two up. Speaking of which, Arthur is still asleep."

"Oh, right," Thomas remarked. He dug his elbow into Arthur's back, and Arthur opened his bleary eyes.

"How long was I out?" He yawned. "I was dreaming, and then I heard horrid laughter like a hyena. And that elbowing was unnecessary, Thomas."

Thomas shrugged and settled back into his seat.

Arthur turned toward Marissa. "Did you manage to get some rest, too? I know you didn't sleep well last night."

"Yes," Marissa stated bluntly, refusing to turn her head away from the road.

"Anyway, Arthur," Sienna continued. The dirt road underneath them had turned to cobblestone, which thumped loudly under the mare's hooves and caused the cart to rattle. "We're approaching the southern gates. Are you three ready?"

"Yes," they all replied in unison.

"Here is my sister's address." Sienna handed Arthur a slip of paper, which he folded and placed in the breast pocket of his vest. "It's already noon, but since the black market doesn't open until late at night, you should have plenty of time. Stay safe. I'm rooting for you."

The huge iron gates stretched toward the sky as they approached. A guard signaled to the watchtower, and the gates rattled forward with a loud creak, welcoming them and several other waiting carts into the bustle of the city. Sienna gave the guards a quick nod as the cart passed.

"Alright, I'm gonna let you off here." Sienna stopped in the middle of a small square where traffic was light. "Nearest carriage house is about half a mile north, just past a little bookstore on the corner."

A strange unease crept through Marissa's scales as they waved to Sienna. The cart clip-clopped back toward the kingdom's edge and slipped through the massive gates, disappearing down the dusty road back to Vale. Marissa knew that Sienna's departure signaled that there was no turning back; the three of them were alone to complete their daunting, dangerous task.

It was a quick walk to the carriage house. They passed by the bookstore Sienna mentioned, and Marissa realized why she used it as a landmark—it was easily identifiable with its giant mural of a gray horse galloping out of an open book, misty stardust scattered around its hooves.

"Three please." Arthur approached the small window next to the carriage house. "Here is the address." He handed the slip of paper to a well-dressed man with an oddly slick mustache. The man unfolded the paper and scanned it, his eyes flicking from word to word. He nodded.

"Autumn Leaf Tailoring in southern Augustree? Not a problem. That'll be two silver."

Arthur paid the man from his seemingly never-ending bag of coin, and the three of them settled into an elaborate carriage made of a dark, exotic stained wood with plush maroon seats. Thomas entered through the side door and sat in the back, facing the carriage driver's seat.

Marissa opted to sit in the front so the driver couldn't see her masked face, and Arthur took a seat next to her.

Thankfully, the driver seemed oblivious to them, focusing on the road as he ushered his two gray geldings forward. Marissa pressed her forehead against the window, watching the busy streets of Brennan ripple past them.

"So... Arthur?" Thomas suddenly spoke up after a few minutes of silence. His tone was accusatory. "I realize now how ya are able to help me and my wife. That's an awfully large bag'a coin yer carryin' around."

"Indeed." Arthur raised an eyebrow with his usual cool disposition.

"Yer not gonna tell us where ya got the money from?" Thomas gestured toward Marissa. "Does she know?"

"She does. My name is Arthur Brennan. My father in the king's cousin."

"Wait up now, yer royalty? What're you doing outta the castle hangin' 'round with common folk, 'specially a reptilian?"

Arthur grumbled, "This is precisely why I do not tell people. The word royalty elicits some peculiar reactions."

"Sorry." Thomas's shoulders sank. "Well, either way, I'm glad a man of yer standin' decided to help us."

This only seemed to irritate Arthur further. He fixed his gaze on the window, signaling that the conversation was over.

"I am not close with my family," he remarked after a few seconds of silence. "And I haven't lived in the palace in over a year. My parents throw coin at me to stay out of their business. And I can't exactly say no to more funding for my shop."

"Ah, I see," Thomas responded, crossing his arms and leaning back in his seat. "I was never close to my parents, either. They 'ere gunsmiths, and expected me to follow in their footsteps. I was their only child, and although they 'ere always kind and respectful, I think it hurt 'em that I became an equestrian."

"You rode horses?" Arthur raised an eyebrow.

"Sometimes. I mostly bred 'em. I had about three dozen at my peak. I bet ya have even seen some of the progeny—I sold several stallions to the royal stables when I was younger."

"What made you become a miner, then?" Marissa asked, realizing too late that her question was insensitive.

"Well, that'sa story for another time. Let's just say life isn't always kind to us, as I'm sure yer aware. So, now let's go to ya—where did ya come from? Like yer parents, how did they..." He clasped his hands together in a suggestive motion.

"Thomas," Arthur scolded. "That is inappropriate."

"I'm serious! Ain't ya a reptile expert? Don't ya ever wonder how a human and a snake beast end up procreatin'?"

"I mean ... I won't lie, I have wondered. With male reptilian anatomy and a woman's reproductive system, I suppose it—"

"Please. Stop."

Marissa clasped her hands over her ears, her face burning with embarrassment. Even though she was eighteen, she knew embarrassingly little about reproduction. *I don't need a biology lesson right now. I don't even know my parents, and I certainly do not want to discuss my conception.*

"Sorry," they both muttered, settling into their seats.

Marissa spent the rest of the carriage ride gazing out the window, her chin resting on the back of her hand. As the carriage slowed or stopped due to traffic, she caught brief glimpses into normal human life—a little boy dipping his fingers into a fountain while his parents watched; a young couple browsing the storefronts arm in arm; an elderly woman adjusting a bow on her little dog's collar. Warmth, kindness, joy ... emotions that until recently were foreign to Marissa. And now she was about to risk her life for the reptilians.

I just pray that one day, if I do meet them, they don't reject me.

"Alright," the driver announced as the carriage pulled to a slow halt. "314 Oak Avenue. It looks like your tailor is right there."

The man pointed to a quaint shop nestled between two large antique stores. A small green sign hung from a pole out front, with Autumn Leaf Tailoring painted in swooping gold letters.

"Thank you very much." Arthur waved to the driver as the three of them exited the carriage. Marissa pressed her scarf against her nose and mouth, hoping that Autumn would be just as friendly as her sister.

"Before we head inside," Arthur remarked, grabbing Thomas's sleeve as he meandered toward the shop. "The Menagerie is just around the corner. We need to drop off Nim and Aurora. I doubt Autumn will be okay with my hundred-pound dog bustling through her shop. And Sienna said her sister is afraid of reptiles."

"Ah. I've been wantin' to see yer fancy pet shop." Thomas grinned.

A few minutes and a couple of street corners later, they arrived in front of the Menagerie. A young, pale blond boy, no older than eighteen, sat at the front counter reading a book next to a snoozing green dragonling. He seemed surprised to see them.

"Hello, George," Arthur greeted. "I know we're back a few days late, but I hope things have been going well. We just need to drop off these two, as we have a bit more business here in Augustree. Are you alright to close the shop tonight? I'll probably be able to take back over tomorrow."

"Not a problem, sir." George grinned. Marissa could tell by his demeanor that he was more than happy to sit in a shop full of mystical creatures all day.

"It is much appreciated. And I told you, you don't need to call me sir. Makes me seem old." Arthur shook his head. "Oy, I can't believe I'm twenty-three this year."

"I'm thirty-one," Thomas grumbled. "I don't wanna hear it."

"Anyway, this is George," Arthur introduced. "He'd been hanging around the shop for a while, and after he finished school, I made him my official assistant. He's a big fan of dragons. Wants to venture outside the valley and study them."

George sighed and patted the dragonling next to him. He seemed attached to the little creature, who Marissa imagined was very expensive. Dragonlings were from far beyond the valley, and being no larger than a cat at full size, they were the ultimate exotic pet for wealthy keepers.

"This place is amazin'," Thomas remarked in awe, his head swiveling around the store. "Where do ya get all of these beasts?"

"Some are field collected from the valley and other regions, and the rest are from local breeders," Arthur replied. "But as much as I'd love to discuss these beauties, we don't have time to chat. It looks like Aurora has settled into her bed. Marissa, could you please put Nim in that open tank?"

Nim seemed to resist as Marissa unwound him from her neck. Sadness flooded Marissa's body as she placed the little snake in the glass-doored enclosure. He slithered up a branch and settled in the middle of it, his head resting on his coiled body. Marissa could sense his emotions, and while he was a bit sad, he surprisingly seemed to understand their situation.

"Alright, let's be off," Arthur announced as Marissa slid the glass enclosure shut. "George, thank you again. Come along, you two. We have clothing to obtain."

INSIDE THE SHOP, A SINGLE TINY ROOM WITH forest green wallpaper was crammed with clothing racks, mannequins, and sewing machines. A petite woman with glossy red hair looked up from the front counter where she was counting change. As she looked up, Thomas's jaw dropped.

"Why hello," she greeted. "Welcome. How may I help you?"

"Wait'a minute," Thomas exclaimed. "Sienna didn't tell us y'all were identical twins."

"We're not, actually." The redhead chuckled. "I'm a year older. We just look so much alike that everyone thinks we're identical. So, I take it you're acquainted with my sister, Sienna?"

"Yes," Arthur spoke up. "She's an old friend from university. My name is Arthur, and this is Marissa and Thomas. We were looking to acquire some cloaks and scarves for the winter, and your sister says you are the finest tailor in Brennan."

"Well, I don't know about finest, but I appreciate my sister's compliments. My name is Autumn, by the way. Any friend of Sienna's is a friend of mine."

"Thomas, why don't you go browse some of the nearby stores?" Marissa suggested. "We won't be long."

"Ah, I see. Ya want me out of yer hair," he grumbled as he walked toward the front door. "Well, I have no business here, so I s'ppose I can do some browsin' while y'all get yer clothes."

"I've had quite a few customers come in asking for cloaks and scarves lately." Autumn led Marissa and Arthur into a back room. "Perhaps it'll be a cold winter, though I would never expect snow in the valley. Now, would you like me to take measurements for a custom cloak, or would you like to browse the racks?"

"Racks, please," Marissa blurted out. She did not want Autumn to get any closer to her than necessary. One slip of her scarf or blouse sleeves and they would learn how terrified of reptiles Autumn truly was.

"Of course, right this way." Autumn gestured toward several short aisles of clothing in the middle of the shop. Every style, color, and fabric imaginable poked through the tightly packed racks. Autumn fumbled through the coat hangers. "Cloaks are ... right here. We have mostly dark colors, as we are coming into winter. Please feel free to browse."

Marissa peered down at a soft gray cloak that appeared to be her size. She grabbed the price tag on the shirt sleeve and grimaced.

"You know," Marissa whispered to Arthur as he flicked through the racks. Autumn had settled back behind the counter. "We can just get a cloak for you. I already have one."

Arthur stopped browsing and locked eyes with Marissa. "Yes, one that is torn and filthy. You don't think the wealthy scoundrels in the black market will notice?"

She shook her head sheepishly.

"Is this about money?"

"N-no."

He sighed. "Relax, Marissa. I just told you that my parents toss far more coin at me than I need. This is important. Besides, I can't stand to see you walk around in vagrant's clothing."

Marissa grumbled.

"Sorry ... that was insensitive. What I mean is, you're a wonderful person and ... well, you deserve to wear clothes that aren't dirty, that's all."

Marissa stepped away and continued browsing. Out of the corner of her eye, she could see Arthur blushing and shaking his head over his conversational blunders. *So many colors, so many styles... I have no idea what would look right on me.*

She was drawn to a silky black cloak with ruffled shoulders and silver clasps. She pulled it off the rack, its long fabric sweeping across the floor, and examined its tag.

I think this will fit.

"That looks nice," Arthur commented. "Dark colors suit you."

Marissa approached the front counter, where Autumn looked up from a pile of inventory sheets.

"Do you happen to have someplace private where I could try this on?"

"Of course." Autumn ushered Marissa into the back of the shop and opened a small closet door. "In here. Come out and model for us once you've changed."

Marissa's scales shivered as Autumn closed the door behind her, leaving her alone in the stale, windowless room. A single glowing lamp illuminated her dark figure in the wall-length mirror. Marissa grimaced. It had been a while since she'd seen her full reflection, and Arthur was right—her light brown cloak was tattered at the bottom and caked in a layer of dirt.

She unbuttoned the cloak and tossed it on a nearby bench. She rolled up her sleeves, examining the inky black scales cascading down her arms. She unwound the black scarf from her neck and tapped her reptilian nose with her finger, enjoying a few breaths of fresh air without so much fabric over her nose. She liked her smooth scales, but her face had always looked so misshapen. *Not quite human, not quite reptilian. A bizarre in-between.*

Marissa huffed and tossed the obscuring scarf back over her face.

"Oh, that fits you perfectly!" Autumn clapped as Marissa emerged from the dressing room. "I must say, though, between your scarf and dark hair, that's a lot of black. Maybe—"

"I like black," Marissa interrupted. *Besides, with the dangerous place we're going, the more we blend in with the shadows, the better.*

"I agree," Arthur announced as he stepped toward Marissa, another black cloak wrapped over his folded arms. "Look, we'll match."

Autumn seemed perturbed by their color choices. Marissa and Arthur resembled ghastly reapers as they stood side by side in their cloaks. *We will look a bit peculiar walking the streets of Augustree, but in the black market, we'll blend in perfectly.*

"Well, that's certainly a fashion statement," Autumn remarked. "Are you two ready to check out?"

Marissa watched Arthur dig several silver coins out of his bag and hand them to Autumn. He gathered up both cloaks, plus a black scarf that matched Marissa's, and the pair left the store with a cheery wave.

"Thank you again for your help!" Marissa smiled.

"Of course. Tell Sienna to come visit soon. I miss her!"

They stepped out the creaky front door and onto the busy streets. But as they took a few steps forward, Arthur paused, biting his lip.

"Listen, I need you to find Thomas and head back to The Menagerie for an hour or two," he announced. Marissa read the troubled look on his face and immediately knew why.

"You need to speak with the king, don't you?"

"Yes," Arthur sighed. "Quite frankly, I'm dreading it. My last meeting with him did not go well. The king is not fond of the reptilians, and I fear that this isn't the end of the conflict. I have my doubts, but I really hope that he concurs that this was a minor incident and that he needs to back down and leave the reptilians alone."

"I hope so, too. I wish you the best of luck," Marissa responded. "I hope you return with good news."

"Thank you, Marissa. Here are my keys. Stay safe while I'm gone."

As Arthur handed the cloak and his keyring off to Marissa and departed down the street toward the palace, a deep discomfort washed over her. Like Arthur, she wanted to believe that all the reptilians wanted were the remains of the slain Varan. She wanted to believe that the mounting tensions would dissipate and that the deeply divided valley wouldn't succumb to chaos.

But despite her vain hopes, the foreboding warnings of the snakes in The Menagerie still panged through her heart.

Something is coming. And I feel powerless to stop it.

Chapter 18

A DEEP FEELING OF UNEASE CREPT OVER Arthur as he stood outside the entrance to the throne room. The king had surprisingly agreed to speak with him; maybe he was pleased that Arthur was no longer trudging through the outer villages in search of the troublesome Naga. The serpentine creature had returned to reptilian territory, which Arthur hoped meant that this whole conflict was over. But the harrowing thought that it wasn't still snaked through his mind, and Arthur hoped that his conversation with the king would provide more clarity. If the king agreed to call off his search, then clearly he was unaware of any further malevolence.

But if he doesn't...

Arthur's worried thoughts were interrupted by a loud creak and sudden whoosh of air as the heavy throne room doors crept open. He'd heard faint voices while he waited for his turn to speak with the king, but he'd been too lost in thought to decipher their conversation.

As a lone figure stepped through the doors, Arthur suddenly wished he'd been paying more attention.

Lorenzo Castella? What's he doing here?

The olive-skinned man, who had graying black hair and was about the same age as the king, acknowledged Arthur with a polite nod as he departed down the hallway. The Castellas were one of the wealthiest families in Brennan, with close ties to the monarchy and a large amount of influence. Arthur's throat soured at the thought of them. He knew the visit was likely just political banter, insignificant to his current concerns, but he still wished he'd paid more attention to their conversation.

As Lorenzo's footsteps echoed down the hall before fading away, a guard snapped Arthur's attention off the wealthy aristocrat.

"The king will see you now. Right this way, please."

As Arthur entered the cavernous room, King Gabriel shifted in his throne, looking just as irked as when Arthur interrupted his conversation in the library a few days earlier. The strange female guard was once again pressed against the far wall, her bright blue eyes locked on Arthur as he approached.

He took a deep breath. *Be polite, but direct. His reaction will tell you all you need to know.*

"Your Majesty." Arthur cleared his throat. "I appreciate you taking the time to speak with me today."

"I appreciate the formalities, Arthur." The king's tone was sharp. "But I'm well aware of why you're here today. I take it your little expedition to find the Naga was unsuccessful?"

"I did not encounter the Naga, no. But I discovered what he was after. I believe this was all just a poaching incident; the reptilians were looking to retrieve the hide of a slain Varan. They returned to their territory shortly after."

"I see." The king replied flatly. "And if you never encountered the Naga, how do you know this? Did you see him leave the outer villages? How do you know he won't return?"

Arthur opened his mouth to speak, but no words trailed out. *Crap. I certainly can't tell him that I was accompanied by a half-reptilian girl who sniffed out the Naga's trail.*

He took a deep breath, his eyes locked on the king. *The researchers ... the tablet ... what did they find out? You're hiding something.* But he knew he couldn't demand answers. He was a distant, ostracized royal, already on thin ice, and hurling accusations at the king would get him kicked out of the palace, perhaps for good. He huffed, trying to hide his anger. The king's expression was a sour mixture of disgust and pity.

"Arthur." The king's voice softened. "This no longer concerns you. In fact, I wanted to speak with you today to give you a very firm warning; if you interfere in this matter again, I will have no choice but to have you arrested. You are part of this family, and I do not want to see it come to that, but I will not let your traitorous love for those beasts endanger this kingdom."

Arthur's face fell. "Your Majesty, I—"

"Go home, Arthur," the king commanded. "Focus on your pet store and stop throwing yourself and everyone else into danger. Consider yourself lucky you didn't encounter that Naga; it very well could've killed you."

"Your Maj—"

"This conversation is over."

King Gabriel lifted a hand, and the female guard stepped forward, her palm perched precariously over her sheathed sword. Arthur stepped back, not wanting a confrontation, and dejectedly plodded out of the throne room.

Arthur's shoes stomped through the halls as he departed the palace at a brisk, irritated pace. His mind swirled with the dreadful reality that his worst fears about the conversation with the king had come true. If the king refused to heed Arthur's warnings, it meant that this wasn't just a poaching incident. There was another mysterious, possibly frightening, reason why the king was so intent on hunting the Naga down.

As he stepped onto the bright midday streets, he remembered his earlier warnings about visiting the black market. *I tried to talk Marissa out of it, telling her it was too dangerous...*

But now he was grateful for his friend's stubbornness. If Arthur couldn't get the truth out of the king, the black market was their next best chance. He knew the increased poaching and the Naga's presence were likely linked; some root cause was generating all this conflict.

Arthur took a shaky, nervous breath. As determined as he was, it was him and Marissa against everyone else, seeking the impossible resolution of peace.

Gods, both human and reptilian, please ... help us find answers tonight.

MARISSA SAT CROSS-LEGGED ON THE FLOOR IN Arthur's apartment, perched in front of his wall of reptile tanks. The faint tick of the wall clock was the only sound in the eerily still room as Marissa locked eyes with one of Arthur's boa constrictors. She'd been there for over an hour, her mind focused intensely on the serpentine creature in front of her, desperately trying to decode its primitive emotions.

The large, heavy-bodied brown snake, nearly eight feet long, gave off the same sinister emotion as the snakes downstairs in The Menagerie. It came in rhythmic waves, like a heartbeat. But as hard as Marissa focused, digging into the depths of her reptilian soul, she couldn't figure out the vague warning that the boa was pulsing into her mind.

She'd considered retrieving Nim for company, but he was huddled away in his rock cave. He'd had quite the adventure the past few days, and she knew that carpet pythons normally slept most of the time. She decided it was best for him to get some rest.

Thomas had been quiet the entire time Arthur was away. They'd engaged in some small talk, but Marissa was still wary of the remorseful poacher, which Thomas seemed to understand. He paced around the apartment, both fascinated by the home's valuable treasures and freaked out by the array of reptile tanks.

"Beasties," Thomas grumbled as he locked eyes with a judgmental-looking bearded dragon. The lizard opened its mouth, its slimy pink tongue protruding between its toothy jaws, and Thomas sneered in disgust. Marissa peered up from her spot on the floor and chuckled. The squat, broad-faced creature appeared to be smiling.

Suddenly, the jiggly old door handle rattled from the outside, and Arthur pushed the door open with a loud squeak. Marissa's eyes immediately shot over to her weary-looking friend, and her heart dropped when she saw his despondent face.

Arthur closed the door behind him, his gaze still locked on the floor. He took a deep breath before looking up with a forced smile.

"How did it go?" Marissa asked apprehensively.

"About as I expected." Arthur huffed, taking a seat on the couch. "The king only wanted to see me so he could threaten to throw me in prison if I further intervened.

Which can only mean one thing—this wasn't just a poaching incident. He's hiding something."

"Do we have any idea what that is?" Marissa asked.

"Well, hopefully, we'll figure it out ourselves." Arthur snatched up the black cloak that was draped across the back of the couch. He rubbed the silky material in his fingers, a tense expression on his face. "This must be connected to the poaching. I'm hoping we'll be able to find answers at the black market. You were right, Marissa; we must infiltrate those scoundrels and put an end to this."

"Well, my contact won't be available until midnight," Thomas interjected. "It's only six o'clock."

"The night is still young." Arthur peered outside at the melting orange sky. "We still have some of that blue flower tea..."

"Nah, let's do a proper dinner," Thomas objected. "I wouldn't mind goin' into this with a bit 'a mead in my system. I saw a lil' inn 'round the corner. Blue Birch, was it?"

"No," Marissa and Arthur exclaimed in unison. Thomas looked bewildered, and Arthur sighed.

"Marissa was unmasked there a week ago," he continued. "Luckily, I heard that once the gossip got out, the rest of the district regarded the tavern patrons as nothing more than drunk buffoons making up fairy tales. But still, we should roam the streets of Augustree as little as possible. Plus, Marissa cannot eat without removing her scarf."

Marissa had initially recoiled at the thought of going to a restaurant, especially with a poacher in tow. But they had a long night ahead of them, and Arthur's cupboards were bare. Her stomach rumbled, and she thought back to the night she went to the Blue Birch Inn and how much she wanted to enjoy a nice dinner—eat a hot meal and not roasted rats.

And as much as I resent Thomas, we're all stuck together for the next few hours. I may as well go into this with a full stomach. I must be brave tonight.

"Actually, I bet I can. Watch this." Marissa tossed her cloak over her shoulders and draped her scarf across her face. She then peeled apart two layers of her scarf, revealing a small hole over her dark lips.

Arthur raised an eyebrow, amused. "I suppose that could work. But Marissa, I don't want to put your safety—"

"Safety? We're about to sneak into the black market!" She huffed. "Please. I can do this. I want to have dinner at a nice inn like a normal person."

"Very well," Arthur agreed. "We can always explain the scarf as hiding scars or burns or some other malady. Let's pack up these cloaks and head south to Everwind for dinner. It's a lot closer to Alistar, where we need to be later tonight, anyway."

"The industrial district?" Thomas remarked. "I bet they have some interestin' bars."

As they stepped outside and strolled down the cobblestone streets, Marissa was relieved to be leaving Augustree. She told herself to be brave, but she was even more paranoid than usual. She walked with her head down and kept her scarf pressed tightly against her nose and mouth. Arthur placed a hand on her back as they approached the carriage house.

"Steel Forge Inn in Everwind, please." Arthur handed the attendant a few silver coins that chimed in his palm.

Marissa was quiet the entire carriage ride. Her nerves raced faster as midnight approached. She swallowed, trying to calm the deep knot in her stomach. The sun slipped under the horizon as if bidding them a final goodbye.

Marissa shuddered as they passed the palace grounds. The giant, looming spires were normally awe-inspiring, but tonight they looked menacing.

"Here we are," the driver announced not long after.

They were just past the palace, in western Everwind. They were near the Alistar border, which was a sea of lit windows. The churches were always open to weary patrons looking for a warm meal and a place to pray. Everwind, on the other hand, was a dark graveyard of factories that were closed for the night. Only the homey inn in front of them showed any signs of activity.

"Have a lovely evening." Arthur waved at the driver as they exited the carriage. The elaborate vehicle wheeled away, hooves clacking against the craggy cobblestone.

Marissa had heard that industrial district inns were boisterous, but she wasn't prepared for what awaited them as they pushed open the heavy oak doors. Every table in the brightly lit restaurant was full of wily patrons. Several ornate wooden tables in the far corner seated groups of disheveled workers engaged in gambling. Every time the dealer tossed the dice, and they settled to a fumbling halt on the velvet-lined table, screams of either joy or disgust rang throughout the entire establishment. Coins flew in the air, and waitresses carried huge trays of drinks between the rowdy tables. The bar was even more crowded than the one in Orchid.

Marissa buried her face in her scarf, wondering if she'd made the right decision to go out. Meanwhile, Thomas's eyes lit up like fireworks.

"Now, this is a fine place for dinner." He joyously stepped forward, but Arthur grabbed his collar before he could venture off toward the gambling tables.

"Do calm yourself, please," Arthur scolded. "We are here to have a nice meal, not watch you pawn away the last of your copper coin."

Thomas seemed deflated as they settled at one of the dining room tables, but he perked up again once a waitress passed with a large tray full of mead.

"I recommend everyone limit themselves to one drink, please." Arthur lifted a menu off the table and inspected it, adjusting his glasses. "Grapefruit mead, interesting..."

As her companions scanned their menus, Marissa instead scanned the crowd. The inn was so full of activity that no one even glanced in her direction.

I can do this. She opened her menu, reading the different items and their mouthwatering descriptions. She so rarely had a nice meal, and there were so many delicious options that it was difficult to decide.

A cheery, freckle-faced waitress dropped several large mugs of water at their table and took Arthur and Thomas's alcohol orders. Marissa lowered her head, studying her water glass. *Ice? I've never had ice before.* She lifted the mug to her lips and brushed aside part of her scarf. The deep frostiness of the cold water seeped through her entire body. She shivered. She normally disliked the cold, but the ice water was pleasant and refreshing.

As she set the mug down, Arthur gave her a small thumbs up.

This is working. No one noticed a thing. It is amazing how normal, mundane parts of human life are so foreign and intoxicating to me.

"This place reminds me of the gamblin' hall in my hometown," Thomas remarked. "Such a nice place to unwind after a long day at the stables. I remember the year I won a big pile o' coin right before Marian's birthday. She wanted that 'lil wooly rabbit for sale at the feed shop. A year later, we had six of 'em and more yarn than we knew what to do with."

A deep chill set in over Marissa and Arthur. Thomas seemed lost in thought; his eyes glazed over with nostalgia. Marissa knew that he hadn't given up his stables to become a miner on purpose, but she didn't dare bring up what happened.

But it didn't take long for Thomas's tone to shift. "I said I'd tell ya my story another time, didn't I?" The light in Thomas's eyes faded, and he set his drink down on the table. "I guess now's as good a time as any. I know y'all met me and thought I was a pathetic drunkard, always at odds with my wife. Truth is, that wasn't always the case. Up until two years ago, I had my life set. A stable full of animals, a cozy home, and the best wife I could'a asked for."

"But ... what happened?" Marissa asked timidly. The waitress appeared and set two large mugs of mead on the table. Thomas reached for one and took a large gulp, foam settling on his mustache.

"Ellie happened, and then we'd never be the same again. We'd wanted kids for years, and we kept tryin', but with Marian havin' so many health issues, it never happened. Finally, one year at Christmas, when Marian was doin' better, she announced she was finally expectin'. We were overjoyed. My parents, who I was never close with, started comin' 'round more often. Our whole lives revolved around gettin' ready for the baby. But later on, Marian started gettin' sick again. Nothin' major, but she needed to rest more. She was so worried about the animals, especially the horses, since she couldn't care for 'em like she used to. I kept tellin' her to stay in bed, away from the stables, but she kept comin' out to visit 'em."

Marissa's gaze fell to the table, anticipating what could go wrong.

"Then it happened. She was almost due, and she came walkin' out of the house while I was workin' with a young colt. I told 'er to stay back..." Thomas choked up. He took a sip of his mead, taking a moment to recollect himself. "He kicked 'er right in the belly. I rushed 'er inside, and for a few hours, everythin' seemed fine ... then it happened. Marian gave birth that night to our daughter. She came out perfect, just like any other lil' baby, but we didn't hear a sound from 'er. She wasn't breathin'. We tried for hours to revive 'er... it was no use. We named 'er Elizabeth, Ellie for short, and buried 'er behind the stables the next day."

Marisa and Arthur sat frozen, their eyes shifted downward and glazed over with sad sympathy.

Why are you feeling bad for him? He's still a killer...

Marissa shook the thought out of her head.

"Ya can imagine what happened after that," Thomas continued. "We couldn't bear to even look at the horses. On top of bein' sick, Marian was depressed, hardly gettin' out of bed. Instead of comfortin' 'er like a good husband, I lost myself to gamblin' and drinkin'. Within a year, we were barely speakin' to each other. Our money dried up, the farm was sold, and I was forced to become a miner with crappy workin' conditions and low pay. I won't lie. I can be a terrible person. I just wanted ya to know I wasn't always this way. Ya have every right to be mad at me for what I did. Even if I did die from that snakebite, I wouldn't have blamed ya. There's no excuse for murder. I'm realizin' too late that the reptilians ain't the monsters we believe 'em to be."

"Do you think Marian's doing okay at her parents' house?" Marissa asked.

"Ah, I'm sure she's alright. She does this all the time. I left 'er a note on the counter. She'll probably be mad at me for a bit, but we always manage. I look forward to seein' 'er when I get home tomorrow."

Marissa peered up at a nearby wall clock. It was almost eight. *Four more hours until midnight ... when Thomas will approach his contact and ask them to direct us to the black market. Then Thomas will leave, venturing back to Copperton in the morning, and Arthur and I will be alone.*

"Well, we appreciate all of your help," Marissa thanked Thomas. "I really hope you and Marian can find peace."

Marissa shook her head. She knew her sympathies were futile and that it would take a lot more than hope to heal Thomas and his wife's pain.

"We will eventually," Thomas replied. "'Specially now that we can get the cure. But even after her disease is gone, we've still got a lotta mental healin' to do, and that starts with me. In fact," he pushed his mug of mead across the table in Marissa's direction, "no more drinkin' tonight. Feel free to take the rest o'mine."

Marissa eyed the amber-colored drink suspiciously.

"I promise I ain't got cooties," Thomas teased.

Marissa lifted the sour-smelling beverage to her lips. Arthur raised his eyebrows and grinned, surprised that she was willing to take a sip.

As the drink hit her forked tongue, it was sweet and tangy with a faint hint of citrus. But it was the bitter stinging aftertaste that made her entire face crinkle and sent her into a violent coughing spasm.

Thomas cackled, slapping a hand on the table. Arthur shook his head and rested his temple on his palm. A small, amused smile crept across his face.

Marissa huffed and took a larger gulp just to prove them wrong. She went into another coughing fit, and Arthur swiped the drink from her hands.

"Alright, that's enough for you," he muttered. "I don't want to find out tonight if you're a lightweight. What time is it, anyway?"

"Just past eight." Thomas glanced over at the wall clock. "We got a few hours. How 'bout we try to enjoy ourselves a bit before y'all descend into that crime pit?"

Marissa spent the rest of the night fighting down her nerves and relaxing as much as possible. Just before nine o'clock, the waitress set an enormous steaming plate of food in front of her.

"Us village folk call that fish n' chips," Thomas commented. "Deep-fried goodness. Best comfort food around."

Marissa had never seen so much food in her life. Several long strips of crispy mead-battered fish sat on a bed of fried potatoes that was so large that some of them spilled off the plate.

"Here." Arthur handed her a glass jar full of red paste. "It's ketchup. You're gonna need it for the fries."

CHAPTER 18

The crispy, oily food was incredibly rich, and she was full after eating only half of it. But she couldn't stop eating—she didn't know when she'd be able to have this sort of meal again.

"Careful, you're getting crumbs on your scarf." Arthur chuckled.

The two men were amazed that Marissa managed to finish her entire meal. She even plucked the crumbs off the grease-stained plate.

"Haven't y'all been travelin' together?" Thomas turned to Arthur as the waitress took their empty plates away. "Do ya ever feed this woman?"

Arthur looked off to the side and shrugged. "To be fair, our first night of traveling was spent in an abandoned inn."

They were in no rush to leave the restaurant. If they stepped outside the cheery racket of the inn, they'd be greeted by the cold, dark, empty streets, and the reality of their mission would hit the bottom of Marissa's stomach like a rock. Instead, they sat at the table, talking the time away. Arthur even ordered dessert for the three of them to split—a huge brownie mountain dripping with vanilla ice cream.

"I'm so full," Marissa grumbled, resting her head on the table.

"We call that a food coma." Arthur laughed. "I'll be right back. I need to use the restroom."

Arthur stood up from his chair and brushed past Marissa, leaving her and Thomas alone at the table.

Marissa peered up at the clock—it was nearly ten. *Two more hours.* Her heart pounded in her chest.

She turned to face the pink-cheeked man in front of her. He gave an awkward smile, trying to loosen the tension between them. *It's unsettling how normal he seems. Sometimes it's hard to believe he killed a reptilian.*

"Ya know," Thomas interjected. "Yer foolin' yerself if ya pretend ya don't see it."

Marissa tilted her head. "See what?"

"What we all see. Arthur's got feelins' for ya."

Her stomach dropped. Embarrassment quickly burned through her body, reddening her cheeks. "He does not."

"What makes ya think that? I see 'im givin' ya that look all the time. It's the same look I used to give Marian when we first met. Also, ya slept on his chest on the way to Brennan."

"I... I..." Marissa stuttered. She cleared her throat, regaining composure. She lowered her voice to a whisper. "You're insane. I'm a reptilian. Half-Naga. Snake-person. Humans are terrified of me. What makes you think a human man, much less a member of the royal family, would have any interest in a monst—"

Marissa stopped.

You're not a monster, Marissa. You're special. I know it sounds corny, but I genuinely believe that you exist for a reason.

She swallowed hard, forcing back her emotions. "It doesn't matter. There is no way that a royal could be with a freaky-looking snake girl who lives on the streets. Ever."

Thomas gave an unconvinced frown, shifting back in his seat. "Alrighty then. Whatever ya say."

Marissa folded her arms on the table and rested her head between them. *Feelings!?* She knew little about emotional connections. She grew up in an orphanage with a headmistress that tolerated her at best and kicked her out as soon as she turned eighteen. She had never been hugged, or kissed, or experienced true warmth from another being. She figured that she was destined to be alone.

"Excuse me, Marissa."

She felt a hand on the back of her chair as Arthur slid past her and returned to his seat. He peered over at Marissa, who still had her head still buried in her arms. "Are you alright?"

"I'm fine," she mumbled.

Arthur shot a glance at Thomas, who shrugged.

The waitress came by with three cups of hot water. She had been confused by Arthur's earlier request, but obliged.

"What, did you three bring your own tea bags or something?" she joked.

"Sort of," Arthur responded. "But thank you."

As the waitress walked away, Arthur pulled the packet of blue flowers out of his pocket and dropped a few petals into each of their cups.

"Drink up quickly. We need'ta get goin' if we have'ta get all the way to the southern gates," Thomas noted. "We're gonna have'ta walk; carriages don't run this late at night."

As Marissa finished her tea, a deep feeling of relaxation crept over her like a warm blanket. It felt like the stormy nights spent in the storeroom as a child, warm and dry despite the leaky roof, reading her favorite books. *Let's see how long this feeling lasts.*

The waitress returned, and they paid for their food and departed out the front door into the eerie chill of the night. Since they were in the closed-down industrial district, the streets were mostly empty, and a sinister stillness hung in the dark sky.

Arthur pulled his cloak out of his satchel and slipped it over his head, fumbling with the buttons. Marissa pulled the hood of her cloak farther over her forehead. The atmosphere changed as they ventured into Alistar. Gone was the merry bustle of daytime activities. The sky was veiled in a thick cloak of darkness, and the faint, flickering streetlamps did little to fight it off. Odd shadows stretched across the ghostly orange light.

There were far fewer people out this late at night, and the ones they did see wore jackets or cloaks that heavily shrouded their figures. They walked at a brisk pace with their heads down, drawing as little attention to themselves as possible. Marissa's eyes clung to Arthur and Thomas walking ahead of her on the narrow stone sidewalk—she didn't dare lose sight of them. *At least my warm cloak and stomach full of food and tea make me feel more secure.*

"We're comin' up on the gates," Thomas whispered after almost an hour of walking through the gloomy streets. "Keep quiet and let me do the talkin'."

The large iron gates stood like quiet statues in the pitch-dark air. They were firmly sealed shut; few carts dared to travel through the outer villages so late at night. A couple of weary vagrants hung around the nearby churches, clutching bowls of watery porridge; their figures illuminated by the light radiating from the stained-glass windows.

Marissa pressed her scarf against her nose as they approached a lone figure standing under a glowing streetlamp next to the gatehouse. The man was quite short; he wore a black jacket and a brimmed hat that shielded his lowered gaze. The dark silhouette of a cigar hung from his mouth, and soft tendrils of smoke wafted in the air around him.

"'Ey Thomas," the man greeted in a gritty voice. He lifted his head, revealing beady black eyes under the shadow of his hat. "I see ya brought friends. And where are the goods I asked for?"

"I'm sorry, but the mission wasn't successful. However," Thomas quickly changed the subject and gestured toward the two dark figures beside him. "I've brought some patrons who are very interested in yer wares. They'd be grateful for an escort to the market."

The man stepped closer, circling and eyeing Marissa and Arthur like cattle at a feedlot.

"Well, I'm certainly pleased to take on new customers. But Tommy, ya can't just go tellin' every buddy out in the villages about the market."

"We're from Brennan," Arthur spoke up. The scarf wrapped around his nose and mouth shifted as he spoke.

The squat man raised a hairy eyebrow. "Ah, I see. I can tell by yer accent that yer city folk. Very well, come with me. And Tommy," the man pointed at Thomas, "I appreciate ya bringin' me new customers, but next time I want my goods. Understand?"

"Yes." Thomas's body was stiff as he forced a polite response. Marissa had seen his face twitch when the man called him Tommy.

"C'mon, follow me." The man pointed at Marissa and Arthur.

As they left, Marissa turned back around to Thomas. He grew more and more distant as they walked, yet he remained still under the glowing streetlight. Once they were almost out of sight, Thomas waved and disappeared into the darkness. He would return to the Steel Forge Inn and rest for the night. Arthur had already given him the coin for his wife's cure, plus some extra to travel back to Copperton in the morning.

I wonder if we'll ever see him again. Murderer or not... I am grateful for his help.

Marissa and Arthur followed the man through the narrow alleyways between the main roads. He shuffled along with a hunched back and stumbling pace. Marissa noticed a slight limp in his right leg. Eventually, they reached a worn-out carriage parked along a side street. The driver nodded as the three of them approached but otherwise did not move.

"Hop in." The man opened the door. Marissa took a step back, perplexed.

"What'ya lookin' at?" he grumbled. "We certainly ain't gonna walk all the way to Augustree."

Augustree? The black market is in the merchant's district? I suppose it makes sense...

The man sat across from Marissa and Arthur in the carriage, silently puffing on his cigar.

"May I ask you something?" Arthur's soft voice broke the silence.

"Depends on what that somethin' is," the man grumbled.

"We've heard that the prices for full hides have increased recently. Do you happen to know why?"

"Ah," the man grumbled, lifting his cigar and raising the brim of his hat. Marissa tried her best not to recoil as the bitter smoke stung her nostrils. "Let me introduce myself. Down here, I go by Miles, and I specialize in Varan goods. A big buyer's been comin' in and purchasin' hides off all the vendors. Just started happenin' a few days ago."

"Do you happen to know who this buyer is?"

"Why do ya need to know?" Miles looked annoyed, and Marissa shuddered. "My clients generally don't take well to their names bein' thrown around. Everyone knows about the big buyer, but I wouldn't go around askin' for details once we get to the market. The buyer is very keen on keepin' their identity a secret, and vendors don't like nosiness."

"My apologies," Arthur replied in a very formal tone. "You'll have to excuse us, as we are new to the market etiquette. Since we were looking to purchase hides, I was just wondering if there had been recent changes to supply or quality. I did not mean to intrude on your client's privacy."

"Ah, understood." Miles's tone softened, and he leaned back in his seat. "As far as I can tell, nothin's different about the hides, other than the prices shootin' up."

Marissa's eyes shifted over to Arthur. *He seems acquainted with dealing with these sorts of formalities. He probably spent a fair share of his childhood tiptoeing around snooty royals and their etiquette.*

Miles seemed content to silently puff on his cigar, so Marissa took the opportunity to lean her head against the carriage window and close her eyes. In between energetic bursts of fear and anxiety, she was quite tired since it was nearly midnight.

Just don't fall asleep.

Chapter 19

$\mathcal{M}$ARISSA'S STOMACH CHURNED AS THE SOUND of hoofbeats slowed, then stopped.

"Alright, hop on out." Miles waved them along as they exited the carriage. The driver clicked to the horses and disappeared down the road without a word.

Marissa's eyes widened as the three of them rounded a corner.

I recognize these streets... wait, is that...?

Miles stopped at the back entrance to an abandoned storefront. He dug out a set of keys and fumbled over them for a few moments, forgetting which key was the correct one. On his third try, the lock finally clicked open, and he grumbled in relief.

They entered a dark, empty storeroom full of nothing but dust and cobwebs. But through the single open door, Marissa could see out the front windows and into the road. Off to the far left, a lacquered gold sign was barely visible. It was so far out of view that she could only see the last four letters of the store's name, E-R-I-E.

But she knew what store it was. She had been there several times.

The Menagerie is this close to the black market? I've been staying just a few blocks from here...

A horrid sickness crept through her stomach as she realized how near she'd been living to such a revolting place, so close to certain death. Arthur noticed the sign, too—his gaze fixed on it for a moment, and Marissa could hear his breath slow. But he quickly looked away and turned his attention back to Miles—he couldn't let his emotions slip. Marissa couldn't either, so she took a deep breath and followed Arthur, her face hidden behind his shoulder.

Miles pulled the keyring back out and unlocked a small cellar door in the far corner. Beyond the creaky hinges was a set of old, ominous-looking wooden stairs leading into a pitch-black room. Miles pulled a box of matches out of his pocket and lit an old oil lamp sitting on a nearby shelf.

"C'mon, let's go."

As they descended into the darkness, Marissa felt a deep sense of dread, as if she were about to jump off a cliff. *This is it. No backing out now. I, Marissa, a half-rep-tilian, am going into a pit full of Brennan's most dangerous criminals.*

She knew an unmasking was possible and that if her scarf fell over her reptilian nose or her cloak sleeves rolled up a bit too far and revealed her scales, she would be dead. She was venturing into the lair of the humans who killed her kind to help the half of her that she'd never met.

Yet, as scared as she was, she was even more concerned about Arthur.

He lives a comfortable life, surrounded by his animals, with all the money he could ever need. And now he's risking everything for the reptilians.

So far, he hadn't faltered—no hint of emotion had crossed his eyes. But Marissa knew that he was just as afraid as she was. *I must protect us both.*

Ya know, yer foolin' yourself if ya pretend ya don't see it. Arthur's got feeli—

No, Marissa shook the emotions out of her head. *Don't think about that right now.*

"I didn't even know that Brennan had basements," Arthur remarked as they reached the bottom of the stairs. "I thought the Valley of Scales was all swampland?"

"It's difficult." Miles waved the lantern around the room. He appeared to be searching for something. "But possible. Everythin' is reinforced with limestone. It's still a flood risk, since we're sittin' right at the water table and limestone is full'a holes, but the patrons were insistent that the market be built underground. Makes it much easier to keep away from pryin' eyes."

Miles tapped the wall in several places, then his eyes lit up. "Aha, found it. False wall, let's just push this aside..."

Beyond the hidden door was a narrow underground alley. As they crept down the cool, musty path, Marissa could hear rattles of activity coming from the end of the tunnel. Her heart pounded as blood rushed through her ears. She shifted closer to Arthur, who was in front of her, as they walked single file.

The tunnel eventually led into a large open hall, cascading onwards for what seemed like miles. Marissa spun around and realized there were several more tunnels coming from other parts of Brennan that led into the massive space. *It's like a giant underground root system, but full of infection and rot.* The hall was faintly lit by hanging wall lanterns, and the dim, clammy air of the underground hung over the wandering patrons. They all wore dark cloaks with scarves wrapped around their faces, just like Marissa and Arthur. Small groups of them shuffled quietly through the stalls like specters in a graveyard.

A large central aisle separated two rows of vendor stalls. Marissa's stomach fell as soon as they came into view. Bits and pieces of reptilians were for sale at every one—rows of teeth on a shelf, processed hides hanging from coat racks, even bags of shed skin that had been ground into a fine powder.

Every one of these hides... Marissa stared in horror as they approached Miles's stall. *Was a living, breathing reptilian.* The eerie aura of death seeped through the wares and crawled across the vendor stalls. Marissa's mind buzzed inside her skull as if she could hear the screams of the victims. She wondered how the wretched patrons managed to wander around, gazing at reptilian parts as if they were trinkets in a tourist shop, and ignore the hundreds of tormented souls that haunted the market.

What a nightmare. This place is cursed.

"I notice ya lookin' at the hides." Miles gestured toward Arthur, who stood near the racks and ran his fingers along the scales. "Naga hide is prettier, and Gharian hide is tougher, but nothin' beats Varan when it comes to versatility. Check out how small and uniform the scales are. It's the lightest reptilian hide of all..."

Marissa stepped away from Arthur and Miles, wandering around the stall and examining its wares. Varan teeth and claws were perched on tiered shelves, and their dorsal spines hung in bunches from the stall's roof. Marissa tilted her head back. Behind the stall, next to the register, was a small, worn notebook.

Arthur, please ... keep him distracted.

As Miles continued blathering on about his wretched wares, Marissa crept around the back of the stall, pretending to be enamored by the rows of Varan teeth. She picked one up, holding it up to the dim light of the lanterns and studying it while her other hand fumbled with the notebook's pages. She waited for a moment when Miles had his back turned and looked down.

The book was a collection of purchase receipts for the past year. Marissa flipped through the dates until she reached October. As Marissa had expected, Miles's sales had increased nearly threefold over the past few days. His scraggly handwriting was barely comprehensible, but Marissa noticed the same signature repeated on most of the orders.

Cac... cas... rell... Castrella. No... Castella. I think? That must be a last name. I need to tell Arth—

"What'cha doin' back here, m'lady?"

Marissa jolted upward, nearly knocking the Varan teeth off the table.

"Oh, hello, Miles," Marissa greeted. She straightened her posture. *Be like Arthur, cool and calm...* "I was just admiring these teeth. I didn't realize Varan had such long ones."

"Indeed, they do. 'Ere longer than Naga fangs, and a lot wider." Miles lifted a large fang off the table and admired it, the enamel shining in the dim light. Marissa's shoulders softened. *That was close.* "My clients use 'em for all sorts of things. Potions, teas ... or even just wearin' 'em under their clothes. It'll give you the strength of the lizard beasts themselves. For ya, I'll do a special. Two for one gold."

Marissa froze. *He'll be suspicious if I don't buy something. I don't have any money. Arthur has—*

"Here you go." Arthur dropped a gold coin in Miles's palm. Marissa noticed a Varan hide draped over his arm. "We'll take two of your largest teeth, please."

"Excellent." Miles grinned, revealing a mouth full of silver teeth. "May I interest ya in anythin' else?"

"I think we're all set here," Arthur responded, clutching Marissa's arm. "We plan on browsing the rest of the market while we're here. Thank you again for your assistance."

"Not a problem." Miles waved as Marissa and Arthur wandered down the aisle of stalls. "Come back soon, ya hear?"

Marissa fought down the urge to shudder in disgust as they walked away. Arthur's whisper buzzed low in her ear. "What did you find?"

"Let's leave," Marissa whispered back, hesitant to give away too much information in the middle of the black market. "We have what we need."

"You found out who the buyer is?"

"I think so." Marissa's head swiveled around, trying to make sure no other cloaked figures were nearby. "But it's too dangerous to talk about it here."

Arthur nodded in understanding, and as they walked back toward the underground alleyway, Marissa stopped. She took in one last gaze of the market, the stalls, and all the reptilian wares. She lowered her head and clasped her hands down at her hips.

"What're you doing?" Arthur whispered harshly, attempting to pull her away.

"There, I'm done." Marissa looked up. "We can leave now."

As they exited the black market and returned to the surface, Marissa felt like she could finally breathe again.

Even though they were in a musty old storeroom, it didn't compare to the thick, ghastly air of the black market choking her lungs.

"Okay," Marissa sighed, her chest heaving. "Now that we're out of that hell pit, let's get back to The Menagerie. I need to discuss what I found with you in private."

"Okay, sounds good. But why did you stop back there?"

Marissa lowered her head, her voice somber. "I'm not religious, but … I felt that I needed to pray. I asked that reptilian god to help them, the one you had a portrait of on your wall. I could feel them, Arthur—so many tormented souls haunted that place. Those filthy criminals see exotic goods; I see a slaughterhouse."

"I know." Arthur placed a hand on Marissa's shoulder. "But there's nothing we can do for them. Not yet, anyways. Let's get out of here."

Chapter 20

"**C**ASTELLA."

Arthur's eyes widened as Marissa mentioned the name.

"Do you recognize it?" she asked. "It was on most of the receipts. Miles was right—his sales have tripled over the past week."

"I do." Arthur's expression was grim. They stood alone in the kitchen, a soft glowstone lamp on the table the only source of light in Arthur's small apartment. "The Castellas are one of the wealthiest families in Brennan. They're not royalty, but they may as well be. I've had my fair share of encounters with them. The truth is, I saw the patriarch of the family when I went to speak with the king. I couldn't hear their conversation, but maybe it had something to do with this. The Castellas love to flaunt their money, but I have no idea what they would need so many reptilian hides for."

"I mean..." Marissa paused. She shivered at the thought of sneaking around a powerful family's estate. "We must do something. We now know who the culprit is—is there any way to investigate this further?"

"Actually." Arthur gestured for Marissa to follow him out of the kitchen. In the far corner of the living room was an old writing desk. "The Castellas are having a party tomorrow night. Celebrating their son's engagement or something. Just another reason for them to invite a bunch of nobles over and smooth-talk them while they're drunk."

Marissa gulped. Sneaking into the black market was one thing, shrouded in cloaks and scarves, in a place where people wanted their identity to be kept a secret. Infiltrating a party and interacting with the other guests without raising suspicion the entire night would be impossible.

"Are you suggesting we sneak in?" Marissa asked. "That's—"

"Relax. We don't need to." Arthur opened the drawer underneath the desk and pulled out a crisp, folded envelope. Inside was a small card inked with elaborate calligraphy. "I was invited. The whole royalty thing has its perks. You can be my plus-one."

Marissa's scales quivered at the thought of going to a fancy party and pretending she was a full-blooded human. *And a high-class one at that.* She imagined the Castellas and the rest of the wealthy entourage as snobbish, bloodthirsty wolves, ready to devour her once it became apparent she wasn't one of them.

"The good news is that it's a masquerade ball, so we can disguise you. But even with that," Arthur's voice lowered, "this is dangerous, even more so than the black market. Do you want to do this?"

Marissa was both terrified and furious. The black market was scary enough, and now she'd have to face down one of its most lucrative buyers. All she could view them as were secondhand killers, farming their dirty work out to the peasants, their dainty hands stained with the blood of the reptilians. *And I must walk into their estate and pretend to be a gracious guest.*

"We've come so far," she remarked. "We can't give up now. We need to figure out why they're buying all those hides and maybe even learn the truth about that Naga."

"Indeed, we do." Arthur wandered across the living room, tracing his fingers over the Varan hide spread across the couch.

"I still can't believe you bought a hide."

"Hey, it was for the same reason you got those teeth. Miles wasn't going to let us leave without some of his wares. It was an unfortunate necessity to complete the mission."

Marissa reached into her cloak pocket and pulled out the Varan teeth. They gleamed like precious stones in her palm. "What're we going to do with them?"

"I was thinking about that. I want to give them a proper burial. But it'll need to wait until we're closer to Varan territory. I want to lay them to rest in their homeland, not on the grounds of their killers." Arthur peered over at the wall clock. "Regardless, it's two a.m., and I'm exhausted. Let's go to bed and discuss things further in the morning."

DESPITE HER WORRIES, MARISSA WAS SO EXHAUSTED that she slept until nearly ten o'clock. She opened her vivid blue eyes, yawned, and crept over to the window. A thin ray of light crept between the gauzy curtains and into the guest bedroom, and soft hums of birdsong and market activity echoed from outside. Sizzling and crackling sounds came from the kitchen. Marissa got dressed, ventured into the hallway, and spotted Arthur cooking breakfast. He smiled warmly at her.

"Did you sleep alright?" Arthur asked as he slid two fried eggs onto elegantly patterned plates and lined them with buttered toast. Marissa took a seat at the kitchen table. Arthur placed one of the plates in front of her, but she was too weary to acknowledge him. "I guess not. It's a lot to process, isn't it?"

Marissa poked her egg with her fork. She wasn't hungry, but she ate a few bites to show her appreciation. *This is far from over. Even if we discover why the Castellas are buying so many hides, what are we supposed to do about it? We're just two people...*

"What happens if we can't find anything? And even worse, what if we get caught?"

Marissa's sudden, heavy questions broke the silence in the air.

Arthur set his fork down and sighed. His gaze shifted to the floor, unable to come up with a reassuring answer.

"If we don't find anything ... I'm not sure what our next plans are." Arthur frowned. Marissa wasn't sure either; she knew that if they went chasing after the Naga again, Arthur could end up in prison. *And I could be killed.*

"Let's just focus on tonight," Arthur continued. "If it's unsuccessful, we'll cross that bridge when we get there. As for being caught ... we can't let that happen. There's no way around it. We know how dangerous this is. But..." Arthur straightened in his seat. "We're more likely to get caught if we go into this stressed. The party isn't until seven, but we still need to get you a dress. We've done a lot of traveling lately, so let's just relax and try not to worry for a few hours."

Arthur is right. It's just a party. It'll be fun. Marissa doubted her last thought, but she had to resist the fear that choked her throat.

"Should we go back to Autumn's? I bet she—"

"Unfortunately," Arthur raised an eyebrow, "going to a wealthy family's party requires a certain dress code. Autumn's shop was lovely, but we'll need to visit a very different type of tailor for this event. In fact, it's already ten-thirty, so we should probably get going."

Marissa raised her eyebrows and peered down at her plate. *I really do need to eat.* She quickly gulped down the remainder of her egg and two slices of toast.

Arthur laughed. "That was fast. I suppose that's a snake thing; you're very good at swallowing your food whole."

Marissa stopped eating and shrugged, embarrassed. "I'm ready. Let's go."

GEORGE GREETED THEM WITH A FRIENDLY WAVE as they ventured downstairs and into the shop. The green dragonling sat next to him on the counter, playing with a small skein of yarn. Aurora sat by the front door and lifted all three heads as they approached.

"Good morning." Arthur nodded. "We have an errand to run, but I'll be back to mind the shop later today. Marissa will be assisting me, so feel free to take the afternoon off."

As Arthur spoke, Marissa walked over to an enclosure on the back wall. Nim awoke as soon as Marissa appeared in front of the tank. He stretched his long neck out to greet her, his black eyes glittering. Marissa went to open the enclosure door when Arthur stepped behind her.

"Marissa," Arthur whispered in a soft, scolding tone. "We can't take Nim with us to a tailor. You'll have plenty of time to spend with him later."

"I know," Marissa sighed and removed her hand from the glass. She followed Arthur to the front door, where they stepped out into the cool, damp morning air.

"It's just a few blocks this way." Arthur pointed. "Closer to the palace."

Marissa's head spun as they walked, wondering what sort of dress she would need to wear to fit in with Brennan's wealthy elite. *I need to be able to cover my neck and arms... I hope no one gets too suspicious...*

"You need an alias," Arthur interrupted Marissa's swirling thoughts. "Let's start with a fake name."

"I don't know many female names. But there was a little girl at the orphanage named Cecelia. I always liked that name."

"It's a nice one. It suits you well."

Marissa's mind wandered back to her childhood days at the orphanage. Cecelia was a small, pale brunette the same age as her. In fact, she was one of the only children to show her any kindness. They occasionally played together, even if Cecelia was hesitant to let Marissa get too close. Marissa scoffed. *Thanks to Jack and his rumors of me having diseases.* But Cecelia kept her distance for good once Marissa was unmasked in the garden and forced to live in the storehouse. Marissa would never forget the look of terror on her only friend's face when she discovered the truth.

Marissa shuddered. Remembering Cecelia's horrified reaction reminded her of what the consequences would be if she were unmasked at the party.

"You're a shopkeeper that runs the bookstore across from The Menagerie," Arthur pondered. "That's how I know you. But there's just one thing ... we can't pretend to be a couple or even remotely interested in each other."

Marissa's stomach dropped. "Is there a reason? Wouldn't I be your date for the evening?"

"Plus-ones don't have to be romantic. We can pretend you're there to chatter with the nobles about literature. And my relationship status is ... complicated. Let's leave it at that."

Marissa shivered, feeling her heart sink. She recoiled at the unfamiliar emotions that swirled through her head. *Stop it. Why do you care? You're a snake, and he's royalty. Enough with the jealousy.*

"Here we are." They rounded a corner, and Arthur pointed to a large shop across the street.

Marissa noticed that this section of Augustree seemed fancier than the rest. The shops were more elegant, and so were the people. Marissa watched a woman in a silky coat and fur scarf stroll by with an enormous mastiff on a metal leash. Even the dog seemed to hold its head up as they passed. They were close to the palace; its magnificent towering spires peeked over the tops of the stores.

The tailor, Imperial Thread, was much different than Autumn's little shop. While Autumn Leaf Tailor was a cozy, homey mess, with wares shoved into every corner, this shop was immaculate. Fancy glowstone lights illuminated a row of mannequins in the front window, and there were no sewing machines or clothing racks in sight. In fact, the shop was mostly empty, except for a few lacey ballgowns in the center of the store.

"Good morning," Arthur greeted the receptionist. Marissa stared wide-eyed at the elaborate dresses in front of her. *I've never seen such fancy clothes in my life.*

"Yes, hello." The receptionist, a tall, wiry woman with graying hair and a long nose, eyed them above her tiny reading glasses. "Do you have an appointment?"

"I do not." Arthur cleared his throat. "But I was hoping you'd be able to squeeze us in. Under Arthur Brennan, please?"

The woman's demeanor immediately changed upon hearing the royal surname. She brushed the loose strands of hair out of her face and stuttered, "Oh, yes, of course. One moment. Let me fetch an attendant for you. And are we shopping for you both today?"

"Just her." Arthur waved Marissa over, diverting her attention from the fancy dresses. "We're in a bit of a rush; we have a last-minute party to attend tonight, and she needs something to wear."

"Tonight? That's cutting it a bit close, but I'm sure we can help."

A young woman with pale brown hair and thin eyebrows stepped toward the front desk. "Hello. My name is Agnes. I will be your assistant today. What sort of formalwear are we looking for?"

"We need a ballgown for tonight," Arthur responded. "However, it's a bit of a tricky situation. My dear friend suffered some burns as a child, and she's terribly self-conscious about her scarring. It's a masquerade ball, but she still needs her arms and neck fully covered. Do you have something that would work for us?"

"Let's see," Agnes pondered. "Unfortunately, without time for tailoring, we have limited options. We have some fine scarves, but she'd also need a high neckline and long sleeves, which aren't really in fashion right now. Only one dress comes to mind that fits the description. It's a bit dated, though. Let me contact some of the other local shops and see if they have anything—"

"No, that's alright," Marissa spoke up, uncomfortable with inconveniencing them. "I'll try on the dress you have."

"Very well. Back here, please."

Marissa nervously followed Agnes into the back of the store, where next to a small row of dressing rooms was a large storeroom.

"Let me go fetch it. I'll be right back."

Marissa stared at her reflection in the mirror, smoothing the shoulders of her cloak. The day before, the black garment was the fanciest piece of clothing she owned... *until now. I just hope I don't look like a fool.*

"Here it is!" Agnes carried the long maroon gown out of the storeroom, careful not to drag it across the floor. The dark dress was made of heavy silk, with long billowy sleeves down to the wrists and black flowers embroidered onto its hefty train.

"I also found this scarf to go with it." Agnes gestured toward the thin lacey cloth draped across her forearm. Glittering black beads were sewn into the scarf's tassels.

Marissa gazed at the dress in awe. *I can't believe I get to wear something so beautiful.*

"Do you need assistance?" Agnes asked as Marissa took the dress and walked into a fitting room. "It's a bit cumbersome, and—"

"I'm fine, thank you!"

Marissa saw Arthur's eyes widen as she stepped out of the dressing room, holding the edges of her dress up so she wouldn't trip. She turned around and peered at herself in the mirror. Even with her face and neck covered by the beaded, black scarf, she felt so glamorous that she could barely contain her excitement. For a moment, the fear of investigating the criminal Castella family faded away. She, a half-snake street urchin, was going to live like royalty for a night. *I may as well enjoy it.*

"You look lovely."

Arthur stepped toward her. Marissa beamed, grinning, with her full fangs exposed underneath her scarf. She took a deep breath and sucked down her overwhelming emotions. She thought her heart would explode with happiness or float out of her chest and up toward the ceiling. She stood silently in the back of the store, gazing into his forest-green eyes, her hands just inches away from his.

"Marissa, I—"

"Oh my goodness, I must say, that dress suits you so well," Agnes exclaimed, interrupting them. "Who says you need the latest fashion to look stunning at a party? So have we decided on this one?"

"Oh, yes, of course. I love it." She nodded eagerly. Arthur chuckled.

Marissa shook her head, pulling it back down from the clouds. Arthur followed Agnes up to the register, leaving Marissa alone to change into her regular clothes.

She huffed as her normal, darkly cloaked form appeared in the mirror. *At least I get to wear it again tonight.* She exited the dressing room and glanced at Arthur at the register. He smiled and nodded at Agnes, and Marissa saw a gold glint in his palm as he handed her the payment for the dress.

What were you going to say to me? I want to know.

But at the same time, she didn't. She wasn't ready to confront the emotions that were still so new to her. A horrifying thought crept into her skull. *What if they catch me? I could die at the hands of the elite and never see Arthur again.*

Marissa was quiet as they left the store. Her head was full of excitement over the dress, terror for the upcoming party, and complicated affections for Arthur.

"You seem tense," Arthur remarked as they walked the streets of Augustree. Marissa's dress was tucked in a garment bag and slung across his shoulder. "You worried about tonight?"

"Yes," Marissa replied, relieved that she could blame her nerves on the party and not acknowledge her other emotions.

"Well." Arthur looked up, admiring the clear blue sky. "It's noon. Do you mind helping me mind the shop for the rest of the afternoon? Don't forget my promise before—consider it your first day on the job. I'll pay you well for your time."

Marissa beamed, and Arthur could tell she was smiling behind her scarf. He chuckled.

"Well, it'll be a short day," he noted. "I'll have to close shop early; we have a party to attend."

Chapter 21

*A*S RAMSEY APPROACHED THE PALACE DOORS, he could tell that the guards were bewildered by his disheveled state.

After two days of nonstop travel back to the safety of Brennan, he was dirty, exhausted, and traumatized by his companions' deaths. When he had first stepped out of the temple, he was greeted by the stagnant bodies of their horses, each with lifeless, bulging eyes and gushing arrow wounds in their chests. Thin rivers of blood flowed from their fatal injuries, staining their watery graves with a red tinge.

He ended up having to make the journey back to human territory on foot. He spent an eternity trudging through the dense, foreboding swampland, with muggy clothing and the persistent fear that a Naga would shoot an arrow through his skull at any moment. Thankfully, he didn't come across any, and he nearly wept with relief many hours later when tiny flickers of civilization crept into view against the darkening sky.

Now, he had finally made it back to the palace. Relief washed over his weary body as the massive doors heaved open, revealing the glittering foyer. He had completed his mission, but he was anything but proud. All he wanted to do was rest without the constant empty-eyed stares of his deceased companions flashing through his mind. But he still had to give the king the dreadful news that his guardsmen were dead, he was correct about the idol's existence, and, most importantly, that the Naga most likely had a piece of the idol and was plotting to summon a god.

Too stressed and exhausted for formalities, he plodded across the foyer and marched straight up to the king's throne room. The guards were startled by the dreadful somberness in his eyes, but they seemed to be expecting him, as they immediately pulled the doors open and let him through without an introduction.

"Ramsey." The king's voice was soft with concern. He stood up, stepping away from his throne and approaching his unkempt heir. "You have returned. Are you alright? What happened to yo—"

"It's all real," Ramsey uttered in disbelief. "The temple … the idol … the Naga…"

"It's alright, Ramsey." The king placed a sympathetic hand on his shoulder. "Deep breaths. I need you to tell me what happened."

"The tomb was empty, and it was clear that someone had been there recently. It had to be the Naga. That's why he's been acting strange, breaking into homes ... he's searching for something ... maybe even another piece of the idol."

The king's eyes widened; a distressed gaze crossed his face as he processed Ramsey's words.

"I'm afraid that confirms my worst fears. But Ramsey ... where are the others?"

Ramsey's face paled, turning a deathly shade of white. King Gabriel took a step back, his face somber with realization.

"A pair of Naga caught us in the temple." Ramsey's voice quivered. "I ... I was the only one who made it out alive."

The king lowered his head, taking a moment to absorb the news. He seemed both deeply saddened and disappointed at his guardsmen's deaths.

"This means war, doesn't it?"

Ramsey's dire question hung heavy in the still air of the throne room. He began to tremble as the king's despondent eyes met his.

"I know the humans and reptilians have always been at odds," Ramsey continued. "We've always had tension, always on the brink of conflict. But is this it? We can't let them summon their god; it could destroy Brennan."

The king nodded slightly, taking a deep breath.

"Yes. But it's alright, Ramsey. You don't need to do anything more right now. Preparations are already in place, and you need rest. In fact, isn't the Castellas' party tonight? You should go and enjoy yourself. These heavier conversations can wait until you've recovered."

Ramsey sighed. The king was right; he needed to recuperate after his harrowing experience. He longed to take a nap in his own bed. Spending the evening having a few drinks with his wife seemed like a pleasant respite from his tormenting journey.

"One last thing—please do not go about discussing this matter with others. We cannot risk a kingdom-wide panic before we're ready to deal with the reptilians."

"Of course. I understand."

"Excellent. Now go upstairs and rest," the king said softly. "You deserve some leisure time this evening. We can meet tomorrow to discuss things further."

"Thank you, Your Majesty."

As Ramsey turned to leave, the king clutched his shoulder again, this time with a much firmer grasp.

"And Ramsey," the pleased glimmer had returned to his eye, "you did well. I'm proud of you."

"So let's go over food next. The Castellas mostly serve hors d'oeuvres and other small appetizers at their masquerade balls, so people can eat neatly without removing their masks. If offered one, pick it up cleanly between your thumb and index finger..."

Marissa found it funny that Arthur was lecturing her on formal etiquette while she was elbow-deep in a dirty reptile tank. She took a deep breath, trying to focus both on Arthur's lesson and scrubbing every square inch of the enclosure. The sour scent of vinegar burned her nostrils as it seeped out of her cleaning sponge. The tank's occupant, an albino ball python, was draped around Arthur's shoulders like a necklace as he dusted the shelves behind the register.

"But why do they all wear masks?" Marissa asked.

"It goes back to the old days. Back when Brennan was first founded, masquerade balls were held to allow the royals to let loose without revealing their identities. But some ... scandals emerged, and now the masks are just a formality, holding on to tradition. But it's still forbidden to remove someone's mask at these sorts of parties, which works out well for us. No one will suspect that you're half-reptilian."

"That does make me feel a bit safer. Alright, I'm done." Marissa crawled out of the vinegar-scented enclosure, careful not to hit her head. The back wall of the Menagerie had nine tanks arranged in a three-by-three cube. The ball python's enclosure was on the bottom left, less than a foot from the floor.

"Excellent." Arthur smiled, stepping toward Marissa and letting the curious ball python slither into her arms.

It crawled up her shoulders, its tongue flicking her cheek, before settling around her neck. Arthur sneered. "They all like you more than me. When I first pulled that little guy out, he was all balled up, refusing to budge."

Marissa lifted the python's head up to her ear, pretending she could hear him whisper.

"What's that, little snake? You say Arthur should let George clean the rest of the reptile tanks?"

Arthur smirked. "Fine. You did do all of them except the top ones. I won't make you haul the stepstool out." He turned Marissa around, so she faced the reptile tanks. "Alright, let's hope I've taught you enough with my lecturing this afternoon. Quiz time."

Marissa giggled. In between discussing what to expect at the party, Arthur had filled her head with plenty of reptile knowledge. He was like an encyclopedia, full of facts about nearly every species.

"Let's start with the top left." Arthur pointed.

"That's easy. Corn snake, also known as a red rat snake."

"Excellent. Now name off the rest."

"Let's see, blood python, bullsnake, a lavender morph hognose." Marissa's gaze flicked across the reptile tanks as she recited each species. "Another ball python, but that one is a female piebald, and..." Marissa grinned as she stepped toward one of the middle enclosures. "My favorite little carpet python, Nim!"

"Excellent." Arthur smiled proudly. "You've got 'em. The bottom tanks are all ball pythons, anyway."

All nine snakes sat at the front of their tanks, their eyes locked on Marissa. She smiled. "I'd own them all if I could."

"Well, maybe, someday, if you make it to Naga territory, you can," Arthur remarked. "Lots of snakes live in that area in a sort of symbiotic relationship. I've seen some of the chieftains wear them around their necks like jewelry, just like how you wear Nim."

Marissa's face fell. "I hope that Naga will be alright."

"I know," Arthur replied sympathetically. "But we're going to figure this all out; that's why we're going to that party. Speaking of which, I can't believe it's already five o'clock. We should get ready soon."

Five?! Marissa's gaze shot outside. She'd been so preoccupied with cleaning the reptile tanks that she hadn't noticed the time pass. The cobblestone streets were cast in a hazy orange glow, signaling the impending sunset.

Marissa swallowed hard, her chest shaking. She'd had such a relaxing afternoon cleaning the reptile tanks and conversing with Arthur. She didn't want it to end. She knew that she'd have many more days like this if she continued working at the Menagerie, but she'd have to make it through the party first.

I'll make some sort of etiquette blunder, and they'll get suspicious. What if my fake identity falls apart? What if my mask slips, or...

Arthur placed a hand on her shoulder. "It's alright. I'm scared, too. Let me go ahead and close the shop, and we'll head upstairs. I'll put on some tea; I still have a few of those butterfly pea flowers. Your dress is hanging upstairs in the guest bedroom."

Marissa nodded. She stood silently next to the front window as Arthur counted out the register, locked the front door, and turned off the lights. The darkened storefront rattled Marissa's nerves. *Our relaxing day is over.*

She followed Arthur up the stairs, the old wooden boards creaking with every footstep. He fussed with the finicky lock until the old wooden door crept open with a loud groan.

Marissa felt nauseous. She was unsteady on her feet and had difficulty keeping her balance. She felt Arthur grab her as she fell backward.

"I... I..." Marissa stuttered, unable to stand. She trembled as Arthur picked her up and carried her down the hallway, setting her down on the guest bed.

"It's okay." Arthur's soft, reassuring words caused Marissa to burst into tears. Arthur pulled her closer, and she pressed her face into his chest and sobbed.

"I'm scared they'll get suspicious, or I'll be unmasked... I can't let my life end like this while the whole valley plunges into chaos." Marissa's words quivered, her voice rising and her chest heaving. "Whatever's coming, all this tension between the humans and reptilians... I must stop it. I can't die tonight!"

"And you won't!" Arthur shouted, grabbing Marissa's scaled cheeks and pulling her out of her panic. "We'll get through this together. I promise. Nothing will happen to you."

Marissa froze, unfamiliar with the feeling of human hands brushing against her face. Arthur leaned in closer, pressed his forehead against hers, and closed his eyes. His arms wrapped around her back, pulling her into a firm embrace. Marissa shivered, and Arthur squeezed her tighter in response. They sat silently on the bed, seeking comfort in each other's arms, refusing to acknowledge their impending fate. For in that moment, they were alone and at peace.

For the first time in her eighteen years of life, Marissa had been hugged, and she never wanted it to end. She was almost brought to tears by the immense comfort that a sincere, warm embrace had given her. *All those nights alone, as a child... why couldn't I ever experience this? Is this what it means to feel human emotions?*

Marissa had never known her parents. She had pushed them out of her mind a long time ago, but now she wondered what it would've been like to grow up with them. She knew that her family never stood a chance; a human mother and a Naga father together in a world that forced them apart. She decided that if she ever met them, the first thing she'd do was give them a hug.

"I'm scared, too," Arthur whispered, his voice soft in her ears. He pulled away, his gaze drifting down toward the bed as if he knew their embrace was wrong. Marissa's scales went cold. *I'm not ready to let go yet.*

But she had to. It was five-thirty, and the party was fast approaching. Marissa would have to confront her emotions once they made it through the night.

MARISSA STEPPED IN FRONT OF THE WALL-LENGTH mirror in Arthur's master bedroom. She wanted a moment to observe her true self, dressed up in her silky ballgown, before trying on her mask. She studied the face reflecting back at her, a face that had a reptilian nose and was half-covered in smooth black scales that trailed up her throat and faded away near her cheekbones. But beyond her peculiar features, Marissa glowed like royalty. The dark maroon of the dress complimented her pale skin and long black hair, which was immaculately combed and fastened with a silver clip.

"That's a lovely color on you." Arthur appeared in the mirror behind her, dressed in a full black suit atop an embroidered brown vest. He gestured toward his maroon bow tie. "Look, it matches your dress. Now, where are those damn masks...?"

As Arthur strolled away, his hands resting in his suit pockets and his tailcoat trailing behind him, Marissa couldn't help but stare. *He looks handsome...* she shook her head. *Stop gawking and focus.* She wound the beaded, black scarf around her neck and forced a prim smile onto her lips.

Tonight, I am no longer Marissa, the half-reptilian girl. I am Cecelia Burton, wealthy literary expert and bookshop owner. I must embrace the world of the elite to uncover

their murderous secrets. I will be successful; no one will sus-
pect a thing.

"Found them." Arthur emerged from the closet, clasping several elaborately painted masks. "They were buried behind some old boxes. Here, this is the only full-face one I have."

Marissa traced her fingers across the glossy white mask. Swirling patterns inked in gold and silver danced up the nose and across the forehead, and tall wafting feathers sprung from its sides. Its hollow, empty eye sockets glared back at Marissa. She held the mask up to her face, the cold ceramic sending a chill down her spine.

"Looks good." Arthur nodded. "Perfectly disguised. Now, you remember everything I taught you? Backstory? Etiquette?"

"Yes, and yes." Marissa fastened the mask to her face and took a deep breath. Having almost every part of her body covered made her feel secure. Arthur wore a lacey black half-face mask that left his lower cheeks and mouth exposed.

"Alright, my lady." Arthur did a cheesy bow and held out his folded arm. Marissa giggled. "Off we go. I sent word to my parents at the palace about my last-minute attendance. Thankfully, they were thrilled that I wanted to participate, and they sent a carriage which should be arriving..." Arthur peered out the window. "Right now. Quickly, let's head downstairs."

Marissa's eyes widened behind the mask as they stepped outside. The sleek purple carriage was far flashier than the city-owned ones, embellished in gold trim with delicate carvings along the doors and wheels. It was driven by a royal carriage driver dressed in full purple-and-gold regalia. As the carriage stopped, the driver stepped down and held open the doors, bowing as Marissa and Arthur approached.

Marissa nodded and gave a quick thanks before climbing into the carriage. The interior was lined in a silky material the same shade of deep purple as the driver's uniform. Marissa sat down gently across from Arthur, afraid to ruffle the delicate seats.

"Quite different from the city carriages." Arthur chuckled as two pearly-white horses pulled the vehicle down the street. Marissa gazed outside the window but quickly pulled away when she realized the passersby were staring in awe.

"Very different." Marissa shifted in her seat. "I'm glad your parents were able to send a ride for us so last minute."

"That's the thing." Arthur scratched his head. "They sort of don't know that I'm bringing a plus-one."

"Why not?"

"Well..." Arthur shook his head, his expression tense. "Remember how I mentioned my relationship status was complicated? Truth is ... I'm sort of betrothed to the Castella's youngest daughter."

"Wait, what?"

Marissa was glad her face was covered by a mask so Arthur couldn't see her sickened expression.

"I apologize. I should've mentioned it before. My parents arranged it back when I was a child. I was supposed to formally propose two years ago when she turned eighteen, but I've been dragging my feet. I have no interest in marriage right now, especially to a vapid witch like her. She doesn't like me either; she just pretends to pine for me because she wants to marry a royal. It's a whole ugly mess. It's part of the reason why I don't have a good relationship with my parents and why I tend to avoid these sorts of events."

"I'm assuming she'll be there?"

"Most definitely. She's probably preening in her dressing room as we speak. Just don't be alarmed if my parents drag me away to be with Adeline for most of the evening. That's why it was so important to teach you proper etiquette—you may end up needing to face the guests alone."

Marissa's stomach clenched. Not only did she dread the thought of an uppity heiress swooning over Arthur, but she doubted she'd have much to contribute to the wealthy partygoers' discussions. *Maybe it'll give me a chance to slip away and investigate the estate...*

"One last thing," Arthur mentioned. "There are six Castella children, four of which are boys. The two youngest ones, as far as I'm aware, are single. So, what I'm saying is, um ... don't be afraid to engage them in conversation. They love to show off their home; see if they'll give you a tour so you can investigate. They're yearning fools whenever they're in the presence of a young lady, even one behind a mask."

"You want me to flirt with them? Arthur, I—"

The carriage came to a halt.

"Ah, we've made it just in time." Arthur pointed outside. "Luckily, it's not far of a ride."

Marissa peered out the window. They were in Silverkeep, the residential district on the border just outside the palace grounds. The carriage had stopped in front of a magnificent estate, smaller than the palace but dwarfing the humble townhomes surrounding it. A set of large wrought-iron gates, with a similar design to the ones in Alistar, towered outside the multi-story estate. A large, curled letter C crowned the top of the gates, which swung open as the carriage passed through and came to a halt in front of a sweeping staircase.

"Eleven o'clock pickup time, sir?" the driver asked Arthur.

"Indeed. Thank you for the ride."

The driver bowed again before climbing into his seat and taking the reins. The elaborate carriage wheeled away toward the palace, disappearing in the distance.

"Well, here we go." Arthur straightened his bowtie and offered his arm for Marissa to hold. "Walk right next to me and keep pace."

Marissa clasped Arthur's arm as they strode up the staircase to the front doors, the soft fabric of his suit gliding across her palm. A few feet in front of them was another couple, also dressed in fine evening wear. The sheer outer fabric of the woman's teal ballgown seemed to sparkle under the soft light of the entrance.

A pair of guards were propped on either side of the open doors, their posture stiff and alert. They gave a firm nod as Arthur and Marissa passed.

"Here we are," Arthur remarked as they entered the estate. They stood in a brightly lit foyer lined with glittering chandeliers, fine oil paintings, and intricately upholstered furniture. Beyond the massive room, a swirling cacophony of music and chatter echoed down the hallways.

Marissa's eyes nearly popped out of her head. *I had no idea such a lavish place existed.*

Arthur smiled. "I hope you enjoy the party, Cecelia. Now, if you don't mind, I should find my parents."

Chapter 22

*T*HE MAIN BALLROOM WAS DARK, WITH THE soft yet rich tones of the live orchestra floating through the heavy air. The massive space, with its towering ceilings and glossy floors, was full of chattering guests clustered in tight circles. Light from large, ornate sconces glittered across the wall, casting eerie shadows across the patrons and making their elaborate masks even more sinister. Marissa clung to Arthur's arm as they strode through the room, determined not to lose sight of him.

Through the crowd, a woman in a dark blue gown waved them over. She wore a matching mask that covered most of her face, but Marissa could tell by the spidery hands clasped around her drink that she was an older woman. Puffy chestnut hair, the same color as Arthur's, was pulled into an elaborate updo above her head.

"There you are," she announced, her voice stern. Marissa and Arthur approached the woman's circle, which contained four other masked guests. Her ominously dark eyes locked on Marissa. "And who is this?"

"Hello to you, too, Mother," Arthur responded curtly. His head circled around. "And Father. Ramsey. Charlotte. Adeline."

Marissa's scales prickled at the mention of the final name. The petite young woman, barely older than Marissa, stood on the edge of the circle. Her crimson gown and mask were the most elaborate ones Marissa had seen so far, speckled in glitter and gemstones, with intricate beading trailing down the bodice of her dress. An aura of callous superiority radiated from her, and her masked gaze was locked on Arthur. Arthur's father and brother waved at Marissa, but this woman did not acknowledge Marissa's presence or even glance in her direction.

Marissa also noticed that while Arthur's parents were alert and lively, his brother looked exhausted. His posture was slumped, and he seemed to lean on his wife for support. Even behind his half-face mask, she could see his weary, saddened gaze, as if something dire was on his mind. Arthur noticed as well; Marissa saw him study his brother's strange demeanor out of the corner of his eye.

Arthur shook his head, diverting his attention away from his brother, and placed a hand on Marissa's shoulder. "I would like to introduce you to my friend, Cecelia Burton. She runs the bookstore across the street from The Menagerie. Cecelia, this is my mother, Regina, my father, Frederick, my brother, Ramsey, and his wife, Charlotte, and the Castella's youngest daughter, Adeline."

Regina narrowed her eyes and opened her mouth, but her husband cut her off.

"Ah, a fellow literary enthusiast," he remarked. There was a warm tone of sincerity in his voice that contrasted his wife's shrill gaze. Regina gave him a sharp, knowing glance, and he nodded. "Come with me. I have some fellow acquaintances who I'm sure would enjoy your company."

Marissa's shoulders quivered. She wished she could disappear as Arthur's father led her away from the others. Her reptilian ears picked up on the discussion behind her as Arthur's mother pulled him aside for a lecture.

"A betrothed man inviting a peasant girl to a ball!" she hissed her harsh words in a low whisper. "What uncouth manners have I raised my son with? How are you going to explain this to Adeline and her parents?"

As Marissa walked away, the conversation faded from her ears before she could hear Arthur's response.

"Here we are." Frederick pulled them into a small circle near the orchestra. Four masked faces, all men, peered curiously at Frederick's strange guest.

"Gentleman," Frederick announced in a strong tone. The others ceased their chatter and lifted their heads. "I would like to introduce you to Cecelia. She runs a bookstore in Augustree, so I figured she should join some fellow admirers of literature for the evening."

Marissa swallowed, her fear burning her throat. *I was hoping I wouldn't be questioned about my book expertise. All I've ever read are old children's novels in the storeroom—how am I supposed to contribute to this conversation?*

"Pleased to meet you, Cecelia," the shortest man, whose puffy graying mustache poked beneath his half-face mask, greeted her. "Gregory Altman. I am employed by Frederick to help run the royal library. We were just discussing our favorite new novels. I'm curious. What have you stocked your shop with lately?"

"I..." Marissa's brain scrambled to come up with a coherent answer.

I've only read one non-children's book...

"Well ... I recently finished reading *Crown of Fangs*." She winced, hoping that her answer would please her companions. *Is that even considered literature? What if they think it's—*

Frederick and the two men next to him wore blank stares, but the young olive-skinned man on the far side of the circle's eyes lit up. "I just finished reading that, too. Quite an interesting take on the myth. I always enjoy a good story about a great hero triumphing over evil. What did you think of the book?"

A great hero triumphing over evil? Marissa's face stiffened as she hid her disgust.

"Well ... to be honest, I think that Perseus isn't a hero, and Medusa isn't a villain."

Marissa shivered as soon as her sudden thoughts escaped her mouth. *Why did you do that!? Now is not the time to spit out your personal opinions.* She took a deep breath, awaiting her companions' reactions as if her life depended on it.

"Oh?" The young man's eyebrow raised. His expression was one of curiosity, not distaste, and the knot in Marissa's stomach loosened. "And what in the book made you come to that conclusion?"

Marissa's eyes flicked around the circle. Frederick gave her a wary glance, as if warning her to choose her words wisely.

"Well..." Marissa's mind searched for the right phrasing. "When I read the book, I didn't see Medusa as evil. I actually liked her. She's not a monster—she's just cursed, and not even for good reason. And Perseus beheading her and using her head as a weapon is just cruel."

The man raised an eyebrow. "I must say ... that is fascinating. In fact, some people believe her image wards off evil—I've heard of townsfolk wearing amulets of Medusa's head. I believe you are correct—it could be argued that Medusa is not the villain the book believes her to be."

The others nodded in approval. Marissa's chest lightened, proud of her newfound ability to fool the guests with her literary knowledge.

I can do this. I just have to play their little game until I can sneak off and investiga—

The previously quiet, humming background tunes of the orchestra grew louder and more animated. Several couples strode into the center of the room atop the large, intricate parquet floor, swaying and twirling with precise elegance.

"Cecelia." The young man stepped forward and stretched out his palm. "May I ask for a dance?"

The others gave approving smiles as Marissa nervously stepped forward and placed her hand on top of the young man's. Her eyes flicked toward the far side of the room, where Arthur led Adeline out to the parquet and began to dance.

Marissa gulped as they reached the center of the prancing guests. "Sir, I..."

"Oh, pardon me." The man let go of Marissa's hand and turned around to face her. Underneath the bright chandeliers, Marissa could see his sharp cheekbones, dark swirling hair, and deep brown eyes. "I haven't introduced myself. My name is Antonio Castella. I'm very pleased that you could make it to my family's party tonight."

Castella?!

Marissa forced back a shudder as Antonio placed his hand on her waist. *I do not want this criminal touching me.* She sighed, remembering Arthur's words.

They love to show off their home; see if they'll give you a tour so you can investigate.

Marissa shook off her disgusted nerves and forced a polite demeanor. "Pleased to meet you, Antonio. Pardon my clumsiness. I'm afraid I'm not much of a dancer. Will you teach me?"

Antonio perked up at Marissa's request. He seems more than happy to teach a supposedly naïve damsel the basics of ballroom dancing. Within a few minutes, Marissa pranced and twirled around the room with the elegance of an esteemed noble, her refined yet repulsive partner following her every move. His firm gaze was somewhere between a warm romantic and a thirsting debauchee. Marissa sneered behind her mask. *How ironic. His family buys the murdered hides of reptilians, yet he has no idea he is preening over a half-snake girl.*

There were brief moments where Marissa caught Arthur dancing with Adeline in the corner of her eye, but as much as her distasteful envy snaked through her mind, she had to focus on Antonio. But Marissa did notice in those few brief glances that Arthur's movements were stiff and his eyes devoid of emotion.

The orchestra bellowed out a few melodic symphonies before pausing for a brief intermission. Antonio's movements ceased; his hand still pressed against Marissa's waist.

"I must say, for a novice, you are quite the dancer." He led Marissa toward a nearby table, where he offered her a thin rippling glass full of a strange, rosy-colored liquid. The sharp, sour scent of alcohol burned her reptilian nostrils. She plucked a straw from the table so she could slip the drink underneath her mask and recoiled as the sweet yet searing concoction trailed down her throat.

She knew she shouldn't refuse his advances, but she had to be careful of becoming intoxicated.

That might be exactly what he wants. Marissa scowled in disgust.

"It's so refreshing to talk to someone who isn't afraid to speak their mind," Antonio remarked as they stood by the beverage table and watched the crowd. "All of the royals and elites are so proper. They surround themselves with ninnies who do nothing but echo their praises. I never dare speak my own opinions around them, especially my parents."

"Well, I would certainly be interested to hear them." Marissa discreetly set her drink on the table behind them. "For example, is it me, or are these glasses far too small and fragile?"

Antonio chuckled. "They're horribly impractical. But the thin glass is expensive and, therefore, highly desired among these sorts of partygoers. Personally, I prefer a large mug for my alcohol. In fact," he raised his eyebrows and leaned inwards, "what do you say we slip away from this whole charade, and I'll show you where my folks keep the truly first-rate drinks?"

Marissa's stomach fell in conflicted horror. This was exactly what she needed, yet incredibly dangerous. But she knew she had to take the risk and hope her illusions of courtship would hold up when they were alone.

"I would love to. In fact, would you be willing to show me around your beautiful home?"

Marissa's anxiety hung in her chest. She hoped that Antonio would heed her request without becoming suspicious.

"Of course. I'm happy to give such a fine young lady a tour." He offered his arm. "Please, come with me."

As they strode through the crowd, several pairs of eyes fell on Marissa. The passersby seemed curious about Antonio's newfound companion. Marissa held her head up high, pretending to be the proud darling of the host's son. Her reptilian ears picked up faint whisps of gossip, but no one addressed them directly as they strolled out of the ballroom.

"There are nine bedrooms and six bathrooms, most of which are upstairs on the second and third floors," Antonio explained as he led Marissa through the elegant, cavernous hallways of the estate and showed her its many spacious rooms. The halls were empty and quiet, and their voices echoed off the tall, ornate ceilings. "Downstairs is the foyer, two dining rooms, my father's office, the ballroom, and two of the bedrooms, including the master. And the main kitchen, which is this way."

Antonio led her through the massive kitchen, which was nearly the size of Arthur's entire apartment. A small crew of cooks fluttered around, scrubbing dishes and plating tiny hors d'oeuvres, but none of them acknowledged Antonio's presence. He pulled Marissa along, seeming to sneak past the chefs, and led her down a heavy wooden staircase to a cool, dark wine cellar.

"May I interest you in a glass of my family's finest strawberry rosé?" He pulled a slender bottle off the shelf. "It was cultivated in the fields my family owns in the outer villages and has won several awards. We can take it upstairs."

"That sounds lovely," Marissa agreed, masking the terror in her voice. "But do you mind if we finish the tour before treating ourselves to some wine?"

Antonio raised an eyebrow. "I see. It would indeed be best for me to show you the rest of the estate first. Let's start with the upstairs."

He led Marissa up a wide, towering staircase to the second floor, where a large sitting room awaited them at the top. Antonio suddenly pressed a palm to his head and placed the wine bottle on the coffee table.

"Shoot, I forgot a bottle opener. Should've grabbed one downstairs, but I know there are a few around here somewhere. I'm not sure where those damn servants left them..."

As Antonio fiddled around in the sitting room, Marissa noticed a small door down a thin hallway on the opposite wall. Its frame was small and inconspicuous, making it appear to lead to some sort of storage area that wasn't meant for prying guests. She had no idea what was within it, but she couldn't leave any room unexamined. This was her only chance to infiltrate the Castella home.

He's distracted. Now's my chance. Marissa stepped away as Antonio dug through a wooden chest perched next to the couch. *If he catches me, I'll just chalk it up to innocent curiosity.*

Marissa didn't take her eyes off Antonio until she reached the door. It was unlocked, but it opened with a rather loud squeak. Marissa jolted, but thankfully, Antonio was on the far side of the large room and completely oblivious.

As the door swung inward, the contents of the room crept into Marissa's view, and she nearly screamed. Intense horror and panic flooded her body as she'd never felt before. She strode wearily into the room, so stunned that she was barely able to keep her footing. Her eyes circled around the small space, her mind reeling. She could only see a small part of the dark room, but it was so shocking and distressing that Marissa could barely comprehend the full scale of it.

Hides. Hundreds of them slumped haphazardly in crates like discarded blankets. But that wasn't what terrified Marissa—it was what the hides had been made into. Dim light crept through the doorway, illuminating the scales that glittered across the centerpiece of the room: a full set of armor that towered over Marissa's slight frame. It seemed to leer at her, its presence mocking and intimidating her. It seemed to whisper, *take it all in, snake girl. Look at what the humans have done.*

"There you are," Antonio exclaimed. His presence nearly made Marissa jolt. He held up a shiny metal object.

"I found the bottle opener. And it must've taken me a while because I see that you got adventurous."

Marissa gulped. Antonio laughed, stepping forward as the glowstone lights flickered on around them. The few crates of hides turned into dozens. "We're not supposed to be in here, but I'm sure we'll be fine. This is the ingenious work of my father. Once those damn reptilians started creeping around the outer villages and scaring the locals, he had an idea. He approached the king and received hefty funding to commission a full legion's worth of armor at our family's blacksmith."

Antonio stepped forward, and Marissa followed. She stepped in front of the armor set and pressed her fingers against the cool scales. She swore she felt them quake under her touch. *These are Naga scales. They feel just like my own.*

"This is the key to exterminating those reptilians for good," Antonio continued. Marissa kept her fingers pressed against the armor, too stunned to respond. "The hides are incredibly strong and a lot lighter than traditional armor. Our men don't stand a chance fighting in those clunky metal suits. This gives us the advantage we need. This is just a prototype, but once it's approved by the king, we'll be making hundreds, maybe even thousands of these. Isn't it magnificent?"

Marissa turned toward Antonio. He wore the same warm, unassuming smile he'd given her all night. Marissa seethed behind her mask. *You ... callous ... murderers ... you expect me to be impressed!?*

She knew this was just the first armor set, and they already had the hides to make hundreds more. All those reptilian lives lost, just to become an accessory to further violence. *Do you not see what you've done!?*

Marissa knew that this was it. Humans and reptilians had always been at odds, always on the brink of violence ... but now it was inevitable. War was coming, and Marissa was powerless to stop it.

The king ... the royal family ... they really were behind all the poaching...

Arthur...

"Are you alright?" Antonio reached for Marissa. "You look a bit faint."

"I..." Marissa shifted, her legs unsteady. "I think I'm just a little warm. Here, let me sit down for a moment."

Antonio helped her back into the sitting room, where she plopped down on the couch. She clasped her knees in her palms and took several deep breaths, the haunting sight of the armor set still flashing in her head.

"Here." Antonio crouched next to her. "Let's take your mask off."

"No," Marissa swatted him away. "I'm fine. Let me just catch my breath."

Antonio's hand reached up for her mask again. Marissa's scales ran cold, and she shifted backward.

"But I haven't seen your face all night," he pleaded.

Marissa recoiled in horror. Antonio pressed his body toward hers, placing his other hand on the couch.

The more she moved away, the closer Antonio crept toward her.

"No, please." Marissa's voice quivered as a last begging resort.

"Why not?" Antonio's soft pleas grew more forceful. He had Marissa pressed against the wall, his body blocking any path of escape. He reminded Marissa of a spoiled child that wouldn't take no for an answer. Her eyes veered wildly around the room, searching for something—anything—to get her out of this situation.

"If you're after that pathetic royal you came here with, don't bother," Antonio growled. "He's engaged to my sister. Besides, I've had a lovely time tonight. Haven't you?"

His hand reached for her mask, and Marissa squeezed her eyes shut.

I have to do this.

It's my only option.

It's my only means of escape.

Antonio began lifting the mask off her face. Marissa felt the cool air of the sitting room waft against the scales that lined her chin.

I haven't bitten anyone since I was seven years old...

She didn't wait until the mask was all the way off. As soon as her black-lipped mouth was exposed, she sank her fangs into Antonio's neck. The metallic tang of blood crept into her mouth and dotted the hardwood floor as Antonio's screams pulsed through Marissa's ears. She bit him for less than a second, just long enough to inject him with venom, before refitting her mask and bolting downstairs, leaving the injured man crumpled on the floor.

She dove past the servants and out into the hallway. It wouldn't be long before Antonio's screams alerted the staff, and she needed to be as far away from the estate as possible. As she ran for her life toward the foyer, Marissa thought back to the orphanage—the thought of that horrible bully, Jack, lying on the ground, screaming in pain with two puncture wounds on his collarbone, and the look of horror on Beatrice's face as she rushed outside.

You bit him! You... you monster!

"Marissa?"

She came to a sliding halt. Arthur stood in the hallway, a bewildered expression on his face. He stepped closer and recoiled in horror.

Marissa looked confused, until she tasted it. She pressed a finger to her mask and realized it was wet, as were her lips. She caught her faint reflection in a nearby wall hanging, and she noticed a small bloodstain dotting the edge of the mask near her chin.

Time seemed to slow around them as the panicked shouts of the staff echoed from upstairs. Through the chaos, Marissa could hear Antonio's clear screams.

"She's a reptilian! Get her!!!"

Arthur heard them, too, because his eyes widened in terror.

"Good gods, Marissa... what have you done?"

Chapter 23

MARISSA DIDN'T HAVE MUCH TIME. THE alarmed staff could come sprinting down the stairwell at any minute, and she needed to escape before that happened. Yet as she stood in the hallway, her eyes locked with a horrified yet worried Arthur, it felt like it was just the two of them.

"Arthur," Marissa panted, her chest heaving and her hands clasping into fists. "When you visited the king, did you overhear anything about armor?"

"What are you talking about?"

Marissa's expression fell. *He doesn't know.*

"I found out what the Castellas have been buying all those hides for. They're making armor for the Brennan soldiers. Armor that your family paid them for. This can only mean one thing—the kingdom is preparing for war."

"Wait, what? My family? Marissa, I—"

The shouts were followed by rapid footsteps down the stairs. *They're coming for me.* Marissa glanced back at the stairwell, then at Arthur.

"I have to go." Marissa brushed past him. "You can't go after that Naga again, or you'll end up in prison. But I can, alone. I'm going to reptilian territory and telling them what the humans are doing."

"Marissa, wait!"

Arthur's shouts echoed down the hallway as Marissa ran. She bolted as fast as she could until she reached the foyer, her fancy shoes skidding across the slippery floors. It had only been a few minutes since the bite, and the panic was still contained farther within the estate. The guards near the front door didn't seem alerted. She stood up straight, took a deep breath, and cordially strode past them as if nothing had happened.

The cool, dark air of the city streets was a welcoming relief, and Marissa took a deep breath as she stepped outside. The entrance was quiet, as all the guests were still cavorting inside the estate. She untied her heavy mask, slipped it off her face, and tossed it into a dense tangle of hedges. With her burdensome disguise gone, she slid her lacey black scarf over her nose and mouth before taking off into the dark maze of Silverkeep.

She kept running until she was out of the residential district and back in Alistar. She peered behind her;

all she could see were churches. She couldn't even see the palace. Her mind settled now that the panic was over, and she took a seat on a bench in a nearby park to catch her breath. She needed to get to Varan territory as quickly as possible. *But how?* She had no money and the Castellas likely wanted her dead. The horrid memories of Antonio's screams pierced through Marissa's skull, and she shook her head. She could handle the emotional consequences of the bite later; for now, she needed to keep moving.

I'll find that abandoned inn and sleep there for the night. Then I'll travel to Varan territory in the morning. Marissa didn't have the money to rent a cart, so she'd have to make the entire journey on foot. But she wasn't afraid. She was so resentful and angry that she'd bite down every bandit in the Valley of Scales if she had to.

A soft rustle in the nearby bushes startled her. She shook her head, thinking it was a squirrel or lizard, or some other wild creature. But as it rustled again, Marissa noticed a flash of bright yellow. She stood up and stepped toward the bush. Her eyes nearly popped out of her head as a familiar face poked out between the leaves.

"NIM!?" she exclaimed, stepping backward. "What are you doing out here? HOW are you out here!?"

The little yellow-and-black snake flicked his tongue. Marissa shook her head, feeling dumb for expecting Nim to explain himself. He stretched his neck toward Marissa, expecting to be picked up. Marissa placed him around her neck, where he settled in a happy coil.

"All I can say with certainty is, you are no ordinary snake." Marissa rubbed the top of his head. "C'mon, let's get out of here. I may need your help fending off some bandits tomorrow."

ARTHUR STOOD FROZEN IN THE HALLWAY AS THE servants brushed past him. Their hazy, panicked shouts swept across his stunned ears. *Where is she? The snake girl, find her!*

It had been several minutes since Marissa fled down the hallway. Arthur had watched in disbelief as her once elegant maroon dress became a billowing hindrance to her escape. The panic in her eyes and the tense gravity of her voice haunted his frazzled mind. Less than an hour ago, she was an elegant guest, shrouded under the guise of wealth, that had captured the alluring attention of the hosts' youngest son. Arthur remembered the way she charmed Antonio as they swept across the ballroom; Arthur had been watching Marissa out of the corner of his eye as he danced with his dreadful fiancée. He was sickened by not only the thought of them together but also Antonio's inevitable fury if he discovered who Marissa really was.

You pig. Arthur growled. *You don't deserve her, anyway.*

The knot in his stomach had clenched even tighter when he saw them slip away from the ballroom. He knew this was important; after all, he'd been the one to suggest flirtation as a means of investigating the estate. But he couldn't help but feel like he'd thrown Marissa to a hungry lion.

But what went so wrong in such a short span of time?

It didn't take him long to find out. Antonio's cries could be heard halfway across the estate, but Arthur didn't realize the full extent of the situation until he ventured upstairs.

A crying Antonio was sprawled across a couch in the sitting room, surrounded by a swarm of fawning attendants. He howled as the family's apothecary administered a large dose of antivenom. Arthur scoffed. *He's being a bit dramatic. Her venom isn't deadly, and he has access to the finest medicine in Brennan. He'll be fine.*

Antonio alternated between moaning sobs and tirades of vengeful anger. Arthur watched as the man's crinkled, tear-stained face turned an irate shade of red. But as much as Arthur mocked the pitiful sight, he was terrified for Marissa. The Castellas would show her no mercy. Not only had a reptilian entered the home of one of the most powerful families in Brennan, but she dared to endanger the life of their son.

Arthur grimaced. *This won't bode well for the reptilians' reputation as monsters.* But he knew that the attack wasn't unprovoked. He shuddered at the thought of the sort of domineering behavior that would force Marissa to sink her fangs into Antonio. *He trapped her. Biting him was her only means of escape.*

Antonio caught a glimpse of Arthur standing in the corner. His head lifted, and his weeping voice turned shrill. "Him!! He brought her here!!"

Arthur panicked and bolted down a nearby hallway. As he slipped away, he noticed the servants hush Antonio with soft, soothing voices. Clearly, they were acclimated to his hysterics and were more concerned with healing him than heeding his vengeful requests.

Arthur stepped backward, not taking his eyes off the now-distracted Antonio and his swarm of servants, and bumped into a hard surface. He turned around and discovered a small door tucked at the end of the hallway. Arthur was confused by its subtle, modest appearance—most of the doorframes in the Castella estate were tall and elaborately decorated.

It's probably just a storage closet, Arthur reasoned. *Or ... it's discreet because the Castellas don't want anyone venturing in there.*

His mind flicked back to Marissa's panicked question. *Did you overhear anything about armor?*

Arthur took a deep breath, pushed the door open, and immediately stepped back in horror. Amidst the boxes of hides, the glorious, shining suit leered like a demon in the dim light of the storage room. Arthur felt sickened, as if he'd just walked into a morgue. In the shadow of the Castella's magnificent achievement, all Arthur could see were dismembered bodies, even if they weren't human.

Marissa wasn't kidding. This is horrific.

His terror morphed into a frenzy of anger. *The Castellas ... even my own family. They're all murderers.* He wanted to pull apart every piece of the cursed armor and take the hides far away from Brennan. Then he'd come back and tear the Castellas to pieces.

His anger softened. He knew there must be a reason why the humans were so adamant about war. But regardless of the cause, killing hundreds of reptilians to equip an army wasn't the answer, and he didn't want to watch the valley fall into chaos. He felt just like Marissa when she said she was only one person. How could he possibly stop the reptilians, the Castellas, and even his own family, let alone an impending war engrained in hate that ran back centuries?

I can't. Marissa is the only one that stands a chance. But I must help her however I can.

He eyed the single musty antique window in the back of the room. He fiddled with the latches, and to his surprise, it creaked open on its ancient hinges.

"Don't do this."

Arthur jolted and spun around. Ramsey stood in the doorway, the blaring chaos in the rest of the estate a faint echo behind him.

"What do you want?" Arthur hissed.

"I want to reason with my brother." Ramsey stepped forward, and Arthur's body tensed. "You've always been a bit odd, Arthur, ever since we were kids. But bringing a reptilian into Brennan? I think the cries in the other room prove that those monsters don't belong here."

"You're wrong," Arthur growled. "Antonio provoked the attack. You're only calling her a monster because it fits your twisted beliefs."

"We can still fix this," Ramsey reasoned. "You're my brother; I don't want to see you banished. Arthur, I wish I could explain, but … there's a lot more to this than you realize. Our kingdom is in grave danger. Those reptilians aren't who you think they are."

Ramsey took another step forward, extending a hand toward his brother. Arthur gulped, his throat choked up with adrenalin.

"Tell me what's going on," he demanded in an accusing tone.

"Arthur…" Ramsey's face fell. Arthur realized just how frayed his brother's sanity was; his weary eyes were glazed over with a pained hopelessness. "I… I can't."

"Then I don't believe you."

Arthur pressed his back against the armor set, tilting it partway out the window.

"Arthur, I'm warning you." Ramsey's somber tone deepened. "If you go through with this, the king will show no mercy. You will never step foot in the palace again."

Arthur's chest heaved, nervous sweat beading down his forehead. *Those reptilians aren't who I think they are? What do you mean? What did that Naga really want?* He peered over at the boxes of slaughtered hides, his mind drifting back to the Varan that Thomas killed… *Whatever is going on here, murdering reptilians for their hides is still wrong.*

The consequences of his next move would be grave, but he knew deep in his conscience what he had to do.

"You leave me no choice." Arthur narrowed his eyes. "Even if the reptilians are hostile, I won't support slaughtering them to build an army. I will stop this war, somehow... even if means being exiled from this family."

"Arthur!!!"

He hoisted the heavy armor set out the window, his body tumbling after it. The armor clattered into a heap at the base of the building, and Arthur curled into a tight ball and rolled across the grass. He lay still for a few moments, blood pounding through his skull and his shoulders and ankles burning from the impact. But he didn't have time to grovel over his injuries; he stood up, stumbling on shaky legs, and picked up the fallen armor set.

He hauled the heavy hide over his shoulder. *Somehow, I must get this back to reptilian territory.* He rubbed the smooth black scales and realized it was Naga hide.

Marissa...

His mind drifted back to just a few hours earlier. He still felt Marissa's fearful yet comforting embrace, with her soft scales pressed against his skin, just like the ones draped across his shoulder. He thought about his family and wondered what would make them suddenly want to enter a war that could destroy the entire valley. *Why? Why are you doing this? And why won't you tell me?*

His brother's vague warning continued echoing in his mind.

CHAPTER 23

Those reptilians aren't who you think they are.

He shook the frenzied questions out of his head. He needed to move quickly; he knew that Marissa was not the only one the Castellas were after. As Arthur stumbled around the side of the estate, he came across a row of tall, dense hedges immaculately trimmed into perfect ovals. He looked closer and saw a bright white object denting the otherwise flawless barrier.

Arthur's hands shook as he lifted Marissa's mask from the brush. He glanced up at the rows of townhomes beyond him and forced his emotions back, refusing to let tears slide down his cheeks.

Marissa, please... run far away from here. Get to Varan territory as fast as possible and find that Naga. Don't look back. I know I won't.

IT WAS A LONG WALK TO THE ABANDONED INN, which gave Marissa plenty of time to ponder her current situation as Nim napped around her neck. What most preoccupied her mind was how she would approach the Naga. She had never met another reptilian; she wasn't even quite sure what they looked like. She wondered if they appeared as monstrous as the humans portrayed them to be or if they were just strange, misunderstood beings trying to survive in a twisted world.

Marissa knew humans weren't the only ones with blood on their hands. As a child, she'd heard stories of reptilians slaughtering humans that ventured too close to their territories. She remembered Thomas describing them as beasts, more animal than human. *That's how people rationalized poaching them without remorse.* She agonized over her upcoming encounter with the Naga, wondering what she would do and say or if she'd even be able to communicate with it at all.

But there was one question that haunted her the most; would they accept her? Humans hardly tolerated her existence, and she wasn't sure if the reptilians would be any different. *I am still half-human, after all. It's always the other half, whether human or reptilian, that makes me an outsider.*

Marissa pressed on through Alistar, her mind and body growing weary as the night hours deepened. She was determined to face the reptilians without fear. She had spent her entire life hiding in the deepest corners of society, keeping her identity concealed behind a mask and avoiding human interaction, and now was her time to act. *If the reptilians shun me, or worse, so be it. I now know that war is coming and what lies ahead. I won't be afraid.*

It was nearly three o'clock in the morning. Alistar was a silent, stony maze, and Marissa had only the soft lights of the always-open churches for company. The dark night air was heavy and crisp, and Marissa's dragging ballgown did little to obstruct the cold from seeping into her scales.

I wish I had my cloak.

She was exhausted; her thoughts were beginning to collapse, and her footsteps felt like lead. She couldn't quite remember the location of the abandoned inn, but she knew she was close. *Not much farther ... I'll get some sleep ... soon...*

As she plodded gloomily along the dark cobblestone streets, a raucous burst of voices rose above the murky buildings. Marissa paused. *It's coming from the next block over.*

The voices were too jumbled for Marissa to pick apart their words, but she could tell by their unnervingly somber cries that something awful had happened. She picked up pace, her tiredness fading away as adrenalin set in. She hobbled down the street, her elaborate but stiff shoes carving blisters into the back of her heels, until she came across a busy church.

It was brightly lit, just like every other church in Alistar, but this was the only one bustling with activity. A swarm of at least a hundred disheveled people crowded around the entrance. As Marissa stepped closer and the weary patron's faces were illuminated by the windows, Marissa recoiled in horror.

Burns. Some worse than others; the frantic nuns clustered around the ailing visitors and dabbed their oozing faces with cloths. The ones who were uninjured clumped around the edges of the chaos, their dirty faces heavily lined with anguish.

Wait, those are miners' uniforms...

"Marissa? Is that you?"

A distant silhouette jogged toward her. As it came closer, Marissa's eyes widened in shock. "Thomas!?"

He stumbled to a halt a few feet in front of her. His miner's uniform was dirty, as it was before, but this time it was covered in soot and ash. A chalky black substance was smeared across his face and stained his fingertips. The skin below his eyes was bloated, and his pale face was streaked with fatigue.

"W-what are you doing here?" Marissa stuttered.

Thomas wiped sweat from his forehead and gave her an exasperated gaze, as if he was in too much emotional pain for an explanation. He peered over his shoulder, and Marissa noticed his wife Marian slumped across the church steps, having her wounds treated by the priest.

"We just evacuated. Copperton ... my home ... it's all gone."

"What happened?"

Thomas's grimaced, his weary face drained of all color. "It was the reptilians. They burned the whole place to the ground."

Chapter 24

MARISSA FROZE, HER MIND SWIRLING WITH anger and shock at the mounting situation. In her eighteen years of life, she'd never heard of reptilians attacking human villages. *They want revenge. They've gone blind from their own fury.* Marissa knew this was all the reason the kingdom needed to unleash its army; the inescapable war had been set ablaze.

"What on earth are ya wearin'?" Thomas eyed Marissa's dirty gown as it dragged across the cobblestone. "Ya look like ya came from some sort'a fancy party. Don't tell me ya went there with that 'lil beast around your neck."

Marissa frowned and patted Nim's head. "He's not a beast. And where I was is not important. I need to know what happened."

"It was that Naga and its horde of lizards—they waited for the sun to set, then the monstrous army came boundin' through the village. They tossed bits of burnin' wood into every building and terrorized the villagers, lungin' and hissin' at 'em as they fled." Thomas's eyes were glazed over in disbelief, and his face was heavy with sorrow. "I can't believe it. I know I called them monsters, but this was nothin' like when they came searchin' for the hide. They turned into vengeful, wild devils gone mad with rage."

"This is bad." Marissa's eyes scanned across the exhausted, injured crowd. "This is the first time I've ever heard of an attack on a human village. The reptilians are getting angrier, and the royal family is hell-bent on war; this is the perfect excuse for the slaughter to start."

"I mean, what can we do?" Thomas asked, a hopeless expression on his face. "I'd rather not watch this whole valley tear itself to shreds."

"I found out who was buying all the reptilian hides and why. They're being made into armor for the soldiers to fight in. I still don't know what's causing this conflict or what that Naga wanted, but I do know that this war is going to cost thousands of lives, both human and reptilian. I need to get to Varan territory and tell them the truth."

"Are you sure? If you're lookin' to stop a war, makin' the reptilians even more angry ain't the way to do it."

Marissa's shoulders wilted with realization.

"They deserve to know what happened to their kin, even if it makes tensions worse. I'll still find a way to make peace."

"That's a colossal task," Thomas remarked. "But maybe not impossible. I need to deal with the aftermath of the fire, but lemme know if I can help."

"Actually, you can." Marissa pointed beyond the church. "Did you drive here?"

"Yeah. We used our cart to evacuate the wounded. It's parked 'round the corner."

"I need to borrow it."

Thomas grasped his chin with his soot-stained hand. "Ya sure? It's awfully late, and ya look exhausted. Ya should stay at the church with us tonig—"

"No," Marissa refused. She shook her head, forcing away her tiredness. "I need to get out of Brennan and find that Naga as soon as possible. If I leave now, I will still be able to track its scent from Copperton."

"Very well. But Copperton is a several hours' journey, and yer gonna be a lot faster without haulin' the cart behind ya." Thomas waved his hand as he walked away, gesturing for Marissa to follow him. "Have ya ever ridden a horse before?"

"No."

"Well, yer gonna learn." Thomas turned down a dark corner, where his old gelding slumped sluggishly against a light post. He began unhitching the cart as Marissa warily circled the horse. She noticed the old gelding staring at Nim, the eerie whites of his eyes glinting, and decided it was best to tuck the little snake under her scarf.

"Don't worry," Thomas reassured. He pulled an old saddle out of a trunk in the back of the cart and heaved it over the horse's shoulders. "He may be old, but Arrow's still got a lotta stamina left in him. He was the only horse I kept after I sold the farm, and for good reason."

Thomas finished tightening the girth strap and gave the saddle a firm shake. He fed the heavy metal bit into Arrow's mouth as he slid the bridle over his ears, and Marissa winced.

"Relax, the bit's in past his teeth," Thomas explained. "Ya won't hurt him. Here, I'll give ya a leg up."

Marissa hoisted herself over the horse's back and settled uneasily into the saddle. She felt Arrow's round belly rise and fall with each breath. In front of her was a long brown neck draped in a graying black mane and topped with a set of pointed, flicking ears. Her long, impractical maroon dress draped across the horse's rump like a cape. She felt uneasy being up so high, and she gripped the saddle horn in fear as Arrow shifted his weight.

"Hold the reins like this." Thomas laced the braided leather cords through her fingers. "Horses have four gaits; give a 'lil click and nudge his belly with yer foot to get him to move faster. Keep yer hands low and steady. Really sink yer weight into the saddle and use yer leg muscles to balance yourself. I guarantee yer thighs will be burnin' after this." Thomas chuckled.

Marissa nodded. "Thank you. I really appreciate this."

Thomas smiled at Marissa, but his weary grin was quickly replaced by anguish. Thomas took a sharp breath and rubbed his face with his palm as if the reality of the situation had hit him all at once.

"Thomas, are you alright?"

"It's just," he choked on his words, his voice strained from grief. "Life ain't fair, is it? The world can be a cruel and unforgiving place. I'm sure ya know that better than anyone else."

"I guess I do." Marissa frowned and peered down at the cobblestone. "Thomas ... I'm sorry. For your village being burned down, and Nim biting you, and—"

"Hey now," Thomas interrupted. "No apologies. I brought this upon myself. It's not self-pity that's got me emotional. It's my regrets for causin' everyone else so much pain. The whole village had to suffer for my actions, including my wife. But what's done is done. What's important now is stoppin' this war."

Thomas pulled on the reins, and Arrow lurched forward. Marissa's body tightened at the unfamiliar sensation. She took a deep breath, fumbling with the reins in her hands.

"Save travels, snake girl. We're countin' on you. Oh, and one last thing."

"Yes?"

Thomas paused at the end of the street. Marissa twisted around in the saddle and watched him become a faint silhouette in the distance as she ventured toward the southern gates.

"Don't fall off!"

Thomas wasn't lying. My legs are burning.

Marissa managed to keep up a steady canter for several miles before the old gelding lost momentum and dropped to a slow trot. She was desperate to get to Copperton as quickly as possible, but she was grateful for a chance to give her aching thigh muscles a break. She'd been a wobbly mess when Arrow first picked up speed back at the southern gates, and there were several frantic moments where Marissa feared she would lose her balance and fall off. It was a much bumpier ride on a horse's back as opposed to the comforts of a carriage.

Marissa pulled back on the reins, and Arrow slowed to a steady walk. She could feel the sour steam of sweat rise off the horse's back and neck. His snorting breaths heaved with every step of his hooves. *He's exhausted. Better keep him at a slow pace for a while.*

The early hours of the morning crept in, and a subtle hue of daylight slithered up the horizon, banishing the inky darkness. Marissa's mind spun with contemplation as Arrow paced quietly down the misty, dawn-kissed road. She thought about Thomas and the weary souls left homeless by the reptilians' reckless actions. She thought about the royal family and their scheme to arm themselves at the expense of so many lives. She even thought about her parents and wondered what they would think of all this.

But most of all, she thought about the Naga.

What was it really looking for? And why would it cause the humans to start a war?

Once Arrow's hefty breaths lightened, she brought him back up to a trot. She forced her weight into the saddle and pushed her hands down toward Arrow's withers. *It is certainly much faster to travel by horseback.* In half the time it would've taken her to travel by cart, Marissa arrived on the outskirts of Copperton. She couldn't remember exactly where it was, but it couldn't be missed; sooty gray smoke plumes trailed through the sky like a beacon.

Arrow whinnied and stomped his hooves as they traveled down the path to the village, shying away from the stray piles of timber that glowed with still-warm embers. Marissa gasped at the full scope of the desolation as the smoldering remains of Copperton crept into view. The shacks were little more than floorboards surrounded by bits of blackened wood. The remains of the walls were sharp and jagged, and they reminded Marissa of rotten teeth. Her throat tightened as Arrow stepped past a filthy plush doll lying facedown on the ground, its dress and long hair eaten away by fire.

Marissa continued easing her unsteady horse through the debris. She lowered her scarf and stuck out her forked tongue, but all she could smell was the dry, choking stench of smoke. She shuddered and lifted her scarf back over her nose and mouth in a futile attempt to block out the reeking odor. Nim popped his head out to investigate, but after a few tongue flicks full of smoke, decided otherwise and crept back into Marissa's scarf.

How am I supposed to track the Naga now? Are they even still here? What if—

Marissa's thoughts ceased. There were too many of them crowding her mind, making it hard to focus. But what terrified her was that some of the thoughts weren't her own. They trickled through her reptilian brain, and she knew these words weren't being spoken aloud. In fact, they weren't being spoken at all; she could *feel* them, just like with the snakes at The Menagerie. But they were sharper, clearer; conveying thoughts too complex for true reptiles. *Where are they coming from?*

She dismounted Arrow and ventured to the edge of the village, where the dense green forest bordered the smoldering rubble. As she crept closer, the tangled brush began to rattle in rhythmic patterns. *Footsteps.* Marissa stepped back, bracing herself for whatever she was about to encounter.

Several reptilians emerged from the jungle. They had long, thin, lizard-like faces with sharp teeth and brilliant amber eyes. Dense clusters of spines trailed both their spindly necks and down their scaled backs. Their stocky arms ended in scraggly hands with crescent-shaped claws that curled around their spears. Their tall, wiry bodies loomed over Marissa's, and they didn't seem pleased by her presence.

Lizards. These must be Varan.

With a sharp hiss, the reptilians charged. Marissa exhaled sharply and narrowed her eyes, holding her ground with an unwavering glare. Just before they reached her, their jagged spears pointed straight at her chest, Marissa yanked her scarf off and tossed it on the ground.

The Varan froze. Marissa stared them down, refusing to show any hint of fear. A foreign, primitive sensation arose from her mind, and she drove her thoughts into their heads.

<My name is Marissa. I am a half-reptilian, the daughter of a human mother and a Naga father. I mean you no harm, and I hope you do the same. I have an important message to share with your leader. Please, let me speak with them.>

The Varan rose from their leering postures, and their expressions softened. They didn't appear surprised to see Marissa. Instead, they looked relieved. They almost seemed to smile. *It's as if... they've been expecting me.*

<Hey boss,> one of the Varan spoke. His mouth didn't move, but his thoughts sailed through Marissa's reptilian mind as clear as a human voice. <You better come see this.>

Boss. Marissa's blood ran icy in her veins, her soft breath hanging in the air. She knew this was the moment she'd been waiting for her entire life. She remembered her wild dreams as a child, where her mind conjured up images of what the reptilians might look like. There was even one dream, over a decade ago, where the little half-snake child walked together with a towering Naga, her tiny human hand clutching its giant scaled one. In her dreams, they were always kind, gentle beings. Despite her tumultuous upbringing and her difficulties managing her Naga half, reptilians never appeared in her nightmares.

Marissa closed her eyes and took a deep breath. *On this chilly day in October, amid the crumpled remains of a smoldering village, I meet my other half. I finally found the Naga.*

A dark, serpentine silhouette emerged from the forest. A long, slithering tail trailed behind the massive creature, whose mottled black-and-brown scales gleamed like polished stones in the dewy morning light. Marissa saw her reptilian features reflected in the creature, from its snowy-white stomach scales to its flickering pink tongue. Its eyes were a soft shade of brown, its black pupils set in deep slits.

Marissa understood how the reptilian's appearance could be so terrifying to humans. *They are so different...* Her human half tensed in fear, a sudden instinct to flee coursing through her veins. But her reptilian half had always felt a deep sense of calm when in the presence of a snake, and she stood, bold and unwavering, as the Naga slithered toward her. She knew not to let her guard down; one wrong move and he could turn hostile. After all, the reptilians had just burned down a human village.

His gaze ... it's warm. He's smiling at me. But why?

<Hello, my dear,> his thoughts trailed through her head.

Marissa was too bewildered to respond. *Dear?* The Naga's eyes reflected the loving gaze of a longtime companion, and it was the last thing Marissa had expected. Even though they were both Naga, both snakes, something about him seemed too familiar. *His face, his mannerisms, even the patterning of his scales...*

<Your name is Marissa?> The Naga extended a shaking hand. His reptilian eyes glimmered with emotion, just like

a human. <I'm so glad I finally get to meet you. All this time, and...>

Finally get to meet you? All this time? As the flow of adrenalin ceased, and Marissa's exhaustion pounded through her body, the Naga's voice grew soft and fuzzy. Her mind was too fatigued to process his words.

<I'm sorry our first meeting is in a place like this. At least we drove all those damn humans out. Scurrying away like rats, the little vermin... Marissa, my dear? Are you alright?> The Naga noticed Marissa's weakening state and ceased his chatter. He slithered toward her and steadied her in his grasp. Several Varan rushed over and did the same.

As her legs grew less and less stable, Marissa's hazy eyes gazed up at the Naga that loomed over her. His scaly, clawed hands were firm yet gentle. *His scales feel just like my own, even more so than the Naga hide at the Castella's...*

She was so tired that she had to strain her thoughts out, <Who ... are ... you?>

<My dear, let's go back to Komodo. I promise I will explain everyth—>

Marissa collapsed.

Chapter 25

$\mathcal{N}$INE-YEAR-OLD RAMSEY'S STOMPING FOOTSTEPS echoed through the dewy spring air as he plodded down the trailing staircase and into the palace gardens. He grumbled. *Why do I have to be the one to go find him? The blooming maze of foliage, which sprawled in all directions around his towering home, was immaculately trimmed, the skillful hand-iwork of the palace's many expert gardeners. They fluttered around the greenery, snipping dead leaves from trees and pruning bristly hedges into perfect ovals. Not a single blade of grass or splotch of dirt lay on the winding brick pathways that snaked through the grounds.*

At least, not until he ventured farther down one of the path-ways. A few hundred feet from the palace, next to a grove of blooming orange trees, his seven-year-old brother was crouched under a bush. His expensive cashmere pants were scuffed at the knees, and his sleeves were rolled up to his elbows, exposing his dirt-caked forearms as he dug through the damp soil.

"Arthur!!!" Ramsey exclaimed, horrified by his brother's sullied appearance. "What are you doing?! The banquet starts in an hour!"

"Look what I found!" Arthur popped out of the bushes, ignoring his brother's concerns. As he stood up, Ramsey could see more dirt smeared across his rotund cheeks. But as Arthur raised his hand and opened his fist, Ramsey recoiled in alarm. In Arthur's filthy palm was a small, wriggling creature, no thicker than a pencil, brightly banded in yellow, red, and black.

"Are you insane!?" Ramsey shouted. "That's a poisonous snake! If it bites you, you're dead!"

"It's not gonna hurt me, silly," Arthur chided. "First off, you're thinking of venomous, not poisonous. And second, this isn't a venomous snake. My teacher says, 'Red on yellow, kill a fellow. Red on black, venom lack.' This one's black bands touch its red ones. It's a scarlet snake, not a coral snake."

Ramsey's shoulders loosened as his fear dissipated, but his disgust did not. "Even if that snake can't kill you, Mother and Father will! Look at your clothes! You're filthy!"

Arthur huffed, clutching his wiggling prize. The little snake wove between his fingers, more curious than fearful. "I don't care. I don't wanna go to a banquet. They're boring."

"Being grounded will be even more boring, dummy."

"Do you even wanna go?"

Ramsey scoffed, refusing to answer. Truthfully, he didn't want to attend either. As a nine-year-old child, he found royal banquets to be long, tedious affairs, full of droning adults bantering about politics. He hated the formalities of it, needing to recall which silverware to use during certain courses and remembering to keep his elbows off the table. His only source of entertainment during the monotonous event was when his brother made silly mocking gestures during King Gabriel's speeches. But he didn't dare laugh, and he would pretend to be oblivious when Arthur got a scolding from their parents.

But as much as he disliked formal events, Ramsey would never dare act up at them. Even at his age, it was already apparent that his parents favored him. He was always perfectly polite and well-mannered, as a royal child should be. He knew they loved Arthur, too, but his constant antics and misbehaving wore on their patience. Arthur marching back to the palace an hour before the banquet, his fine clothes covered in dirt, would cause his third reprimand in less than a week.

"Do you think that the reptilians can talk to snakes?"

"What?" Ramsey was caught off guard by his brother's random question.

"I bet they can," Arthur continued, running a finger over the tiny, scaled creature. "Especially the Naga, since they are snakes."

"Reptilians don't talk, stupid. They're beasts."

"How do you know? Maybe they communicate some other way. Like how dogs wag their tails. Or how horses stomp their hooves."

Ramsey let out an exasperated sigh. He needed to get his absentminded brother to put the snake down, brush the dirt *off his clothes, and go back to the palace.* And pray he doesn't get a spanking.

"C'mon, Arthur, we need to go inside. Put the snake back where you found it."

"Fine," Arthur grumbled. *He crawled back under the bush—getting more dirt on his pants, much to his brother's dismay—and placed the tiny squirming reptile back in the loose dirt. Ramsey grimaced as his brother stood up.* Now he's soiled his shirt, too.

"You're weird. You know that?" Ramsey teased his brother *as they walked back toward the palace.*

"I don't care. I think weird is good, even if Mother and Father don't. One day I'm gonna be a scientist and study reptiles, just like the researchers at the palace. In fact, I'm gonna—"

Ramsey shook his head as his brother prattled on about his dreams. Ramsey cared about his brother, but his wily behavior drew a wedge between them, and there were many days that he wished Arthur could be more normal. He liked to pride himself on being the better-behaved sibling, but he wondered how their dynamic would change as they got older.

Maybe Arthur's antics aren't all bad, *he reasoned.* At least they will make this banquet slightly more interesting.

RAMSEY REFLECTED ON HIS CHILDHOOD AS HE SAT on a plush bench in the foyer outside the king's private quarters, realizing that his old memories were growing hazier every year. He was surprised that the king had summoned him to his personal study, but he figured that since he was the new heir to the throne, these meetings would become customary.

Arthur hasn't changed. He grimaced. He scoffed at the shameful disaster that his brother had managed to stir up at the Castella's party. Arthur had always been defiant, but Ramsey never expected him to be so brazen as to invite a reptilian to a ball.

Ramsey had never been a fan of the Castellas' pompous, womanizing youngest son, but the sight of Antonio crumpled over a couch while that abomination's venom lurched through his veins made him irrationally angry. Arthur was already on thin ice from his unabashed quarrels with the king, and his semi-reptilian guest sinking her fangs into a human further cemented his fate.

Ramsey's mind twisted as he tried to figure out exactly what she was. *She looked like a normal human earlier in the evening ... she must've had a lot hidden behind that mask.* He continued pondering her origins. *Is she a new type of reptilian? Is she from beyond the valley? Or...* his mind sickened at his next theory. *Is she some sort of hybrid, a cross between a human and a reptilian? Is that even possible? What sort of depraved human would dare produce offspring with those brutes?*

Back at the party, as much as he was focused on digging his brother out of his disastrous situation, he couldn't help but notice the countless boxes of reptilian hides piled in the Castellas' storage room. Although not flaunted in public, poaching was a well-known phenomenon among Brennan's elite. While Ramsey had never cared for the gaudy wares found in the black market, he never thought they would be made into something so sinister. *Fighting against the beasts while wearing armor made from their slain brethren is a bit morbid.*

There had also been recent news of a band of reptilians attacking and burning down a mining camp in the outer villages, not far from Varan territory. It deeply rattled Ramsey's already shaky nerves; he knew that this was only the first in a long wave of violence. And amidst his fears, he kept pondering the reason for the attack. *It might be because of the increased poaching.*

Ramsey had never been fond of the reptilians. Like most of Brennan, he found them to be unintelligible beasts, barely tolerable at their best and savage, vile scourges at their worst. But as he stood alone in the Castellas' storage room the night before, hesitant to leap two stories out of a window to chase his ludicrous brother, even he felt saddened for the hundreds of slain reptilians. *Did they even know what was happening? Do they know that their kin are trying to summon a god?*

He would never admit it aloud, but he wondered if the king had taken the poaching too far.

"Sir." A guard paced forward and stopped briskly in front of Ramsey. "His Majesty will see you now. Please, follow me."

The guard led Ramsey across the foyer and halted in front of a pair of wooden doors, just as tall as the ones that led to the throne room, but far less intricate. *But they're just as heavy.* Ramsey noticed as the guard swiftly drew the doors open and stepped aside for Ramsey to enter.

Ramsey heard the doors creak shut behind him as he entered, and he was left alone in the king's private study. Behind a giant wooden desk, King Gabriel was perched in a plush, high-backed chair, his weary gaze locked on Ramsey, who tried not to grimace. The king was always immaculately fresh-faced in the throne room, impeccably groomed and with an elegant demeanor, but here he looked like he hadn't slept in days. His pale cheeks were sallow and gaunt, his frayed hair uncombed, and drooping pouches of skin hung under his eyes.

The king smiled, and Ramsey noticed it seemed to take him a great amount of effort. Ramsey bowed deeply at the waist, and King Gabriel gestured for him to take a seat across the desk. But as he did, Ramsey's eyes shifted past the king. The female guard from the throne room was perched against the back wall, her eyes locked on Ramsey and her body stiff and unwavering. Ramsey feared that between her presence and his haggard appearance, the king was becoming wearily paranoid.

"Hello, Ramsey." His voice was softer than usual, not out of gentleness but of exhaustion.

"Good afternoon, Your Majesty." Ramsey tried to hide his surprise at the king's current condition. "I take it you've heard the news?"

"Of your brother's abhorrent party guest or of those feral beasts burning down a mining camp in the outer villages?"

Ramsey gulped, and the king pursed his lips in a disapproving manner.

"Let's begin with Arthur. As you know, despite his previous misconduct, I had truly hoped he would turn himself around and become a decent member of this family. I certainly never expected him to have the nerve to bring a dangerous reptilian into the kingdom."

"That's the thing," Ramsey noted. "I met her. She had a mask on, but ... she looked like a human. She's not a true reptilian, at least not the kind that we know of. Is it possible she's some sort of hybrid?"

"She's an abomination, is what she is," the king hissed. "Which brings me to my next point. In addition to the mining camp attack, I just received word from my general that another village in the north was raided, this time by Gharian. And unlike the mining camp, there were fatalities. This is just the start—I cannot fathom the destruction that will occur if they summon their god. I want to do what's best for our people, and that means as long as that idol exists, and they wield that degree of power, we cannot let the monsters remain at our borders. Through this war, we must exterminate the reptilians and conquer the entire Valley of Scales once and for all."

Although Ramsey viewed Arthur as a reckless idealist, deep down, he shared his brother's concerns about the consequences of the war. Even if they succeeded and eliminated the reptilians, it would come at the expense of thousands of human lives. He huffed, tightening his resolve. *It's what we must do. With that idol, the reptilians will be a ceaseless threat capable of killing us all.*

"I understand. What will you have me do, Your Majesty?"

"We're still assembling our forces. But in the meantime, I have dispatched additional fleets to search for the Naga, and I'm currently stationing guards around the borders of all four reptilian territories. If any more beasts dare to enter the outer villages, my men will dispose of them. But right now, our top priority is to secure at least one piece of the idol."

"Do we have any idea where the other pieces are?"

"We do not. But we believe that the Naga has at least one of them, and I now have men patrolling every corner of the valley. It won't be able to hide for long."

"Would you like me to assist the search?"

"Not exactly. Of course, if you do come across the Naga, please eliminate it and secure the idol. But I have another task, one that only you can complete."

"What is that?"

"I need you to track down your brother and persuade him to hand over the reptilian girl. You're the only one he might listen to."

Ramsey's blood curdled at the mention of his brother. He knew that if he encountered Arthur, he wouldn't give up the girl without a fight. *I didn't want it to come to this. You're my brother...* He reflected on their childhood, back when Arthur's antics were just innocent fun, and how much easier both of their lives used to be. *But this was your own doing. You've severed yourself from this family over a bunch of violent beasts. I swear...*

"I'll find my brother. But please ... promise me you won't harm him."

King Gabriel leaned back in his seat and tapped a finger to his chin, contemplating Ramsey's request.

"Very well. If he surrenders the girl without a fight, I'll spare criminal charges, but he is still banished from this family and this kingdom. I don't want that ingrate stepping foot in Brennan ever again."

"And the part-reptilian girl?"

"Whatever she is, for the sake of order in our kingdom, she must be disposed of. We cannot have a reptilian capable of posing as a human lurking in our valley. For all we know, she is a spy for those monsters. But I want her brought to me alive, as I wish to interrogate her before the execution."

Ramsey gulped. It would be much easier to kill the reptilian girl on sight than haul her back to the palace, especially with her sharp fangs and mouth full of venom.

"Ramsey, I know this is difficult for you. I know that you don't want a confrontation with your brother, and I know you're still recovering from the events at the temple. But like I said before, if you want to be king, it will not be easy. I want you, your future descendants, and the rest of our family to live in a world free of this threat. But we must conquer it first."

"Yes, Your Majesty." Ramsey nodded. His mind was frantic with unease, but he didn't dare show any signs of doubt in front of the king. "I will prepare to leave shortly."

"Excellent. Remember, focus on finding your brother, but also keep an eye out for that Naga. And bring the reptilian girl to me, alive."

As Ramsey left the king's study and descended the towering staircase to his own quarters, a deep unease crept through his throat. He wished he could focus on hunting down the Naga, but the king was right; the reptilian girl was dangerous. *Who knows how long she's been hiding among us.*

And if she wasn't with Arthur, the fact that she looked like a human would make her even harder to find.

Epilogue

ARISSA'S MIND STIRRED TO LIFE AS THE SOFT glimmering lights of the Castellas' ballroom twinkled into view. Her unmasked face was bare, and her damaged ballgown had returned to its previously opulent state. She twirled around the ballroom with precise, delicate movements as a shadowy stranger clasped her waist. *Good gods, not this place again.*

Marissa shifted, attempting to bolt away from Antonio and out of the horrid estate, but her legs continued dancing even as her mind pleaded otherwise. It was as if she were a ghost possessing someone else's body. Her hearing and vision were muddled, and she had no control over her movements. Just as her tormented mind began to shriek, begging for release, the shadows on her mysterious partner faded, and a warm, familiar face emerged.

Arthur?

Her panic dissolved like boiling water dissipating into steam. Her tense muscles relaxed, and she allowed her dissociating body to flow freely as she pranced around the ballroom. Her eyes shifted around; the other guests were fuzzy, unidentifiable silhouettes that did not acknowledge her existence. She turned back to Arthur, and his gaze sent a tingling jolt down her throat and into the pit of her stomach. He stared at her with deep, longing eyes, as if she were the only other person in the room.

She matched his tense gaze, studying the flickering hues of green that trailed through his irises. The music swirled into a final crescendo, and Arthur raised a gentle yet firm hand to her cheek. She shivered as his fingertips pressed against her scales.

"Arthur ... you're a human, a royal who's engaged to another woman. I'm a reptilian. A half-Naga. A snake. I can't..."

As she spoke, the warmth in Arthur's eyes faded. The music stopped, and every guest ground to a frozen halt. Their heads jerked in Marissa's direction with inhuman speed, their facial features popping into view, and their mouths gaped open like gawking fish.

Marissa pulled away from Arthur and braced herself for the screams.

But they never came.

She jolted awake, her eyes snapping open. The harrowing faces and Marissa's accompanying panic disintegrated as her waking mind absorbed her surroundings. She lifted her head and realized she was in a small bed composed of wooden posts and a stiff mattress woven from palm fronds. She sat up, realizing her scaled body was clothed in a loose, long-sleeved dress, woven in vibrant stripes of color. *Where am I?*

Her mind flicked back to her last memories before she fell unconscious. *I was in Copperton ... it was in ruin ... surrounded by reptilians ... and they brought me here? Unharmed?* She thought about the Naga, pondering his gentle nature and foreign yet familiar features—how he had called her "dear," as if he already knew her. She had collapsed from exhaustion before she could even get his name, and they'd brought her here to a fanciful woven hut in what was presumably reptilian territory.

She stepped hesitantly out of bed, her legs shifting uneasily under her weight. She walked toward a small dining table, which was lined with a feast fit for a whole family of reptilians. She curiously studied the trays of raw, fileted meats stacked in tasteful pyramids and skewered with thin strips of bamboo. Marissa's eyed gravitated toward the whole, fresh rats, their plump brown bodies piled in a crisscross formation. Her stomach rippled violently, flooding her brain with thoughts of devouring everything in sight. *I'm starving. I didn't get a single bite of food at the party. Maybe I could just take ... no ... what if it's...*

<Oh, hello,> A sudden voice caused Marissa's hand to jolt away from the trays of food. She spun around, and a timid Varan hurriedly made Marissa's bed, fluffing out the pillows against her belly scales. <Don't mind me. I'm just here to tidy up. I hope you don't mind the dress; it's one of our ceremonial outfits. Funny enough, you're the same size as my little niece.>

The Varan noticed Marissa's dumbfounded expression as she stood in disbelief in the middle of the hut. <Oh, I should probably explain. My name is Aina. I'm the chieftess of the Varan. You're currently in our territory, in the capital village of Komodo.>

Marissa's head spun. *We traveled that far while I was passed out? And where did the Naga go?*

<I have a lot of questions,> Marissa responded, her tone uneasy. <But I guess my first one is ... how can I understand you? Until yesterday, I'd never met a reptilian in my life, and I could communicate with them perfectly. But it wasn't through speech or any sort of language ... it was like I could feel their words. How does it all work?>

Aina chuckled. Although the Varan's demeanor was friendly and gentle, Marissa could sense a deep sadness in her eyes, as if she were trying to hide a great amount of pain.

<Language is a human invention,> Aina explained. <I know you've never met a reptilian, but I imagine you've spent some time around other reptiles?>

Marissa nodded.

<You know how you can feel their thoughts? Well, with reptilians, it's similar but on a much greater scale. While true reptiles can express only basic emotions, reptilians can convey complex conversations. Here in Squamata, reptilians are all deeply connected. We don't hear each other's thoughts. We feel them.>

<In Squamata?>

<Oh, yes, that's the true name of this valley. I imagine the humans call it something else, don't they?>

Marissa nodded. *The Valley of Scales is actually called Squamata. Interesting.*

She pondered the Varan chieftess's explanation. She was relieved that she was able to communicate with the reptilians so easily, but she was disheartened that their method of communication was so intrinsic to their kind. *That means learning to communicate with humans would be incredibly difficult.*

Marissa's stomach rumbled, echoing in loud, churning sounds throughout the hut. Marissa clutched her abdomen in embarrassment, and Aina smiled.

<The food is for you, by the way. Help yourself.>

Marissa eyed the table, her ravenous stomach tempted by the assortment of foods, when she suddenly clutched her bare neck. Her eyes widened, an instant panic over-taking her body. <Where is—>

<Oh, your little python?> Aina interrupted. <He's in the gardens being doted on by some of the other Varan. Cute little munchkin. I've never seen a snake like him before. We noticed he was coming into shed, so we gave

him a nice soak. And if you were wondering about the Naga, he'll be in shortly. Please, do eat. He assumed you would be quite hungry after you awoke.>

The Naga left this food here for me... Marissa's gaze shifted back toward the dining table. *It's all raw...* She eyed a small furnace in the corner of the hut.

<Excuse me!> Marissa waved down the Varan as she turned to leave. <Do you have matches?>

A few minutes later, her scales tingled with warmth as she huddled around the crackling fire. Rats cooked quickly, so she wouldn't have to wait long to eat. She sat patiently in front of the furnace, twirling the crispy rodent on one of the bamboo skewers, when a sudden slithering sound startled her.

She twisted her head around and found herself staring at the same towering, serpent-faced Naga from the night before. He smiled and nodded. <I didn't mean to interrupt. I know it's a lot of food, but I wasn't sure what you liked. What ... exactly are you doing?>

<Oh, uh ... I was just cooking one of the rats.> Marissa's voice was soft, fearing she'd done something wrong.

<Hmph,> the Naga hissed, the sharp, guttural noise echoing up his throat. He slithered over to the dining table and plucked a rat off the top of the pile. Marissa tried not to grimace as he gulped the rat down whole, his throat muscles undulating as the rodent snaked its way down his esophagus. <Cooking food. You've been spending too much time around the humans.>

Marissa sat silently, waiting to see what else the Naga had to say. She wanted to bombard him with questions but decided it was best not to interrogate him and let her concerns be answered slowly.

<So, you grew up in an orphanage?> The Naga's deep thoughts broke the silence. <I'm assuming you recently became an adult, and that's why you left.>

Marissa froze. <H-how do you know that?>

<Because I went there. I scoured my way through every village in southern Brennan with little luck. And just when I was beginning to despair, wondering if I'd ever find you ... you pop up in that horrid burned-down camp like you were hunting us down.>

<We... we were trying to find you ... we wanted to know why you were terrorizing those villages ... and the Varan hide...>

<Terrorizing? Those damn humans deserved it. Poaching reptilians like animals ... but finding that little Varan's hide was just a fortunate coincidence. My dear, you were the one we were looking for.>

Me? Her whole life, Marissa had assumed the reptilians knew little of her existence. *The Naga ... the whole Varan tribe ... they were searching for me all along. I don't understand. What do they want with me?*

<Come with me.> The Naga slithered to the doorway of the hut, gesturing for Marissa to follow. <I have something I want to show you.>

MARISSA WALKED SLOWLY, HER EYES LOCKED ON the backside of the slithering Naga as she followed him through the village. She found his legless movements fascinating, how his long tail glided across the ground in a winding s-shape like a true snake. He had to be at least twenty feet long and stood maybe seven feet tall. *Naga are massive, even larger than Varan. No wonder he scared the villagers when he broke into their homes.*

She turned her attention away from the Naga and scanned the activity of the surrounding village. Aina had mentioned they were in Komodo, the capital of Varan territory. While the simple huts, made of thatched palm fronds over a wooden frame, were much smaller than the several-story limestone buildings in Brennan, they seemed to stretch out for miles. In the distance, between groups of huts, Marissa noticed long stretches of damp, marshy swampland peeking out between the trees.

It was early afternoon, and the huts were bustling with activity. Clusters of the spiny lizardfolk huddled around crackling fires, weaving palm frond baskets and fileting fresh animal carcasses into thin strips. Plumes of ashy smoke mixed with the raw, savory scent of fresh meat, wafting past Marissa's nose and dissipating into the forest. She noticed that the Varan didn't cook their food; the fileted strips were passed around on a wooden plank, and the lizards took turns plucking bits of meat and tossing them into their mouths, gulping them down whole in a manner similar to the Naga. Farther away from the fire, a group of juvenile Varan, some already taller than Marissa, scrabbled around an open court, tossing a ball cobbled together from pieces of leather.

But as Marissa walked through the village, she recoiled when she realized the Varan were staring at her. The adults peered up from their campfire duties, and the children froze in place as their leather ball rolled away into the brush. Their amber-colored, reptilian eyes were alight with fascination. Marissa knew they were just curious, but all the gawking made her uncomfortable. She forced a polite smile before focusing her attention back on the Naga.

They finally made it to their destination, a woven hut bordering the swampland. While Marissa's previous abode was a single room, this massive hut was made up of several, sprawling out in all directions. It was by far the largest residence that Marissa could see. *I wonder if this is where Aina lives.*

Inside, a male Varan sat on a wooden bench, his head leaning against the back of the hut and his eyes closed. He wasn't asleep, however, as his amber eyes opened as soon as the Naga slithered into the hut with Marissa in tow.

<Ah, welcome back,> he greeted in a friendly tone. His eyes locked on Marissa. <I can't believe you found her. How fascinating! The body of a human and the scales of a reptilian. I kept wondering what a half-Naga would look like...>

<Rathi,> the Naga spoke up. <I'll be pleased to make introductions later, but right now, could Marissa and I have a moment alone?>

<Of course.> The Varan stood up. He was much taller than Marissa but still shorter than the Naga. <I'll let you two catch up. I'll be with Aina if you need me.>

As the Varan stepped outside the hut, the bright sky bathing his spotted scales in sunlight, the Naga led Marissa through the winding abode. As they passed from room to room, venturing deeper into the hut, Marissa had a feeling that wherever the Naga was taking her, it wasn't meant for prying eyes.

Finally, they stopped. The small room, flanked by two stiff-faced guards, was bare except for a thin, raised platform that came up to Marissa's chest. As she studied the object atop the platform, she grew confused. *An entire room with guards for ... a piece of rock?*

As Marissa stepped closer, she realized the rock was shaped like the bottom of a serpent, its long tail coiling around a pillar. The piece was about eight inches long, simultaneously looking pristine and ancient, and was cut off in a jagged plateau just before the snake's midsection.

<This,> the Naga began, his thoughts booming through Marissa's mind. He lifted the carved rock from its pedestal, and as the Naga pulled it apart, Marissa realized it was two separate pieces stacked on top of each other. <Is the Idol of Vaipera, the patron deity of the Naga. Eight hundred years ago, our ancestors begged for help, and the great goddess of chaos answered, sending

us a tool capable of bringing her to the mortal realm. But the reptilian leaders of the time were foolish, and instead of conquering Squamata once and for all, their indecisiveness caused the idol to shatter into pieces. Since then, this precious gift has been doomed to rot, abandoned, hidden away in each the four territories by the descendants of those reptilian leaders. But thanks to my efforts, that is no longer the case. I have obtained both the Naga and Varan pieces of the idol, and I'm on my way shortly to obtain the third piece from the Gharian. After that, all that's left is persuading those stubborn Testudo. Once we complete the idol, Vaipera will finally be unleashed, and the wretched human's kingdom will be no more.>

As the Naga prattled on, declaring his bold plan to rid the Valley of Scales of the humans, Marissa grew sicker as her horrid realization deepened. Ever since she agreed to help Arthur, she had sympathized with the rogue Naga. She wanted to keep him safe, away from the murderous royal guard ... but most importantly, she kept rationalizing that he couldn't be that bad. She had been treated like rubbish by the humans, and she prayed that the reptilians would be different. She saw them as misunderstood, persecuted souls, treated as monsters just like her. It had foolishly never occurred to her that they could be plotting to destroy Brennan.

She remembered Arthur's words back in Sienna's garden when he mentioned the tablet and how the humans must know something they didn't. *They must've found out about the idol. That's why they're so hell-bent on war.* Marissa knew that the poaching enraged the reptilians, watching their kin be murdered by humans for the sake of vanity. Marissa understood their pain and that the reptilians wanted revenge … but as horribly as she'd been treated by the humans, she didn't want to see them destroyed. *They're not all bad. Marcus gave us a ride when we were stranded … Sienna let us stay in her home and gave us medicine … even Thomas helped us track down the black market…*

And Arthur, he…

A deep, burning emotion choked her throat. Arthur, the man who had accepted her without fear from the moment she was unmasked at the inn. The man who had traveled across the valley with her on the biggest adventure of her life. The man who taught her bravery, kindness, friendship…

The man who made her feel emotions that her lonely reptilian heart had never thought possible.

<Why do you look so upset?> The Naga's eyes glowered with disapproval. <I saw how the humans treated you. When I'm finished eradicating them, Squamata will be a very different place. I will be supreme chieftain, ruler of the reptilians, and you will hold a place of honor amongst our people. You will never know loneliness or rejection ever again. We'll finally be together, me, you, and your mother, at peace for the rest of our days.>

My … mother!? You know my mother?

Wait…

A sudden flood of realization poured through Marissa's body. *No ... it can't be...* She gazed at the Naga, her eyes wild with apprehension.

<Who are you?>

<Oh, pardon me,> the Naga apologized. <I got so caught up in things, I never introduced myself. My dear Marissa, my name is Ezrinth. I am the son of the Naga chieftain Orami, the current leader of the Varan warriors, and, most importantly ... I am your father.>

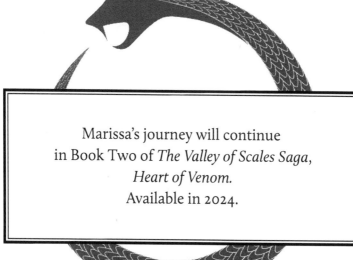

Marissa's journey will continue
in Book Two of *The Valley of Scales Saga*,
Heart of Venom.
Available in 2024.

About the Reptilians

Naga: The Naga are snakefolk native to Squamata. Long and slender, with serpent bodies and scaly arms, they can reach 18-20 feet long and stand up to 8 feet tall. The Naga draw inspiration from several semiaquatic snakes, including the venomous Florida cottonmouth (*Agkistrodon conanti*) and the similar-looking but non-venomous banded water snake (*Nerodia fasciata*). Their name comes from the mythical serpentine creatures depicted in Hinduism.

Varan: The Varan are lizardfolk native to Squamata. Wiry-bodied with thin faces, they have long teeth, a trail of dorsal spines, and are 12-14 feet long, and stand 6-7 feet tall. The varan draw inspiration from monitor lizards, specifically the Ackie monitor (*Varanus acanthurus*). Their name comes from *varanus*, the genus containing monitor lizards.

Gharian: The Gharian are gatorfolk native to Squamata. Heavy-bodied with tough bullet-resistant skin, they are the largest of the reptilians, reaching up to 20-22 feet long and standing 9-10 feet tall. The Gharian draw inspiration from crocodilians, specifically the American alligator (*Alligator mississippiensis*), despite their name coming from gharials, another species of crocodilian.

Testudo: The Testudo are tortoisefolk native to Squamata. Sturdy creatures with heavy, almost impenetrable shells, they are the smallest of the reptilians, standing 5-6 feet tall. The Testudo draw inspiration from tortoises, specifically the gopher tortoise (*Gopherus polyphemus*), which, like the Testudo, are known for digging underground burrows. Their name comes from the Latin word for tortoise, which is also a genus of tortoises found in the Mediterranean.

Book Club Questions

1. At the beginning of the novel, Marissa has difficulty fitting into human society due to being half-Naga. Have you ever felt like an outsider or had trouble belonging somewhere? How did it make you feel?

2. What are your thoughts on snakes? Do you see them as scary, strange, beautiful? How does the portrayal of snakes in this novel compare to how they are portrayed in real life?

3. Arthur is extremely passionate about reptiles, to the point where he is ostracized by his family. Have you ever experienced trouble following your dreams? How did you handle difficulties along the way?

4. Arthur and Ramsey have a difficult relationship due to their contrasting personalities and viewpoints. Do you have siblings (or other family members) who are different from you? How do you resolve conflicts with them?

5. Thomas suffers immense guilt from killing a Varan to save his wife's life. How far would you go to save someone you love? Is it possible for characters to redeem themselves even after committing heinous acts?

6. The humans and reptilians are unable to communicate due to both language and biological differences. Do you believe in the power of words to solve conflicts? How would this novel be different if the reptilians and humans could talk to each other?

7. Ezrinth revealed that he is Marissa's father. Where do you think he has been all this time? And where could Marissa's mother be?

About the Author

SYDNEY WILDER IS A YOUNG ADULT FANTASY author whose inspiration comes from a lifetime of writing, gaming, and caring for reptiles. She has spent many years immersing herself in fantasy worlds through video games, Magic: The Gathering, and Dungeons & Dragons. Growing up in Florida, her love of reptiles, especially snakes, began at an early age. Her first pet reptile was a bearded dragon, and her collection has since grown to include three snakes. Her favorite reptile species are carpet pythons and tuataras. When not writing, she loves bike rides, playing board games with friends, and attending geek conventions. She currently works as a web developer in Central Florida, living with her loving husband and menagerie of pets, both scaled and furred.